Accidental Witness

(Morelli Family, #1)

SAM MARIANO

This is a work of fiction. Names, characters, businesses, places, events and incidents are either the products of the author's imagination, or used fictitiously. Any resemblance to actual persons, living or dead, or actual events is purely coincidental.

*Accidental Witness (Morelli Family, #1)* Copyright © 2017 by Sam Mariano

All rights reserved.

ISBN:1546959351
ISBN-13: 978-1546959359

No part of this book may be reproduced in any form or by any electronic or mechanical means, including information storage and retrieval systems, without written permission from the author, except for the use of brief quotations in a book review.

# DEDICATION

Jen Curtis, this one's for you, lady friend. You are all kinds of amazing. It's hard to believe the Morellis ever existed without you! You've been such a rockstar, and I so appreciate all your help in the promotion of this series! I wish I could give you Vince, but he's fictional. If I had Mateo's wallet, I'd at least buy you some Louboutins to hate. :-D

# CHAPTER ONE

MY MOM always told me not to fall into the "bad boy" trap.

After watching them use and leave her all my life, you'd think I might've learned. As I slip my shoes on and creep out the back door—cringing at the squeal it makes when I try to ease it open—to call Jace Bradford, the friendly neighborhood bad boy who's been flirting with me on and off for a few weeks, it isn't looking so good.

Even as I crouch down beside the stone steps, pulling my cheap coat tighter against my body as a chilly gust of wind whips my mess of dirty blonde hair around my face, I try to talk myself out of it. He's barely off a two week bender with Debbie Reyes, after all. Beautiful, beautiful Debbie Reyes. A chain-smoking, badass bombshell whose facial expressions are limited to bitchy variations of boredom and murderous.

Probably murderous when she looks at me if I go after her sloppy seconds.

But he has such great eyes. And the way he looks when he smiles at me...

"Screw it," I mutter, whipping the phone out of my pocket and taking a couple steps forward, looking back at the house, up at the darkened window of my mother's bedroom. The house has such thin walls you can hear a stream of *piss* as it makes its way to the toilet basin; no way am I calling a guy my mother would not approve of so late on a school night inside those walls. No way.

I practiced what we might say in the mirror earlier, and as my fingers scroll through for his contact name ("Jane babysitting" in case my mom sees his number flash across my screen), I imagine the gravelly "what's up" he will likely answer with.

A flicker of light in the window of the house next door catches my attention. Junkies live there and they're always having people over late at night, so I shouldn't be so startled. Even at eighteen, I'm a little afraid of the dark.

All thoughts of my illicit phone call vacate my head as I watch the orange illumination climb the side of the window, swallowing up the curtain, and my brain slowly processes that I'm not looking at light, but flames.

Fire.

My eyes go wide and for a second, I don't know how to react. I look around for an adult, someone who knows what to do, but of course there's no one. Running around to the side of the house, my eyes dart to their front porch—as if they might be standing outside, laughing at some prank?—but it's empty. I notice a car parked across the street, but that's not unusual, especially outside that house.

Heart hammering in my chest, I fumble for my phone, but then I hear a muffled noise from inside the house and panic makes me blank again, staring at the window. Are there people inside? Should I try to help?

My feet move nervously, trying to debate what to do. I move closer to the front porch, my eyes jumping from the window to the porch, fingers curling tightly around my phone. My brain tells me to call 911, that every moment counts, but something stops me.

"Come on," called lowly, hoarsely.

A shadowy figure slowly backs out the front door, peering inside. I can't tell what he looks like, but I know from his shaggy hair it's not my neighbor or her bald boyfriend.

I open my mouth to call out, but something about the way he's moving—calmly but quickly, hunched, as if trying to hide himself out in the open—gives me pause.

Instead of pushing past the bushes to check on the person emerging from the house, I sink down, hoping the bushy branches are adequate cover. The hand gripping my phone shakes as I push the tab on the side to ensure my phone's on silent. I bring up my camera app, sliding it over to video, and push through the branches of the shrubs. I have a reasonably clear view of the man on the porch—his back, anyway. He looks to his left, then back my way. Ice water pours through my veins, but I don't move, and he doesn't notice me from his quick glance.

A second figure emerges from the house, launching the first guy into motion. Another "c'mon" and then the first guy heads down the front porch steps, making his way toward the parked car.

The second guy lingers at the door longer than the first, peering back inside. He stands there long enough for my thighs to start burning pretty badly from my crouched position. I shift slightly for relief, but lose my balance, falling forward into the shrub.

The second guy jerks in my direction and I draw a quick breath, my heart sinking. His eyes connect with mine through the branches and I drop my phone, seized by terror as he holds my gaze for several seconds.

I know that face.

Not well, but I've seen him around school before, heard the stories about his family.

He's in my English class, and as he takes a step in my direction, I can't wrap my head around what's happening.

He hesitates, looking to the car, then back to the bushes where I'm sprawled. I scurry back, pushing to my feet and running like my life depends on it to my back door, nearly ripping it off the hinges and throwing myself inside. My chest heaves up and down rather violently as I slam the door shut, locking the doorknob and the dead bolt as well. I run to the front door, checking that both are locked—not that a few locks will do me any good if they storm my front door.

"Oh, God," I whine, slowly inching my way to the front door. I have to see if he went to the car. If he hasn't, he's outside my house somewhere.

I've never known dread until this moment.

The car is gone, and I see it—the tail lights, down the road.

He's gone.

I consider my phone, outside in the bushes.

I think of the house next door, of the fire I just saw inside.

If I run back outside and grab it, I could call 911.

If I did, they would know I'd seen it first. They'd ask me questions, investigate what happened.

I would have to tell the police that Vincent Morelli, of the famously criminal Morelli family, had been inside that house when the fire started.

It feels like my heart beats inside my roiling gut as I make my decision and head back to my bedroom, as if I hadn't seen a thing, and hope like hell someone else will call for help.

# CHAPTER TWO

MY EYES burn and my stomach churns as I stand at my open locker, staring blankly at the books inside.

It's been three days since I last ate or slept.

The fire happened on Friday. After an eternity cowering in my bedroom, I finally heard sirens.

By the time help arrived, rushing us out of our house as they worked to extinguish the flames, it was too late. The woman who lived next door—Crystal, her name was Crystal—and her boyfriend were both dead.

I shook violently as my seven-year-old brother clung to my legs, listening to my mother blathering about how it could have been us, how the fire could have spread, clutching my four-year-old sister close and placing terrified kisses on her mop of pale blond hair.

I wondered if they were still alive when Vince Morelli spotted me in the bushes.

I wondered if my phone was still *in* those bushes, incriminating me.

Incriminating him.

The queasiness I felt in that moment never left. In fact, it only got worse. After the workers had all left the scene and night had fallen, I ignored my terror and snuck outside, kneeling by the shrubs and searching for my cell phone.

I didn't find it.

Which meant someone else had.

Every moment since, I've waited for the police or a Morelli goon to show up on our front porch.

It hasn't left much time for sleeping. My nerves can't handle food. My hands shake like a drug addict in withdrawal.

At this point, I'm a pale, exhausted, nervous wreck.

My stomach makes an angry noise and I close my eyes for a moment, wondering how I'm going to make it through the day. I grab the books I need for class, each heavier than the last, and push my locker door shut.

Behind the door, propped against the locker beside mine, stands Vince Morelli. I jump back, squeezing my books tightly as my heart drops out of my rib cage, my back slamming against the cool metal door behind me.

The girl shoots me a dirty look before ducking back inside her locker to retrieve her book, then slams it shut and pivots, heading off in the other direction and leaving me alone with Vince.

He isn't moving, hasn't spoken. He just stands there in his dark jeans with a rip in the left knee cap, the black T-shirt that hugs his biceps, displayed more prominently with his arms crossed. Like all Morelli men, he has luscious, pitch black hair and chiseled features with dark brown eyes that pull you in and threaten to drown you with their intensity.

I'm already drowning, panic clawing at my insides while I try to make my mouth work.

As if he has all the time in the world to wait, he merely watches me.

He must know I haven't turned him in, right? If I told the police what I saw, they would have already called him in for questioning, at the very least.

"Tommy asked me out!"

I jerk back again, turning to face my best friend, Lena Korell, as she beams at me, leaning against the closed locker beside mine and rolling her eyes dreamily.

I turn back toward Vince, but he's gone.

Like my sanity is about to be, I'm pretty sure.

I try to listen as Lena goes on about her Friday night plans. Any other time I would be excited for her, but I do *not* have the capacity to be girly right now.

Hours later, I'm still pale and quiet at lunch, still without much to say about Lena's date, hardly touching the slice of Oreo pie I ordered, dramatically reasoning that if I'm about to be offed by the Morelli family, I should at least have something delicious first.

I can't stop watching for Vince. I imagine him around every corner, search for him at every table. Following lunch is English, the period we have together, and I debate skipping it, but I'm more afraid of him coming to my house to confront me. What can he actually do to me in a school building with security cameras and faculty members milling through every hall?

"What is your deal?"

I glance up at Lena without much enthusiasm. Her dark eyebrows arch expectantly up toward her dark, springy curls, and exhaustion mingled with defeat suddenly sweeps over me. Maybe it would be better to throw myself at Vince's mercy and be done with it.

"You know my house nearly burned down a couple days ago, right?" I ask.

Lena rolls her eyes as she dips a fry in Ketchup. "Your house did not almost burn down."

"It could've."

"No, 'cause you're not a dumb shit who left her crack pipe going by the curtains and then nodded off to the point of not waking up when she's on fire," she states, without sympathy.

"They were human beings, Lena."

"They were gross addicts who broke into your house and stole your television over the summer," she returns.

"She had three kids."

"All of them in foster care. I'm sorry, I know you're a drama queen, but I'm not going to cry over the loss of scum of the earth with you."

I want to tell her, but I can't. I doubt she would be so glib if *she* felt responsible for not saving them, even if they *were* kind of shitty people. I can't say that, so I keep my mouth shut.

Besides, I don't need to bring anyone else into my mess. I haven't told a soul what I saw, but I have an uneasy feeling with Vince lurking around, I'm about to have to tell *someone*.

The sound of a chair skidding across the floor startles the hell out of me. My head jerks up, fully expecting to find Vince Morelli straddling the backwards chair suddenly beside my desk, but instead I see Jace Bradford.

He's giving me that little smile that made me melty a week ago, but I'm curiously unaffected, looking at it now.

"Hey." There it is, the gravelly voice I was all hyped about a few days ago.

I can tell he expects to flirt, but I don't have the energy for it.

Flashing him the least convincing tug of my lips ever, I make a point to look at my desktop, straightening my notebooks. "Hi."

"Lose my number?" he teases.

"It's been a rough few days," I tell him. "There was a fire next door. My neighbors…"

"Oh, shit," he says, rearing back a little. "Is everyone okay?"

Dread trickles through my veins, pooling in my stomach. Just the thought of the house fire makes me queasy—not to mention the lack of food and sleep.

"Pretty sure that's my seat, Bradford."

*I'm* pretty sure my soul falls out of my body as I look up to see Vince Morelli standing at the desk beside mine.

It's not Vince's seat, but Jace doesn't argue. Standing easily enough, Jace swings the chair back behind its desk so Vince can sit down. "My bad, man."

Vince leisurely watches me for a moment before he takes his seat, dropping a notebook and pen on the desktop. It's a perfectly normal thing to do, but somehow it feels menacing.

Jace glances from Vince to me, then skulks away without so much as a goodbye.

My stomach somersaults as I shift in my seat, glancing back at the door. My previous thought about ditching circles back around, but the teacher is already standing at the front of the class. We have a test today, and if she sees me cut out, she may not let me make it up.

Not like I'll be able to focus with Vince sitting beside me anyway.

He normally doesn't sit beside me, and we do have assigned seats, so I wait for the guy who normally sits here to show up, or the teacher to say something about it.

Minutes like hours stretch on before the teacher tells everyone to settle down. She brings a stack of stapled papers and begins doing a head count at each row, passing them back. I wait for her to notice Vince next to me and say something, but if she does, she doesn't seem to care.

As the tests are passed back, I dare a glance over at Vince. He isn't looking at me, but he must sense my eyes on him, because he turns to meet my gaze.

I break eye contact immediately, looking down at my paper. I fidget with the stapled corner and run my fingers aimlessly over the edge. I try to look at him out of the corner of my eye, then I try to stop my leg from bouncing underneath the desk.

The burning question that's been running through my mind nonstop the previous few days emerges again: why was Vince in that house? Was he responsible for the fire? Had he...wanted my neighbors to die? Had he killed them?

Had I, with my silence?

I try to focus on the test, but I can't even get through the first paragraph.

Pushing back my chair and grabbing the paper, I make my way to the front of the room. The teacher turns, startled, since I should've only raised my hand.

"I think I'm going to be sick. I need to go to the nurse."

It must show on my face, because she doesn't argue, merely nodding her head, her eyes searching my face with a trace of concern. "Okay."

I hustle back to my desk to gather my things. I avoid looking at him, but I can feel Vince's hard gaze on me as I flee.

I don't care. I can't. All I want is to get the hell out of that classroom and never see Vince Morelli again.

# CHAPTER THREE

MACARONI NOODLES stick to the pan and I curse the broken dishwasher. Hand washing dishes is the worst, and I never feel like I get them clean enough.

Screwing up my face, I grab a sponge and begrudgingly knock the macaroni off, scrubbing the mushy noodle residue it leaves behind.

It's been a long, long day.

After I left school I had to pick up my siblings and watch them all night while my mom worked. She went to her boyfriend's house after, so I ended up putting them both to bed. It's not an irregular occurrence, since my mom works late hours a lot, but I'm so exhausted that just dragging myself across the room feels like a workout—making them eat and do homework while not fighting was too much to ask.

I have to get some sleep tonight.

Part of me wonders if I should just approach Vince and be done with it. If I could do it at school, I would feel safer. I'm not sure how much more of the cat and mouse games my nerves can take, and at the end of the day, I could actually be endangering my family.

Unease tickles down my spine at that grim realization. If Vince and that other guy *did* kill my neighbors, what would stop them from doing the same thing to us? They could be planning to burn *our* house down as I stand here scrubbing dishes.

I drop the sponge into the sink basin, bracing my weight on the edge as my shoulders sag, my head falling forward.

I have to stop thinking about this. I'm driving myself crazy, and there's nothing I can do about it right now.

I barely register the movement behind me and I'm pushed forward, my hip slamming painfully against the counter. Someone shoves against my back, one arm neatly trapping both of mine against my body, the other clapping a hand over my mouth to stop me from crying out.

A knowing kind of terror drenches my bones and I can't move, can't think—for almost a full second, everything stops.

Then I start bucking, rearing back in an attempt at head-butting my assailant.

My head connects with nothing, but taking advantage of my movement, he swiftly repositions the hand trapping my arms, locking it around my neck and pulling me back into a painful position.

My hands fly to his arms, digging my fingers into his skin as I instinctively attempt to pry them away from my throat. It only serves to tighten his grip, so I stop fighting, terrified he's going to snap my neck and focus on getting myself under control. I force myself to quiet down, in a show of cooperation. I need to see who's in my home to see if I have a chance. If it's Vince, I might make it out alive. If it's some flunky and Vince isn't there, I'm probably already dead.

I count six seconds before he finally speaks. "Are you done?"

My eyes nearly roll back in relief. It's Vince's voice. I attempt something like a nod and the pressure around my neck eases up, disappearing completely as he lets me go. He remains close instead of taking a step back, and for a wild second, I try to remember if there are any knives in the sink—just in case.

*What are you thinking?* No, that's a bad idea. I can't *stab* a Morelli. Then I really would be dead meat.

Diplomacy is the only way to go.

"Don't scream," he says calmly.

I shake my head, my hand automatically going to my neck. "I won't."

His gaze follows my hand as it brushes across my throat.

I'm fine. I'm fine. I'm fine.

I need to calm my ass down.

Only that's hard to do, with a son of the mob breaking into my house while I wash dishes.

My heart floods with ice water as I consider my brother and sister asleep down the hall. They could've heard the scuffle. They could hear…whatever is about to happen next.

"When does your mother get home?" Vince asks, like he's paying a social call.

"Soon."

What, he expected me to tell him he had the house to himself for a while?

Cocking his head to the side, he regards me with a seemingly solemn expression. "Let's not start off with lies, huh?"

My face flushes, despite the ridiculousness of him expecting literally anything from me. "I'm not—I don't know when she'll be home. She's off work already, but she went to her boyfriend's house after. She really could be home any time. And she doesn't know anything," I add quickly.

Eyebrows rising, he says, "Well, at least we don't have to pretend you don't know why I'm here."

I hug myself, running my hands up and down my arms. "I didn't say anything. I didn't even *see* anything, really."

"That so?" he asks, reaching into his pocket and extracting a thin, rectangular object.

My stomach rolls over as he offers up my cell phone.

"You can have it back," he states, regarding my discomfort with amusement. "Obviously I had to delete the video you took—you know, of that thing you didn't really see."

I don't even reach for my phone, and I definitely can't meet his gaze. "All I saw was you walking out of a house."

"That seems like a boring thing to record. Those cute little videos of your siblings, those seem worthwhile…" Pausing, he jerks a thumb in the direction of the hall and pulls a frown. "I imagine they're sleeping right in there, huh?"

I narrow my eyes at him, but words fail me. The unspoken threat lingers, just because of who he is. "You don't have to make veiled threats. I'm not going to say anything. I *didn't* say anything. I didn't even call in the fire. I didn't want to get involved," I say quietly, my eyes dropping to the floor.

Vince soaks that in, then leans back against the counter, crossing his arms. "Why were you out there in the first place?"

## Accidental Witness

The truth feels too embarrassing, but I don't have a lie prepared and I'm no good at coming up with them on the fly. "I was making a phone call."

Lifting a disbelieving eyebrow, he questions, "In your backyard?"

"We have thin walls. I didn't want anyone to hear the call. It was stupid."

"Ah." A knowing nod. "Boyfriend? It's not that tool bag, Bradford, is it?"

My face burns.

Vince utters a noise of disgust. "Guy's an idiot. You could do better."

Before I can think better of it, I retort, "Yeah, well, there just aren't enough mobbed up arsonists to go around."

His brown eyes narrow and he pushes off the counter, taking a step toward me.

I automatically step back, my eyes not moving from his. I am floored by my own idiocy. That was such a stupid, stupid, stupid thing to say, but I force a wavering smile. "What, you can't take a joke?"

"It's an odd joke, considering you didn't see anything," he reminds me.

Bile threatens to rise up my throat and I curse myself a hundred times. I'm talking to someone who has committed criminal acts, not bantering with a hot guy at school. What the fuck is wrong with me?

"I didn't." My voice sounds weak as he continues to advance on me, taking two steps forward to my one step back and eventually his arm shoots out, grabbing me by the wrist. I squeak, literally squeak, and then his hands are on my shoulders, swinging and pushing until the counter's pressed against my back. It's suddenly harder to draw air into my lungs. Vince stands so close I can feel the body heat roll off his chest.

Even though it couldn't possibly do any good, I implement my four-year-old sister's favorite hiding technique and close my eyes.

"See," Vince says, his voice still low and even, "when you say a thing like that, it makes it seem like you're lying to me."

"It was a stupid thing to say. It slipped out."

"Exactly." His fingers brush my chin and I jump, my eyes popping open and quickly meeting his. "If something like that happened to slip out again, say in front of someone else—"

"It wouldn't," I insist. His fingers are still trailing along the curve of my neck. I catch a shaky breath, distracted by the weirdly pleasant sensation. His hands continue their journey and before I realize what he's doing, his hands, positioned around my neck, begin to squeeze.

I gasp, my wide eyes jumping to his in horror. My hands fly to his wrists as his fingers tighten uncomfortably, but not painfully. My throat feels strangely fragile beneath just the strength of his fingers.

"My father, like most of the men in my family, uses fear to motivate people to do his bidding. Violence. Threats. Personally, it doesn't do much for me to terrify a woman. Not usually," he amends, his fingers tightening ever so slightly. "I have to admit, I haven't hated you watching over your shoulder for me since that night. Could be I'm a sick fuck just like the rest of them. Latent gene, maybe. But I'm also your fucking angel of mercy right now. If you watched any other member of my family walk out of that house the other night, you'd be dead already."

I squeeze my eyes shut, feeling the burn of tears threatening to seep out.

"But it was me. And I don't *want* to hurt you, but my ass comes before yours," he states, one eyebrow shooting up even as his eyes drop pointedly to where my ass is pressed against the counter, "no matter how nice that ass is."

Before I can attempt a response, the sound of someone trying to twist the door knob open startles us both.

Vince drops his hands, his gaze jerking to the door.

Turning back to me, eyes full of threats, he says, "Your room."

I grab his wrist, running down the hall as my mom pushes her key into the lock.

We make it inside, but sometimes Mom comes to my room to check in. My room's tiny, barely enough space to get around the full-sized bed, and my closet is minuscule—and shared, since the room my siblings share doesn't have one.

"Will she come in here?" he asks, his gaze lingering on the door.

"She might," I whisper back. "I guess…the floor on that side." I point to the other side of my bed.

Shooting me a dark look, he says, "If you try to signal her or say a goddamn word, Mia…"

"I wouldn't." Mainly because that wouldn't reassure the nice gangster that I wouldn't rat him out, but I don't add that.

Keeping the light off, I climb into bed, yanking my covers up over me. I watch, transfixed, as Vince Morelli lowers himself to the floor, like a real-life monster beneath my bed.

# CHAPTER FOUR

THE DOOR creaks open and light spills in. "You up?"

I debate faking her out, but she flips on the light.

I force a squint, pushing up on my elbows. "Well, I was trying to sleep."

My mom's a tall lady with dirty blonde hair and a weakness for insensible shoes. She falls on the pretty side of average, but years of putting through one disaster after the next have left their mark.

She holds onto the doorjamb as she yanks her purple heels off and shakes her head. "Men are such assholes."

Oh good, she wants to vent.

"I agree, but could we maybe talk about this tomorrow? I was just about—"

"I have to work in the morning," she interrupts, shaking her head. "Jen called off, of course. I'm gonna need you to drop off the kids before school."

I fail to stifle a sigh of annoyance. We're down to sharing a car, which is a real headache. "Well, in that case I definitely need to get to sleep."

She rolls her eyes, exaggerating her disappointment. "Fine, I guess girl talk can wait."

"Goodnight."

"One last thing. I'm definitely not going to be working Mondays after the next schedule. I was thinking, since now I have set hours Saturday mornings and Mondays off, maybe you could start looking into getting something part-time like we talked about? Save up for another car."

"Fine," I say, admittedly a little shortly. "I'll see if I can find something."

Apparently, I'm not psyched enough, so she tries to sell me on it. "It would be *your* car."

It would be a family car, not mine, but I don't argue. I can't even get an *hour* to myself, let alone a car.

"Brax got suspended from work or he wouldn't even be able to pick me up tomorrow; we'd be really screwed then."

"He's picking you up?" Also, what did she expect from a guy named Brax?

"We're going out."

"So I'm babysitting."

It wasn't a question, but she answers anyway. "If you don't mind. We really need to spend some time together."

I nod, lips pressed firmly together.

"If things keep going the way they have been, we might not need to re-up this lease," she said, as if it's a tempting possibility.

Literally the only thing I want to do less than move in with Brax is have this conversation with Vince Morelli hunched on the floor beside my bed.

Since I'm not being cooperative, she huffs and turns off the light. "You're no fun. Goodnight."

As soon as she's gone, I pull the blanket up to cover my face. I consider, just for a moment, how ridiculous my life is. A minute ago, some criminal mobster I go to school with had his hands around my neck, threatening strangulation, and now my mom wants me to find a job with no experience that would be cool with very specific availability—but don't worry, if things keep going well (despite men apparently being assholes?) we can move in with my new "daddy"—who is seven years older than me.

I feel Vince standing by my bedside, but I don't remove my cover.

"You know what, if you wanna kill me, go ahead and do it now. At least then I'll get some sleep."

The bed sags and creaks and my eyes widen, but he can't see. I feel him warm against my side, and then he's tugging my blanket—and then he's under it with me, turning his head in my direction.

"So, that was your mom, huh?"

"That was her."

"Don't like the boyfriend?" he surmises.

"It would be more normal if he dated *me*—and I get the feeling he's had that thought a time or two. Cohabitation is not a good idea."

"You need a new car," he states.

"I need a new life," I return.

"You might be in luck. I've never met a woman who got entangled with a Morelli and didn't end up with a new life out of it, though I can't say that's always a good thing."

That time I'm the one raising my eyebrows. "Are we entangled?"

"I have a feeling we're gonna be."

It's quiet for about half a minute, then I say, "I'm not going to say anything to anyone. Honest. I have enough of my own problems; I don't need to add a mob beef to the list."

"I hope you're telling the truth. Not just for my sake, but for yours," he adds. "You should think of this like you're covering your own ass just as much as mine."

"I probably am," I mutter. "If I would've made the call instead of cowering in my bedroom that night, they might still be alive."

It must've been clear in the way I said it that it's been weighing on my mind, because Vince considers it for a minute, but not with the cold, hard look he'd worn earlier. After a minute, his tone gentler than I expect, he says, "They wouldn't. There's nothing you could have done."

I let it sink in for a second, but the relief I expected doesn't come.

It's probably verification that the guy lying in my bed right now is a murderer, but that doesn't hit the way I expect it to, either.

"Now what?" I ask quietly.

"Well, looks like you're gonna have to share the covers."

Alarmed, my eyes widen. "What? You can't stay!"

He's already smiling, enjoying messing with me.

"Oh." I blush.

Luckily it doesn't take too long to figure out how we'll sneak him out. My mother goes in to take a shower, and once the water turns on, we're clear to creep down the hall.

I open the door to let him outside, but he hangs back, glancing down the hall we just came from. His gaze travels back to me, still unsure.

"You can trust me," I tell him.

Nodding, holding my gaze he says, "I hope so."

With that, he finally walks out.

"Can we get garlic bread?"

I look over at my little brother, taking a third sample cup from the little 'try me' stand in the grocery store bakery. "No. Allan, no more cake samples. You're only supposed to take one."

"I want cake," my baby sister announces, reaching her hand out toward it. I roll my eyes as Allan grabs another one and hands it to her, flashing me an innocent look.

"It wasn't for me," he defends. "Why can't we get garlic bread? Garlic bread is so good."

"We are only here for a box of spaghetti and a jar of sauce. That is *it*."

"Then why'd we get a cart?" he demands, not unreasonably.

"For Casey—she likes to ride."

"No fair, I want to ride. Make her take turns."

I pull the cart to a sudden halt and take a deep breath. "We are not fighting over who rides in the cart. We're not. Can we please just go get the food for dinner so we can go home?"

"I don't wanna go home," Allan complains as he redirects toward the pasta aisle.

I start moving again as he meanders along, telling me how boring home is. I can't really argue that point. Without cable, there are only so many options for television, and even *I'm* sick of the same kid shows over and over. "Maybe you guys can play with your Legos," I suggest. "Or color a picture to hang on the refrigerator. You've got stuff to do."

"It's all boring," he informs me.

"Just grab the spaghetti," I tell him, slowing to a stop in front of the wall of pasta boxes.

"Spaghetti, huh?"

My heart drops out my chest cavity as I recognize Vince's voice, spinning around to find him standing right there in the aisle with me.

"Kid's right," he says, smirking at my discomfort. "That is kind of boring."

My heart continues to skitter around my chest as I glance behind him, checking that he's alone. He notices, and his smile wilts as he seems to consider it.

"Just me," he says, less amused.

Like that makes much of a difference. I don't say that though. Uncertainty rules me as I try to figure out how I'm supposed to react to him suddenly showing up wherever I am. That seems paranoid, but earlier in class, instead of giving the seat next to me back to its rightful owner, Vince sat there again.

"Okay, can we get some garlic bread now?" Allan asks, not noticing my sudden discomfort.

Instead of answering my brother, I tentatively meet Vince's eyes. "What are you doing here?"

"Shopping."

There's no reason to assume he isn't—everyone needs groceries, after all—but I don't believe him. I nod anyway, turning back to my cart and pushing it to the edge of the aisle without a word.

Wheeling the cart into the narrow space between the registers, I take both items from the cart and place them on the belt. Then, as is natural from that angle, I glance behind me.

There's Vince, in line behind me. He's wearing dark wash jeans and a charcoal gray shirt, and man, for a murderer, he looks good.

Just thinking the m-word causes my stomach to sink, and I look at the cashier, wishing she'd hurry up.

"Who are you?" Allan asks him.

"A friend of your sister's," Vince answers.

I cut a glance his way, since that's not how I would describe him. "Why are you in line?"

"Hm?"

"You said you were at the store because you were shopping." I indicate his empty hands. "You didn't buy anything."

A dark brow raises, then he grabs two snack sized bags of chips from the impulse-buy rack and holds them up for my brother. "Which one should I get?"

I roll my eyes as my brother jabs the orange bag. Vince puts the other one back and holds up the bag, shaking it. "See? I'm buying something."

The cashier rings up my items and gives me my total. I freeze, frowning at the computer screen. I brought exactly $4 with me—just enough to buy a box of spaghetti and a jar of sauce. I'm somehow fifty cents short.

"Wasn't the pasta on sale?"

"Yep," she says, glancing at the screen.

I awkwardly draw my money out of my pocket and count it, knowing there won't be enough. I don't understand why. Did Allan not grab the right sauce?

It's humiliating, especially with Vince standing right there, but I don't know what else to do. "Um, how much was the sauce?"

She regards me with vague irritation and I flush.

"It's just—I didn't bring my purse in," I say, even though there's no more money in my purse. "I thought I brought in enough, but I'm a few cents short."

She digs the jar of pasta out, and sure enough, it's a size larger than the one we usually get. I hadn't been paying attention when Allan grabbed it, because Vince threw me off.

"Okay, I'll just go back and grab the right one," I say, reaching out to take the jar of sauce.

Before I can, Vince is squeezing past the cart, coming toward the register. He drops the chips on the belt and takes the sauce out of my hand, giving it back to the cashier. "Can you just add the chips to her bill?"

"You don't have to do that—I can just go get the right one. I could've paid for it, I just…"

He holds up a hand to stop me, handing the cashier a twenty dollar bill. She quickly adds his chips to the bag and gives him the new total.

"Give her the change," he says, moving past me to grab the grocery bag.

I couldn't be more humiliated as the cashier hands me the money—which is saying something, because I've been embarrassed on several occasions in this grocery store. Being poor sucks.

"You really didn't have to do that," I murmur.

Vince shrugs, like it's nothing. I look at the $14 in my hand like it's printed on gold.

The difference between us couldn't be more pronounced.

"You could invite me to dinner to thank me," he teases, waiting for me to wheel my sister toward the door.

"You want to come over for dinner?" I say, my disbelief evident.

"Well, I haven't eaten any yet," he says, like that makes all the sense in the world.

"With my siblings?" I add, now really looking at him like he's crazy.

"Hey, I work with what I'm given," he states.

I automatically wheel the cart outside, but once we get to the car and I realize we're more or less alone with Vince, my discomfort seeps back in.

Lowering my voice, I tell him, "You don't have to keep an eye on me, you know."

"Maybe I *want* to keep an eye on you," he returns, meeting my gaze.

I swallow. "Why?"

He merely shrugs, opening my passenger door and placing the grocery bag inside. "I'll meet you at your house."

I want to argue—I *don't* necessarily want to be alone with the guy who broke into my house the night before, but I know it won't do much good. If Vince wants to come over for dinner, he'll come over for dinner—whether he's invited or not.

# CHAPTER FIVE

HE DOESN'T get there right away. I hustle my siblings inside and get them situated with drinks and activities, nervously watching the door for his arrival. I start dinner anyway, since I'm cooking the same thing even if he doesn't show up.

But he does. And he brings garlic bread, which makes him an instant hero to my little brother and sister. Had I known Vince was going to give me a twenty at the register, I would've maybe agreed to the garlic bread, but they didn't understand that. Where possible, I try to keep our money problems from them. I haven't always, but one day when Mom and I were trying to figure out how to pay a utility bill in front of them, I noticed my brother listening, his little face anxious.

Since then, I don't mention money problems until they're in bed.

I'm attending the pasta on the stove when I feel him come up behind me. Fear is definitely present, but I try to mask it. He's not going to hurt me, he's just… stalking me.

Sure, that sounds right.

Clearing my throat, I ask, "How'd you know they wanted garlic bread?"

"Gotta have garlic bread with spaghetti," he says, leaning against the counter so he can look at me. "Plus, the boy asked for it on the way to the register."

I don't remember that, but I'd been pretty sidetracked by him. Automatically preheating the oven, I let my mind wander. If he's following me to the store, that means he followed me to the preschool to pick up Casey first, then the elementary school to get Allan. He couldn't have, right? I would have noticed.

I hadn't been looking though. I thought—hoped—that we resolved the matter the night before.

"What's on your mind?" he asks.

I realize I'm being oddly quiet, lost in my own thoughts, but... well, it seems warranted. "You followed me?"

He doesn't confirm or deny, folding his arms across his chest and simply watching me.

Even though it is what I believe, I feel arrogant having spoken the words. "I mean, you said you were just at the grocery store, but you obviously weren't buying anything. And I didn't even go straight there." I stop, suddenly hit with the memory of his insinuation last night about my brother and sister's videos, about them sleeping down the hall. My blood runs cold, realizing if he followed me when I left school, he knows where *they* go to school now.

My eyes shoot to his face for verification, but his expression is carefully blank. Swallowing, feeling vaguely like I'm going to throw up, I say, "You followed me to their schools."

He knew I was picking them up, because he heard my conversation with my mother the night before.

I turn and look back at Allan, who trusts him now, all because he brought a damn bag of garlic bread.

Suddenly angry, I turn back to glare at Vince. "Stop it."

Still expressionless, he says, "Didn't do anything."

Jabbing a finger against my chest, I say, "*I* am the only person involved in this. *Me*. My brother and sister have nothing to do with this, and if you threaten them...." I trail off, because I have nothing to threaten him with. What, I'll go to the police? I'm not a fool. I can't make a threat like that and expect him to trust me to keep my mouth shut. If I'm not careful, I could wind up dead.

Suddenly overcome with the weight of this goddamn burden, I shake my head, shrinking a little. "I'm *not* going to say *anything*."

"So you said."

"And you still followed me! You followed me to their schools." I stop, glancing back to make sure they aren't listening. "I told you that you could trust me, and you still followed me. What am I supposed to take away from that?"

Inclining his head slightly, he takes a moment to formulate a response. Finally, not looking at me, he says, "I am trying to trust you, but a little extra incentive never hurt."

"Threatening my family is not how you get what you want from me," I warn him.

Quirking an eyebrow as if amused, he asks, "Then how do I?"

Exasperated, I say, "You've already *got* it. I swear to God, my lips are sealed. Just… leave me alone."

He eyes me up, but I can't tell what he's thinking. "Is that what you want?"

My eyes bulge. "Yes!"

For a moment, he says nothing, just stands there with his arms still crossed. Eventually he drops them, stepping away from the counter with a nod.

I don't know what he's doing as he steps away, and even as he walks toward the door I don't fully trust it. But then he opens the door, turns the lock, and slips out.

"Where's he going?" Allan demands, leaning over the arm of the couch and looking from me to the door.

I don't answer immediately, unsure myself. "I think he had to go home."

"Why? Did he leave the garlic bread?"

I can't help but scoff at the selfishness of children. I glance at the untouched loaf of garlic bread on the counter, and even though it's *absurd*, I suddenly feel the crushing weight of guilt on my shoulders. I tell myself that's stupid, incredibly stupid—he followed me when I left school, he left unspoken threats on the table *again*, and all this *after* I watched him walk out of a house fire that resulted in two deaths.

It's *insane* to feel guilty that I didn't want him to stay for dinner.

But somehow I still do.


I sit in class, anxiously pulling at the creased corner of my red notebook. I'm waiting to see who drops into the seat beside me—Cody

Miller, or Vince.

Cody comes in first. I don't know whether to feel relieved or disappointed.

Then he cruises right past the open desk beside me to the one he's been sitting in for the past two days.

Vince gets there, just before the bell. He takes a seat, not looking at me, but I can't stop looking at him. I could barely sleep all last night, going over and over and over our interlude at dinner. During one of the rounds, I realized he *hadn't* actually threatened my siblings. He hadn't even confirmed that was why he followed me, though I couldn't imagine why else he would.

But he left when I said I wanted him to. If he wanted to threaten and intimidate me, why leave? It's not like I could've made him leave. Even if he *would* have threatened me, right to my face, I would have still had to sit at the table across from him, in the company of my siblings, if that was what he wanted.

As absurd as it is, I can't shake the idea that maybe I hurt his feelings.

The fact that he won't look at me, even though he has to feel me staring a hole straight through him, is doing nothing to ease that guilt.

The bell rings and the teacher launches into her lecture. I steal the occasional glance at Vince, but he never looks my way.

It feels like the longest class ever. At the end, the teacher finally hands back our assignments and the bell signals our temporary freedom.

Vince is up and out of his seat before I can shove mine in my binder. That's not a problem, I know that rationally, but inexplicably, I launch out of my seat and hustle out to the hall to try to catch up to him.

"Hey!"

He slows, glancing back over his shoulder with a confused frown.

He's really cute when he's semi-glaring, but that's totally inappropriate, so I shove the thought away. My face flames anyway, not because of that, but because he does look mad at me.

But he stops. I guess he wouldn't ignore me though, given our little secret.

My books slip, since I was in such a hurry to leave class. I smile a little awkwardly, shifting their weight and readjusting. He's still watching me expectantly, and I have no idea what to say, so I settle with an inane, "What's up?"

Both dark brows shoot up as he stares at me. "Nothing?"

I feel utterly ridiculous, but I decide just to spill it. It's not like I've been shining my brightest around here up until now. "I'm sorry if I hurt your feelings yesterday. I didn't mean to."

He rears back a little, clearly surprised, but doesn't immediately respond.

"I just… I don't know how to do this. I don't know how to put your mind at ease about me, and it makes me really nervous and fearful when I think you're threatening me. Which, I realize, is the point, but—"

He looks around the hall, grabbing me by the wrist and yanking me into a nearby classroom. It's dark, closed for this period. Once inside, he backs me against a brick pillar, so people walking through the hallway won't see us. Bracing one arm against the pillar and leaning in, he asks, "Want to say that a little louder?"

"Sorry," I whisper. It doesn't feel like fear, but having him braced on the wall like this, so close to me in this dark, abandoned classroom… I'm definitely feeling *something*.

I can't read his dark brown eyes, but after a moment, still hovering near me, he says, "I didn't follow you to intimidate you. I didn't even consider that you'd be driving to their schools."

Swallowing, I ask, "Then why?"

He shrugs one shoulder. "Just wanted to see where you were going."

It's still not normal, exactly, but I get the feeling I can't expect that from him. "Why?" I ask again, still holding his gaze.

Another shrug, but nothing verbal this time. His eyes are so intense, his gaze unwavering, but there's something in the depths of his warm brown eyes, something unexpectedly… sad. It hits me harder than I expect it to, that hint of vulnerability. I don't know if he's showing it to me on purpose or not, but he's been far better at controlling facial cues than I am, so I have to imagine it's intentional.

I try to remind myself of the dark knowledge I have about him, but it doesn't make it through. Right now, I'm not afraid of Vince.

I'm attracted to him.

And I think he's attracted to me.

He leans away from me, his arm no longer on the brick pillar behind me, and a strange jolt of disappointment shoots through me. I don't want him to move away—that's crazy, and there's no reason he wouldn't, but…

Before I can shuffle away, he's grabbing my books. I falter a bit, but he drops them on the desk behind him and comes right back.

I exhale sharply, backing up against the brick pillar, but this time he moves closer, bracing his weight again, the other hand landing on my hip.

He has me pinned against the wall. My heart hammers against my chest, and my mind races, trying to sort it all out—his hand is on my hip. He's really close—really, really close.

And then: "Can I kiss you?"

It sounds like I gasp, but I think I was just trying to breathe. I should speak, but I can't find my words. Instead, I nod.

He leans in almost tentatively, as if giving me time to change my mind, and then his lips connect with mine. At first it's a light brush of his lips, softer than I expect, knocking what little guard I have left away from me. His fingers tighten on my hip and I don't know what to do with my hands so they just hang there awkwardly.

Then he coaxes my lips open and his tongue skates across my lower lip. They open, instinctively, and his tongue sweeps inside, and oh, sweet Jesus, my brain suddenly explodes with adrenaline. My hands move to his sides, pulling him closer, and he obliges, flattening me against the wall. As our tongues find a rhythm that works, he fists a hand in my hair and a helpless sound escapes me. He kisses me like he's going to devour me, and to be honest, I want him to.

My hands slide up under his shirt—I don't know how or why, but it happens. With the desire coursing through me, stoked with each caress of his tongue against mine, I'd be lying if I said I didn't want to rip his shirt right off. I envision him backing me up against the teacher's desk, climbing between my legs…

Whoa, whoa, whoa. I break the kiss, pulling back. I feel a little dazed, but I'm confused and disoriented by the level of *lust* I'm experiencing. I've never been so… caught up.

Then again, I've never been kissed, not like that. Lips brushing, a couple times. Never this.

Distantly aware of the bell ringing, I lean against the brick wall, trying to catch my breath.

## Accidental Witness

No longer swept up in whatever magic his mouth was working on my brain, I'm suddenly embarrassed—not just because I let him kiss me, and I hardly know him, but because three seconds earlier, I wanted him to do more than that.

*This isn't me.*

God, what must he think of me?

"We're late," I murmur, because I don't know what else to say.

"We are," he verifies, but he doesn't seem too worried about it.

My eyes meet his fleetingly, but then I glance down, a little awkwardly. "I don't usually…"

He nods, watching me. "I figured."

"I mean, I *never*…"

His lips curve up slightly and he nods again.

Sliding away from the wall and off to the side, I move around him to grab my books. "I have to go."

He doesn't speak and I don't look back as I scurry out of the abandoned classroom and through the now-empty hall, hoping he doesn't follow.

# CHAPTER SIX

I DON'T expect to see Vince again after that kiss, so when I find him waiting by my car after school, it's a hell of a surprise. Not exactly a welcome one, either. Given the lust-monster he turned me into earlier, I want to keep a little distance from him.

He pushes off the car when he sees me, offering something like a smile.

"Hey," he greets.

"Hey," I say, hugging my books close.

"You kind of ran off earlier," he points out, by way of explanation. "I wasn't trying to follow you."

"I figured." I pause. "I mean, if you were, you probably shouldn't wait by my car and announce yourself. It's not very stealthy."

"Good note," he acknowledges.

I nod, glancing into my driver's side window. "I can't really stay and chat. I have to pick up Casey."

"I know. I'll keep it short." Shoving a hand into his right pocket, he glances down at our shoes, then back at me. "Tomorrow's Saturday."

"That does usually follow Friday, yes."

"Your mom's off, so... I figured you wouldn't have to watch the kids."

"It's weird that you know that," I point out.

Smirking, he ignores my commentary. "Why don't you come out with me? We can grab dinner or a movie or something."

My heart stalls, then drops like a rock. "You mean a date?"

He makes a face that's not altogether flattering, considering we were lip-locked earlier today. "We don't have to label it."

Oh, good, a label-hater. Glancing off in the distance, I say, "I don't think so. Earlier was really nice, but also *really* unexpected, and I don't really know you that well…"

"That's fair. Of course, you could *get* to know me if you came out with me."

That's a good point, but I don't know how to explain that I'm hesitant to trust myself alone with him. What if he kisses me and it sends lightning bolts through my brain again? What if we're alone in his car and I don't want him to stop? What if he doesn't?

"I don't understand what happened back there," I say, as honestly as I can. "And I don't know if we should do it again. Ever."

"Why not?" he asks.

"Because… we're not even dating," I state, since I guess it's the simplest explanation. I don't want to bring up the fact that he sort of murdered my neighbors, and definitely broke into my house to scare the shit out of me, and absolutely followed me home from school yesterday, if not to intimidate me and find out which schools my siblings were at, still for *some* reason.

I don't want to point out that I know he's dangerous, and maybe nurturing a relationship with him doesn't seem like the smartest move. Can't admit that when he kissed me, my brain completely crashed and I turned into a lust-monster *despite* all that.

I don't know what I'm most afraid of, but the fact that there are a host of options to choose from? Probably a good indication I should take a big step back. Especially since immediately on the heels of asking me out, he whips out "let's not label it."

It would be my luck we'd go out, he'd kiss me, I'd lose my mind and let him take my virginity, and then come Monday at school I'd see him in passing, flirting with someone else.

He's not inside my head though, so he's searching for some acceptable placation to offer me. "I just… I don't really date."

"Exactly."

He frowns, uncomprehending.

"Look, I'm not going to pretend I'm not drawn to this whole 'bad boy' thing you've got going on. I am. I have a type, and you're sort of like… the bad boy on steroids, because it's not just an air of danger, you're *actually* dangerous. You're the real deal. And I'm attracted to you anyway, obviously. Even though you've scared the shit out of me and made me lose… just, countless hours of sleep, and that probably means there's something wrong with me. But I've seen my mom turn herself inside out over guys like that, guys who come at you with all they've got, but can't be held. And I *know* it's stupid, no matter how exciting it feels in the moment, and I know it's asking for trouble, and that's with guys who… don't have your last name. With you, it's not just unhealthy, it's also legitimately dangerous."

I force myself to look at him after spilling all that, expecting him to be insulted, annoyed, maybe defensive. Instead, he's pensive, frowning off at a spot beyond me. "I can't argue with that."

If I feel disappointed, it's because I descend from a long line of stupid fucking women.

"But it's not dangerous if we don't label it."

Shaking my head, I say, "How do you figure?"

"Look, I'm not saying we could last forever. I'm not even saying it's a good idea. But I like you, and it seems like you're drawn to me—"

"And a moth is drawn to a flame," I interject.

"*But,* why couldn't we just… try it out for a little bit? Doesn't have to be anything serious. You're not stuck with me. I won't dump you in a ditch if it doesn't work out."

Shaking my head at the sheer lunacy of such a proposition, I say, "*Why?*"

Vince stares at me, that vulnerability from earlier dancing in his eyes again. I can tell he wants to say something, but he's struggling to get it out, and damn me to hell, it gets me. I wait, skittish, but convincible.

He swallows, looking away from me, then meets my eyes again. "You know awful things about me that *no one* knows. That no one may ever know… and you still care if you hurt my feelings."

I can almost hear my brain emit a cry of defeat as my heart swells, seeing something in him that needs me.

*Stay strong.*

Poor brain tries one last time, but it's no use—not with those big, brown pools imploring me to give in.

## Accidental Witness

*Don't do it, don't do it, don't do it!*

When my mouth opens, dumbassery spills out. "What time?"

But then his handsome face lights up, and my heart fills with anticipation. I really like seeing that look on his face, knowing I put it there.

"I'll pick you up at six."

Despite the certainty that this is a very bad idea, I can't help smiling as he winks at me and heads off for his car.

Scowling at my reflection, I rip the shirt over my head, tossing it in the floor with the others, and race to my closet. I settled on a pair of snug jeans and tall brown boots, but I can't seem to find the right shirt. It doesn't help that I really don't know what we're doing.

"Not that one either," I murmur, violently sliding plastic hangers across the pole in my closet.

There's a rap at the door and I gasp, grabbing a shirt and yanking it on. "Don't get it!" I call out, not even wanting to deal with my mom. "I'm coming!"

I pause at the dresser to check my reflection real quick before darting out of the bedroom. The door closes behind me just in time to see my mother open the door, despite my attempts to stop her.

I sigh to myself, hoisting my purse on my shoulder and heading toward Vince.

"I'm Mia's mom, Shelly," she says with an overly enthusiastic smile.

Nodding once, hands shoved into his pockets, he says, "Vince."

"Vince, that's a good name. You know each other from school?"

Sliding past her, as if putting myself between them can erase the exchange, I say, "We're leaving."

"Well, okay, but I guess I should probably give you a curfew or something, right?"

"No need," I assure her. "We won't be out late."

"This is so weird." Looking past me at Vince, she says, "Usually I'm the one going on dates."

It amuses me how she says that like *that's* the normal order of things. Without any further damage, I manage to get us out the door, but my face is already warm. I *had* hoped to at least start our is-this-a-date? without flushed cheeks. High hopes, I guess.

Vince surprises me by opening the door for me when we get to his car. His eyes move over my body, a cute little smirk grazing his lips. "You look nice."

"Thank you," I said, my eyes moving quickly over him, too. "So do you."

Turns out we're doing dinner. I decide I may have preferred the quiet of a movie theater, but we've already pulled into a well-lit parking lot of a steakhouse I've never been to. I don't know why I figured we'd get Italian, but I don't mention it.

I feel girly and awkward as we sit at the tall table across from each other, my fingers dancing across the white linen tablecloth, looking for something to do. I need something—anything—to distract me from the reality of what I'm doing right now. Having dinner with the guy who, just a few nights ago, pinned me against my kitchen counter and wrapped his hands around my throat, making a threat he may actually be capable of following through with.

Yeah. *Good* call.

I'm also legitimately terrified this goes well. If it goes well, he may kiss me, and I'm afraid of him kissing me again, maybe more than I'm afraid of anything else he might do.

"So…you have a big family."

His smile dims and I fight a cringe, wondering what could possibly possess me to lead with *that*.

"Yeah, pretty big," he verifies.

"That's cool. I don't. There's my mom and my siblings, but we don't have a lot of extended family, none in the area. I have an aunt who used to live here, but she moved."

I hear myself being boring. I want to stop, but words just keep tumbling out of my mouth like gumballs from a broken vending machine.

"Your family—um, are they all, I mean—uh…" How does one ask about the mob?

"Bad?" he guesses, with an almost sympathetic smile.

I look around, at a loss. I sort of just want to get up and leave. I'll have to change schools, so I never have to look at him again.

Chuckling, Vince says, "You don't have to be so nervous, Mia. It's not even a real date, remember?"

I'm not sure why he thinks that makes me feel *better*, but I'm not comfortable enough to say so.

I must still be looking like I'm seeking an emergency exit, but he goes ahead and answers the question I didn't completely ask. "Yeah, they're all pretty much… involved. I really don't want to talk about them tonight, though."

"Does anyone know what I saw?" I blurt.

His face clears for a moment, goes completely blank, before a hint of caution breaks through. "No. Nor can they—ever."

I nod, not exactly comforted, but it makes sense.

Luckily, the waiter comes over and saves us from our own conversation, taking our drink orders and telling us the specials. He tells us he'll give us a few minutes to look over our menus, then heads off to grab our drinks.

I turn to the safety of my menu, wishing I could shake my nerves. Maybe subconsciously I figure if I bomb this not-date hard enough, he won't ask again.

Won't kiss me again.

Won't turn me into an unthinking lust-monster again.

Won't draw me any deeper into his crazy life.

We order when the waiter comes back, but his departure then means he won't be coming back to save me again soon, and I'm on my own here.

Vince moves the rolled-up silverware off to the side, then glances up at me. "So, are you this comfortable on all your dates?"

I can't help rolling my eyes. "This isn't a date, remember? Can't fence you in," I joke—but only kinda. I do sort of resent that. It's all the more reason to make sure he doesn't kiss me again. I don't even know why I agreed to this nonsense.

No, that's not true.

That damn peek at vulnerability.

"I am normally much smoother than this, actually," I inform him, lifting my eyebrows.

There's a playful gleam to his eyes as he says, "With Bradford?"

"No, we never got to go out. I was trying to call him… that night, but…." I clear my throat. "Well, I obviously got sidetracked."

Vince isn't impressed with my taste in guys, which is pretty funny. "What'd you see in that guy anyway?"

It seems stupid now. I can't explain it. I sigh and offer a shrug, hoping that suffices.

His eyebrows shoot up and he doesn't look completely satisfied, but he doesn't press. "You still wanna call him?"

"I wouldn't be here with you if I did," I tell him honestly.

"He still watches you in class sometimes."

I frown, pushing the straw into my cup and taking a drink of my Diet Coke. I haven't picked up on a shred of interest from Jace since Vince stole the seat next to mine, so I can't imagine that being true. Also, not-date or date-date, this seems like an odd thread of conversation.

"What about you?" I return pleasantly. "Not-dating a harem of other girls?"

He smiles, shaking his head. "Just you."

That pleases me, even if it shouldn't.

Sooner than I expect, the waiter brings our salads, and thankfully we have something else to focus on. I have a whole host of questions I'd like to ask him that I know I shouldn't, and the instinct to push him away is still pretty strong.

His phone goes off halfway through the salads, but he doesn't answer.

There's more silence than I expect, but it's much more comfortable than I would've thought it would be. I like watching him when he doesn't notice. There are questions I have about him that I can't ask, and in those quiet moments, I seek an answer.

How can someone do what he did and then go on about their life? We're the same age, and I can't even fathom having someone else's life in my hands, let alone taking one. Just the possibility of Vince threatening my family was more than I could take—how does he handle the weight of the guilt? Doesn't he feel it? Doesn't it crush him, as he lies in bed at night, trying to sleep?

Has he done it before?

Will he do it again?

Is he a monster?

Noticing my newly solemn mood, Vince asks, "Everything okay over there?"

I glance up at him, nodding, but I wish I hadn't let my mind wander there. "What's your biggest regret?" I ask him.

I hear his fork drop onto his salad plate, but I don't look up. I expect him to tell me I already know, or to get mad that I would bring it up. If I helped kill someone, I probably wouldn't want anyone to bring it up on a date.

I do not expect him to state matter-of-factly, "Being born."

Wide-eyed, I jerk my gaze up to his. He doesn't look especially depressed, like you might expect of someone who says something like that. He takes a drink of his own pop, as if unbothered.

"Being born?" I question. "That's your biggest regret."

"Being born into the family I was born into, specifically," he says, nodding once more. "But if it came down to being born to them or not being born at all, I wouldn't choose the former."

A little stunned, I say, "Wow."

He shrugs, unapologetic.

"You must really hate them," I say, feeling awkward to word it that way, but what else could I surmise from what he just said?

"I don't hate them. It's just… a trap. A prison. In this day and age, most people don't have a path set out for them before they're even born—before they're even conceived. Most guys would be able to sit here with you tonight and call it a date. They wouldn't have met you the way I did. They could be normal, offer you whatever they felt like offering you. I don't have that kind of freedom."

I'm surprised by his openness, even if I don't understand all of it. "You don't think your family would approve of me?"

"Doesn't matter if they would," he says, simply. "I'd never let them meet you."

A knot forms in my stomach. "Never? Not even if we… moved past not-dating and actually….?"

He's already shaking his head, but he looks a little sad. "That can't happen."

A spark of anger ignites within me. "Why? No one in your family *dates*?"

Instead of answering me, he asks, "What's *your* biggest regret?"

I want to say *trying to call Jace Bradford*, but it's too mean. I'm also not sure it's true, as insane as that is. Even as he's sitting across from me adding foundation to the idea that nothing can ever last between us, I feel myself wanting to draw closer. Wanting to know him. Wanting to be the special person who makes it past his defenses.

Finally, with a faint sigh, I say, "I don't think I've done it yet."

## CHAPTER SEVEN

I MANAGE to end the not-date with my virginity intact, and even though I know logically that's not much of an accomplishment, it feels like one.

I didn't let him kiss me.

He wanted to, I could see it, but I was too afraid. Too much about him acts as a siren's call to me already, and I couldn't risk it.

As I hurry inside the house by myself, shutting the door behind me and leaning heavily against it, it doesn't feel like a win. I wanted a kiss. It was a weird not-date, nothing like I've been on before, but there's something so raw about Vince, so unexpectedly forthcoming.

I want him. Physically I can accept that—I'm human, and he's a damn good-looking guy—but I'm terrified of wanting him on any other level.

It's a bad situation, and I need to get out of it.

But also… I don't know if I want to.

I spend yet another night losing sleep over Vince Morelli. It occurs to me around three in the morning that we should probably exchange phone numbers. The way things are going now, the only way I get to hear from him is in school or if he decides to show up.

Monday morning rolls around and I feel weirdly excited to go to school. I'm tired, having slept like crap all weekend, but I'm eager to see Vince.

"Guess who's going to Costa Rica, baby."

I shove my after lunch books into my locker and look over at Lena as she beams at me. "Me? Say it's me and I'll be your best friend forever."

"No."

I roll my eyes, closing my locker door. "Well, good for you," I say flatly.

"No, not me! My mom and dad—they're going away for the weekend, and *we* are having a party."

"No," I say, shaking my head. "I'm not helping you with that."

"You *have* to. Why are we even best friends if you're not going to help me throw a party? I mean, literally all you have to do is pick up some bags of chips or some shit. I'll get the alcohol."

"I don't have any spare money to buy chips."

"I'll give you the money," she says, rolling her eyes. "We haven't gotten drunk together since Macedonia's graduation party over the summer—and that barely counts, since your weak ass got drunk on two beers."

"It was my first time!" I defend.

"Whatever. I don't even care what you say, you're coming. We're going to get stupid and sing in front of our peers, and take awesome selfies. It's already done. You have no say."

"I'm probably going to have to babysit," I point out.

"Tell your mom to get a sitter for once in her damn life; they're not your kids, Jesus Christ."

We can't afford a sitter, but I don't say that. Foolishly, it occurs to me that I could probably bring Vince to that. "Is it going to be a big group, or just a small get-together?"

"Medium-ish," she says. "I don't really want everyone to stay over, and I'm not inviting anyone with super uptight parents. Don't need that drama."

Hesitantly, I ask, "Would you care if I invited somebody?"

She stops, turning to me with interested eyes. "Jace?"

"No," I say, a little too adamantly. "Are you inviting Jace?"

"Probably. I thought you'd be pleased?"

"Uh uh," I say, shaking my head. "Jace is old news. No more Jace."

She sounds surprised. "Really? Huh. That didn't last very long. Why don't you tell me this stuff? That's literally what I'm here for."

"It's super new and casual at the moment. I don't want to make a big thing of it. But… it might be fun if he could come."

"Who?"

I try not to grimace as I say, "Vince Morelli?"

The smile drops right off my best friend's face. "Vince Morelli?"

I nod, almost apologetically.

"You want me to invite the *mob kid* to my house? For real?" She reaches out her hand and feels my forehead. "Weird, you're not burning up with fucking delusional fever."

"I know he's not part of our usual crowd, but…"

"The fucking governor's son is going to be there, Mia, and you want me to invite *Goodfellas*?"

It's not like Lena's bluntness is news, but she's starting to piss me off. "You don't have to be mean."

Staring at me, she asks, "Are you sleeping with him?"

"Not—" I halt, flushing, realizing I almost said 'not yet' instead of 'no'. "Just forget it."

"Ew, you are!" she says, gaping.

I make a face. "I'm not. But ew? Come on."

"His family does heinous shit, Mia. The package might look pretty on the outside, but Jesus Christ. My dad says they do, like, human trafficking. That's third world bullshit, right there. There's no way in hell I could invite him, Mia. Even if my dad wouldn't lose literally all of his shit if he found out, I wouldn't do that."

"It's not like he would know," I mutter, but at this point, I'm out of steam on this argument. Even if she gave in and agreed to invite him, I would be too afraid she'd make Vince feel unwelcome now.

"No," she says, raising her eyebrows and shaking her head.

"Well, I'm not on board for a party anyway," I tell her with a quick shrug. "If you want to hang out, I can hang out, but I can't get away for a whole night with drinking and… the governor's son's kind of a twatwaffle anyway, so…"

"You won't come to my party because I don't want to invite Vince Morelli," she says, staring at me in disbelief.

"It's not because of that," I say, trying to brush it off.

"Bullshit. Hoes before bros, bitch. What are you doing?"

"I'm always the one that makes sacrifices," I snap. I don't mean to say it, even if it's true. "I'm always the one who comes to the group hangout even though you invited the chick who made out with Jensen when we were dating, or totally overlooks the fact that—knowing how much I liked him, you made out with Jace at the Fourth of July cookout, or—actually, can people just stop making out with every guy I'm interested in? Hey, maybe you can go make out with Vince now, or did I finally pick someone too beneath you?"

Lena's jaw hangs open, disbelieving that her passive bestie is the one being a bitch for once.

"You need to take some fucking Midol," she informs me, before ditching me to head to her first class alone.

Unsurprisingly, after that stupid fight with Lena, my day drags ass. I do finally perk up when I get to my class with Vince, even if he gets there just before the bell again.

At least when class is over, he doesn't rush out again. I walk out with him.

"You look tired," he observes.

"Thanks," I return, dryly. He's not wrong though.

Flicking a glance in my direction, he asks, "Wanna get out of here?"

I blink in surprise. "What do you mean?"

Cocking his head to the side, he says, "Let's bail."

"You want to ditch?"

"We can get some pizza before you have to pick up the kids."

That's an offer too tempting to refuse, and since I *did* alienate my lunch companion this morning, I spent lunch studying instead of eating.

"Will we get in trouble?" I ask.

In response, Vince rolls his eyes.

Twenty minutes later, sitting across from Vince as we split an enormous sausage pizza, I feel confident we made the right decision.

Picking a piece of sausage off and preparing to toss it in my mouth, I say, "Man, I never get toppings."

Eyes wide, he says, "Why?"

Chewing and swallowing the piece of sausage, I say, "Kids. They just like cheese. Or pepperoni, so they can pick it off and still only eat the cheese."

## Accidental Witness

"Makes sense," he says, breaking off a second piece of pizza. A gooey gob of cheese stretches until it finally breaks, and he piles it on top before taking a bite.

"This place is good," I say, taking a drink from the red tinted plastic cup.

"You've never been here?"

I shake my head no. "We thought about trying it a couple times, but never did."

Truth is, they just never have any good enough specials. There's another pizza place nearby where you can get the same size pizza for less than half the price.

"How long have you lived here?" he asks, glancing at me across the table.

"Three years. I mean, we still lived in Chicago before that, but we were in the metro area. Before that, we lived in Boston—my mom's actually from there. And then we lived way the hell outside of Chicago for a little while. My mom moved us in with her boyfriend and his sister and her three kids. It was terrible. Luckily the stress of living in a hell house broke that relationship down in a matter of months, but then my mom met this guy, Frank, and they started seeing each other. Frank lived in this neighborhood, and he wanted my mom to move closer—or so she said, because they were going to live together. Now, I don't want to shock you to death here, but it's outside of what we can afford—literally double what we were paying for our last place, but it was totally fine, because she and Frank were going to be together and Frank made a comfortable living."

"But that never happened," he surmised, nodding.

"It didn't, because Frank? *Married*. So, we were stuck in a year and a half lease, living in a rental house we couldn't afford, and now here we are."

"Why did you guys stay after the year and a half?"

I throw my hands up in a dramatic shrug. "She said she didn't want to uproot us again. I didn't complain, because I like living in a house instead of an apartment, but the stress of living so far above our means is… not awesome. We have to pay so much for rent and utilities that, as you saw at the grocery store, we don't have money to live."

"That sucks," he says, sympathetically.

"It does. And our lease is going to be up here soon, but I don't think she's going to renew again. Her boyfriend now lives in the city, and I don't know how she thinks to cram all of us in his two-bedroom apartment, but it seems like that's her new plan."

"He have kids?"

"No. He's young." I shake my head, fatigued just thinking about my mother's relationships.

"Bet you'll be glad to go to college, get away from it all," he says.

"I don't think we'll be able to afford it. Lena's going to Boston College; she wanted me to go there with her, but there's no way. I'm going to take a year off, get a job, get everything sorted. Then we'll see."

"They have scholarships," he pointed out.

I shrug, not really wanting to talk about it. "What about you? Are you going off to college, or staying local?"

"No college," he says, looking at the pizza instead of me.

Frowning, I ask, "Why?" It's not like his family can't afford it.

His lips tug up in a tiny, humorless smile. "Don't need it in my line of work."

Ah, well… sure. I swallow, watching him as he continues to avoid my gaze. "Is it… um… I mean, obviously I only know what I've seen in the movies and TV shows, but you couldn't just opt out, if you wanted?"

Shaking his head slightly, he says, "No. Mateo would have to let me out, and he never would."

"Why not?"

"Because he's an asshole."

I nod, glancing down at my pizza. "Who's Mateo again? He's the boss? Or…?"

"Yeah, more or less. His dad's still the head of the family from a patriarchal sense, but Mateo's the *de facto* head."

"Is it like The Sopranos?" I ask, immediately feeling dumb when he smirks at me.

"No." He laughs a little, dropping his pizza on the plate. "Actually, my family's not exactly what you're thinking. We're not part of the original Sicilian mafia. Al Capone, all that stuff you've seen—that's not really us."

"Oh. It's not? But I thought…"

"No. My family started it here—not in Italy, I've never been there, I probably never will. We aren't *them*, it's just... we're an Italian crime family that goes back four generations—what are people gonna call us, you know?"

"So you're not...?" I'm frowning, confused. "What's the difference?"

"We just do things our own way. We're like self-made bad guys, I guess. Think of the actual mob like old money, and my family like new money. Outsiders might just have one name for us, but to us, there's a distinction. Like, in the *actual* mafia, it's not as blood-obsessed as my family. We have people—soldiers, associates—who aren't related to us, but the core people? All family. With only one exception, all blood related. Our family has *broods* of children—my father's one of seven. It's patriarchal—Mateo's dad was the boss before him, his dad was the boss before him, his dad was the boss before him. Mateo doesn't have a son yet, but when he does..."

"Next boss," I conclude.

He nods once. "Unless something happened to interrupt the line, of course. If someone ever successfully assassinates Mateo, things might change."

"Jeeze," I say, eyes wide. "No love lost?"

"Hm?"

I smile slightly. "It's just weird to hear someone speak so casually of a family member potentially being assassinated."

"They're all bastards," he says, lowly. "Every man in my family. Mateo's line's the worst though. His dad's a sick fuck, and Mateo didn't turn out much better."

"What about your dad?" I ask, playing with my straw.

"Sick fuck. If the last name is Morelli and they possess a penis, just assume they're sick fucks."

I crack a smile. "*You're* not a sick fuck."

"We'll see," he says, as if it doesn't really matter. Picking up his pizza, he says, "Anyway, we shouldn't really be talking about this."

"I like getting to know things about your life," I tell him.

Nodding slightly, he says, "I understand that, but I don't want to involve you in that stuff. I want to keep you separate."

"I won't say anything to anyone," I tell him, plucking another piece of sausage off my pizza. "It must be exhausting, worrying about keeping your whole life secret and segmented like that. You don't have to do that with me."

I look up and catch him watching me, a fond gleam in his eye that instantly unleashes a swarm of butterflies in my stomach. I offer a shy smile in response, then I ruin it by popping another sausage into my mouth.

# CHAPTER EIGHT

"YOUR BOYFRIEND was talking to some other chick before school—they looked cozy."

I look up as Lena's tray smacks the cafeteria table, noting she looks both smug and bitchy. "Excuse me?"

"Just thought I'd tell you," she states.

"What girl?" I ask, frowning slightly.

"A really pretty one. Think Minka Kelly. I don't have any classes with her, so I don't know." Affecting a fake look of surprise, she says, "I guess I won't have to make out with him after all!"

I roll my eyes, wishing she'd just let it go. We're talking again, but she's still making the odd snide comment. I didn't say anything that wasn't true, and I'm not apologizing this time just to keep the peace.

I ignore her comment, glancing around the cafeteria. "Is she here? Point her out to me."

She rolls her eyes, picking up one half of her turkey wrap. "I don't know, I didn't look."

I wrinkle up my nose, picking at the crust of my peanut butter and jelly. "Great. Well, thanks for that."

Sighing heavily, she says, "Jesus. I'll find out."

"He's not even my boyfriend," I mutter. Our lack of label hasn't come up again the few times we've hung out lately, but I don't imagine he's changed his mind.

"You obviously want him to be," she says, unimpressed. "You have such shit taste in men, Mia."

"You don't even know him," I point out.

"Nor do I want to," she replies, popping the top off her green tea. "Blaine's into you; you should go out with Blaine."

Wrinkling my nose up, I say, "Blaine's too polo team."

"He's not on the polo team. We don't *have* a polo team. I mean, water polo, but…"

"He's on the *rowing* team. He's too…all-American, polo shirt wearing, Harvard-going…"

Nodding in fake agreement, she says, "Yeah, guys with actual futures are the worst. You're right. Good call. Don't know what I was thinking."

"He's just not my type."

She rolls her eyes, clearly unimpressed with whatever my type is. "You should get a prison pen pal, then you can meet someone more your type."

"Why don't we talk about something else," I suggest, growing bored of her criticism.

"Look, I just don't want to see you get hurt—figuratively *or* literally. If they go all *Taken* on your ass, you don't have Liam Neeson to bail you out."

"Hey, Liam Neeson could be my dad, we don't know," I joke.

Shaking her head at me like I'm the novelty of her life, she says, "How did I ever find you?"

The one night I'm not having trouble sleeping, I'm jostled awake by the weight of a body curling up beside me.

I don't immediately wake up—at least, not without a fight. It's dark, I'm bleary, and a glance at my alarm clock shows me it's just after 3am.

I sigh, rolling over. Allan must've had a bad dream, and Mom must not be home.

Only it isn't Allan. It's Vince. In my bed, at 3am.

My eyes go wide, still burning from sleep, but… well, I don't understand what the hell is going on.

"Vince?" I murmur.

"Sorry. Didn't mean to wake you."

# Accidental Witness

I blink, rolling over and double checking the clock. Yep, 3am. I turn back to Vince, frowning in confusion. "Um… what are you doing here?"

"Just wanted to see you," he says quietly.

I want to say he could've called, but he still hasn't given me his phone number. I asked. He said no. Still, I'm not sure how he arrived at "I know, I'll break into her house again and crawl into her bed while she sleeps."

"You're such a creeper," I say lightly, reaching out and brushing my hand along his cheek.

He cracks a smile, but my mood dips when I realize he looks sad.

Curling closer to him, I ask, "What's wrong?"

He doesn't answer, just scoots closer, wrapping his arms around me and pulling me against him. We don't speak for a long time, he just holds me, and I do my best to hold him back. My mind works harder than it needs to, guessing what might be wrong. The night of the fire slips to the front of my mind, and I wonder if he could have done something like that again. I don't want to know if he did, but I'll listen if he needs to tell me.

A wave of fierce protectiveness rolls over me and I hug him tighter.

After I squeeze him, it seems to bring him to life. His grip loosens enough for him to lean back and look down at me, but instead of speaking, he leans in and kisses me. Unprepared, I gasp against his mouth, and he wastes no time, deepening the kiss. Arousal stirs within me again, and I'm hyper aware we're in my bed. I can't afford to turn into a lust-monster at 3am in my own bed. This time it's his hand that slides up my shirt, and because I'm in bed and wasn't expecting company, I'm braless. His hand comes up to palm my breast, startling me, then his lips leave mine and begin a trail down the sensitive skin of my neck instead.

"Oh," I murmur, failing in my attempt to stifle a moan as gooseflesh rises up all over my body. "Vince." I brace a hand on his shoulder, the other on his side, and somehow he's already on top of me. I don't try to move him off, but I open my mouth to tell him we need to keep a lid on things—I don't get to, though, as his mouth is on mine again, sweeping the thoughts clear out of my head. The weight of him against my pelvis has me throbbing between my legs, and we've barely even kissed.

"We need to—" I try again to tell him we need to hit the brakes, but he's kissing me again, and then my hands are in his hair, his hands under my shirt, thumbs brushing nipples, and the common sense is gone. Sensation takes over, each caress of his hand feeding my need.

When his hand slips inside the waistband of my pajama pants, I don't try to stop him. My knees fall apart, anticipating his touch. When his finger pushes inside me, I let my head fall back, closing my eyes. Surrendering my body, without knowing where it will lead. It's terrifying and exhilarating at the same time.

It's harder than I expect to stay quiet while he pleasures me, but when I come, his mouth covers mine, muffling the cry I can't keep in.

Sated, vulnerable, I curl up in his arms afterward. He lets me, embracing me snugly again, but now I can feel a certain bulge that I imagine is probably uncomfortable for him. Squeezing my hand down between our bodies, I rub him through his jeans, enjoying the sounds of his moans for a minute. Then I ease out of his grip, sliding down his body.

He looks down at me. "You don't have to do that."

"I want to," I tell him quietly, tugging his jeans down until I can get between his legs. A moment later, I'm brushing my hair back over my shoulder and leaning down to take him into my mouth.

Before long, he's groaning, coming in my mouth. He didn't warn me, but I don't mind. I swallow, creeping back up until I'm snuggled up next to him again.

He kisses me on the forehead and holds me tight, resting his chin on top of my head.

"Thank you," he murmurs.

"Mm hmm," I murmur back. I wait a few seconds before adding, "Are you okay?"

"Yeah. I just want to hold you for a little longer."

I smile, closing my eyes. That's sweet. "I really like you," I murmur against his chest.

I feel a little laugh burst out of him, then he says, "Yeah, I really like you, too."

The loathsome blaring of my alarm is the next thing to wake me, and I'm decidedly less pleased about that disturbance.

## Accidental Witness

Jerking awake, I realize I have no recollection of Vince leaving. I look at the spot beside me in bed, but it's empty. No Vince.

The whole time I'm showering, doing hair, getting dressed, applying make-up, I'm thinking of the night before. I don't know what it's going to be like to see him in broad daylight, remembering his fingers inside of me the night before, bringing me to sheet-clutching orgasm in my own bed.

That was unexpected. I'm not sure if I'm relieved or disappointed it didn't go any further than it did, but I'm still a little baffled that it happened at all. He never explained why he came over, beyond wanting to hold me. I guess it's a good reason, but I maintain he should give me a way of getting in touch with him instead of breaking in when he wants to see me.

Then I get to school, and this time I'm the one who sees Vince with the Minka Kelly girl. Vince has more of an olive complexion himself, but she's darker—Mexican? I can't tell from this angle, but I *can* tell she's gorgeous… and grinning at him, lightly smacking him on the arm. He smiles back, ducking his head, and they head into school together.

I can't get my feet to move. My brain tells me to follow, to approach him, to say hello. She's probably just a friend, and he won't be weird, he'll just introduce me, and that will be that.

But my body isn't liking the chances, apparently. It stays put, staring at the doors they just walked through. Together.

I don't see him again until English, and I can feel myself being weird. I'm relieved when he doesn't get to class until just before the bell, but I find myself wondering why. Could he have the class before with her? Maybe *all* his early classes are with her, and that's why they're so chummy? Do they go on not-dates? Does he show up in her bedroom in the middle of the night when he isn't in mine?

I torture myself with these thoughts until I'm so stressed out, my stomach actually aches.

I want to ask again if I'm the only girl he's involved with, but I don't want to seem insecure and I don't even know if he would tell the truth. My mother has confronted more than a couple cheating boyfriends in her time, and only one actually admitted to it before being caught outright.

And he isn't even my damn boyfriend.

Suddenly my feelings about the night before are sorted—I'm definitely more relieved that things didn't go any further. I don't even know what I was thinking, wanting someone who isn't even officially mine.

After class, as if nothing is wrong, Vince gives me a warm smile. "Hey, you."

"Hey," I say, but with much less affection.

"How are you this morning?"

"Good."

He nods, seeming to retreat. I guess I can't blame him, since I'm being shorter than I want to be, but he hasn't been stuck inside my head all morning.

Out of the blue I ask, "When do I get to meet your friends?"

His eyebrows rise in surprise. "My friends?"

I go for casual and give him a little shrug. "Yeah. You never talk about your friends. You know who mine are—we haven't hung out with them yet, but you know who they are."

Smiling slightly, he says, "I don't want to hang out with your friends."

Well, they don't want to hang out with him either, but I don't say that. "But you never mention yours."

"I don't really have friends here," he tells me.

"I just… I don't get to meet your family, I don't get to meet your friends…"

He slows down, wariness transforming his expression. "What's going on? Is this about last night?"

I feel so lame, but I can't help feeling weird about missing out on all the normal stuff, about how little he can actually offer me. "No, it's just… You won't even give me your phone number, Vince. You get to do whatever you want, and I get…"

I don't say 'nothing,' but I may as well have. The word hangs, unspoken, in the air between us.

He sighs, looking past me. "I told you that from the start. I told you I didn't have much to offer," Vince reminds me.

And I didn't want to get involved, I want to remind him. I want to revisit how I resisted—but I ultimately gave in, because there's this sadness in him that I feel like I should tend to.

## Accidental Witness

Finally he asks, "What do you need from me, Mia?"

But I don't know what to tell him. I need more than he can give, and yet even as that thought emerges, I shove it away. I'm not ready to give up on this. It might be foolish, it will definitely hurt more the longer I hang on, but… I'm just not.

"I don't know," I say, looking down at the ground instead of at him.

He sighs, and I'm surprised when he wraps an arm around me, giving me a loose hug right here in the middle of the hallway. "I don't want to make you sad."

"*You* don't make me sad," I tell him. "Your circumstances, maybe."

"Yeah, me too," he mutters.

"Promise me something," I tell him, swallowing my doubts. "If you start seeing someone else, you have to tell me. Don't make a fool out of me because I'm trying to make all these exceptions for you."

Vince scowls, but I can't tell why. "I wouldn't do that, Mia."

I nod, feeling a little less anxious.

He catches my chin lightly and tilts it up until I'm gazing into his earnest brown eyes. "I'm not interested in anyone but you. That's not what any of this is about. You know that, don't you?"

"It's what I believe," I say. But that's not the same thing as knowing.

He frowns a little, brushing his lips across my forehead before pulling away. "We should start walking or we're gonna be late again."

I nod, slowly making my way down the hall with him beside me.

It's a long day. I'm worn out from Vince and Lena and my own stupid brain—I'm just depleted. What I want most in the world is to go home and fall into bed, sleeping peacefully for four or five days. What I want least in the world is what actually happens.

"Hey! Hey, are you Mia?"

I slow down at the sound of my name, turning around to see who's chasing me.

And it's Minka Kelly.

I'm able to pretend for zero seconds that I'm pleased to see her. "Yeah."

"Hi," she says, grinning at me. God, she's so pretty.

"Hi," I reply, not smiling back.

"You're Vince's friend, right?"

Hearing her refer to me as Vince's *friend* is maybe the only thing that could piss me off more than I already am at the world today. "Yeah. I'm Vince's friend," I say flatly.

Her smile dims slightly, then she grimaces a little. "Sorry, he told me you guys were having a rough day."

My stomach twists up into a knot, and it takes a Herculean effort to remain there instead of turning and literally running away.

"Do you like cupcakes?" she asks.

I stare at her wordlessly.

"Vince thinks we should be friends," she says, trying again. "Sorry, I know it must be weird to be accosted by a stranger, but he asked me to."

I don't know how to feel about that, but my stomach is still knotted. I did ask to meet his friends. Maybe this is his way of trying.

Thrusting her hand in my direction, she says, "I'm Cherie."

I shake her hand, but warily. "Mia."

"Right," she says, smiling again. "Anyway, Vince's…" She pauses, her eyes rolling up as she appears to think. "Aunt? Cousin? There are so many Morellis to keep track of. Francesca's his cousin. Anyway, she runs this bakery. I thought I'd buy you a cupcake and introduce you."

My eyes widen of their own volition. I don't know if I'm more surprised that this girl has met his family (but I can't?) or that she wants to introduce me to them. My mouth starts to open to tell her that Vince doesn't want me to meet his family members, but I don't know how I can tell her that when it's clear *she* has.

"The Oreo cupcake's my favorite," she adds, trying to bust down the wall of silence.

I already feel like I hate her, but I can't deny she's charming. Her friendliness might be infectious, if not for how deeply and profoundly jealous I am of her.

"Have you met Mateo?" I ask, since it's all I can think about.

Wrinkling her nose up in displeasure, she says, "Of course. We're not going to meet him. You don't want to meet him. But Francesca's fine."

## Accidental Witness

My options are either burst into tears, or go get a cupcake.
So I nod, following this goddamn girl to get a cupcake.

I don't know why I let her drive—why I don't just ask for the address and meet her there. She talks my ear off for twenty minutes, and then finally we pull into a little brick bakery with a green awning.

"Here it is!" she says brightly. She must be so tired of talking to me, carrying the conversation more or less by herself, but you can't tell it from her cheerful demeanor as she hops out of the car and heads inside.

I try to stop thinking about this girl in Vince's life, the one he allows access to all the things he tells me I can't have, because for better or worse, I'm about to meet one of his relatives.

A ring of bells hangs on the door, chiming as Cherie opens it and heads inside. A dark-haired woman, probably in her late twenties, looks up and smiles, obviously recognizing Cherie.

"Oreo cupcake?"

"You know it," Cherie says, stepping off to the side and giving me an encouraging look as I come up to stand beside her. "This is my friend, Mia. I don't know what kind she wants, but you can put that on my tab, too."

The woman scoffs, rolling her eyes as she bends to retrieve a cupcake from the glass display case. "Tab. Right."

Cherie grins, and I can almost see why Vince is going to leave me for her. She's goddamn delightful.

Francesca slides a cupcake on a paper plate across for Cherie, then offers me a smile. "And what kind would you like, Cherie's friend?"

"Actually," Cherie puts in slyly, "she's Vince's friend."

Francesca gaze snaps to Cherie instead of me. "Vince's Mia?"

I'm stunned at that, and my jaw inches open. Why does she say that like she... *knows* of me?

Cherie bobs her head, appearing quite pleased with herself.

"I thought he wasn't going to introduce her?" Francesca questions, still at Cherie, not at me.

"He's not—not to everyone else," she says, her smile dropping. She holds up a hand, as if to slow Francesca down. "And it goes without saying, don't mention this to anyone. But Vince said she was feeling weird about not being able to meet anyone in his life, and I thought… hey, we're a part of his life!"

I have no idea how I feel about Vince apparently spilling all our business to other people when he won't even share it all with me, but I'm still reeling from the fact that his aunt-or-cousin Francesca recognized me as Vince's by name.

"So, Vince told you about me?" I ask her, trying to get my bearings.

Smiling thinly, she nods. "A bit."

"And you're…"

"Francesca," she says, offering her hand.

I shake her hand with more warmth than I shook Cherie's. "Vince's…aunt?"

"Cousin," she amends. "Mateo's sister. We're all cousins."

"Oh."

"Mateo doesn't come around here," she adds, setting my mind at ease. "He doesn't care for sweets all that much."

Clearing her throat, Cherie says, "Actually, that brings me to another point. Vince tells me that Mia is looking for a part-time job. I remembered you saying you wanted to hire someone else to pick up a couple shifts a week. I thought maybe you could help each other out."

Francesca starts shaking her head even before Cherie finishes. "Mateo combs through all the applications."

Cherie scowls, then rolls her eyes.

It's the first time I've seen her be less than pleasant. Does *anyone* like this Mateo person?

Watching me a little more closely than I'm comfortable with, Francesca asks, "How badly do you need a job?"

"Well, pretty badly. But it's fine—I know Vince doesn't want me to meet your brother. I don't even know if he wanted this, and I don't want to push it. Plus I have very limited availability, only like Mondays and Saturdays, so I'm probably not… It probably isn't worth the risk."

"I could hire you under the table, if you're comfortable with that. No paper trail, no application, nothing he could see. I don't really need any extra help on Mondays, but I could use someone on Saturdays."

"Really? Wow, that would be great."

Francesca smiles. "Good. Can you come by Monday for training?"

"I can, yeah. After school?"

She nods, grabbing a pencil. "What's your full name?"

"Uh, Mia Mitchell."

She jots it down on a piece of wax paper. "Mia isn't short for anything?"

"Nope."

"And you go to Vince's school?"

"Yep."

She jots down something else, then drops the pencil, folding the paper up and putting it in her pocket. "All right. Did you want a cupcake?"

As stressed out as I was when I came in here, I'm actually smiling now. Not only am I going to have a little extra income to make life easier, but Vince actually *told* someone about me. For all that he tells me I have to be invisible to his family, I'm actually not.

"Oreo, please."

# CHAPTER NINE

LENA HAS her party, and I don't go.

Instead, I go to the movies with Vince. My mom wasn't pleased, since she wanted me to babysit so she could go to the boyfriend's house, but she ended up having to take the kids with her since I told her I wouldn't be home.

Which means we have my house to ourselves after the movie.

Vince waits on the porch next to me as I fish my key out, jingling it in front of him. "These are keys. This is how you're supposed to enter a house."

He smirks, stepping behind me and wrapping his arms around my waist. I shiver as his lips brush the nape of my neck.

No longer a smartass, I get the door open as quickly as I can and stumble inside, turning in his arms so I can look at him. He backs me up against the wall, raising my hands over my head as his lips work their way down my neck again.

God, I love this.

"Door," I murmur weakly, since it's still hanging wide open.

Without stopping, he kicks his leg out behind him and it slams shut.

I smile, but then I'm lost to the sensations of his hands skimming their way down my body. "We should go to your bedroom," he murmurs against me.

I'm still afraid we're moving way too fast, and I don't think going to the bedroom is a good way to slow down, but I don't have sufficient reason to say so. We have been in that bedroom together before, even alone *in* the bed, and we haven't actually had sex yet. Surely we can make it a third time.

We should probably discuss sex at some point—at least make sure he has a condom, in the event we decide not to stop one of these times.

Not right now though, I decide, as he hauls me toward my bedroom door.

"I want you, Mia," he murmurs before leaning in to kiss me again.

Hearing him say that is like its own brand of euphoria. "I want you, too," I tell him.

It's true—I just don't *want* to want him as much as I do, this quickly.

He steps toward me, backing me up until my legs hit the edge of my bed. Grasping my chin in one hand, he runs a thumb across my lower lip, holding my gaze as he does.

"Kiss me," he demands.

I don't hesitate. Lurching forward, I brush my lips against his, my hands finding their way around his back to pull him close. He takes over the kiss, hands roaming, one down to my hip, the other on my back. He catches the zipper on my dress and tugs it down until my back is mostly exposed and the fabric gapes open at my shoulders. His eyes rake over me, taking me in, and I revel in the warmth in his gaze. It's not just lust; I see more there.

Releasing his hold on me, he takes the gaping edges of the fabric and slides it off my shoulders, down over my arms, and the dress falls to the floor. I try not to feel self-conscious that I'm standing there in nothing but a lacy black bra and a pair of (not matching) black panties, but there's no time for that, because then he's reaching around my back again, unhooking the clasp.

I let out a shaky breath as he tugs that down my arms, too. As he tugs it off, drops it to the ground, and just looks at me.

It's not fair that he's still fully dressed, so I grab at the hem of his T-shirt, tugging it upward. He takes the hint, reaching behind his neck and tugging it off. He drops it in the floor along with my clothes, but he's not as self-conscious about it.

"Have you...had sex before?" I ask, feeling my face warm as I ask. He nods.

I figured, but I still feel awkward hearing it. "I haven't."

A hint of a smile tugs at the corners of his mouth. "I know."

Instead of discussing it further, he kisses me. It feels different skin to skin, somehow even more intimate as my breasts press against his warm skin. My nerve endings come alive as his fingertips skim my bare sides, and the throbbing between my legs begins anew.

He pulls away a moment later, unfastening the button of his jeans. I swallow hard as he slips out of them, and I climb on the bed, sitting back on my heels, uncertain.

Then Vince is on the bed with me, and I'm relieved we were too busy kissing to turn the light on. He takes my hands and tugs me close, and then he kisses me again. He keeps holding one of my hands, but he drops the other and lets his hand drift down between my legs. My knees spread a little wider as he breaches my entrance, and I gasp against his mouth when he suddenly rubs my unprepared clit. Pleasure shoots through me, and it runs over me like a steady stream as he continues to play with me, never breaking our kiss.

It's pandemonium in my body as I try to keep pace kissing him, but I keep breaking away, closing my eyes, riding the wave of pleasure moving through my body. Everything tightens and I can't do it anymore; I can't focus on kissing, and he doesn't make me. He uses his free hand to gently push me back and I follow his lead, lying down and spreading my legs for him.

It hits hard and I cry out, my body arching up off the bed as ecstasy shoots through me.

I collapse against the bed, breathing heavy. Vince moves between my legs, tugging my panties all the way off. He's still in his boxers, but the way his eyes are devouring me, I'm pretty sure he doesn't want to be.

"Do you have a condom?" I ask.

Relief shows on his face before he can wipe it away, and I can't help but smile as he hops off the bed to retrieve it.

I allow myself a moment of anxiety while he prepares. I'm still not sure I'm ready, but I don't know if I ever will be with him. There's no point tormenting both of us for some arbitrary period of time, knowing he may never be able to offer me the security I would want to actually do this. If I'm going to do it anyway, and I'm pretty sure I am, it may as well be now.

Climbing back on the bed, he moves between my legs. His hands run over the outside of my thighs and he looks me in the eye. "You're sure?"

I nod, as sure as I probably ever will be.

He leans down and kisses me again, his hand moving between my legs again. This time he isn't there to toy with me for pleasure, but to prepare my body for invasion. The kisses help ease my nerves—just light, sweet kisses. Eventually they change, become more demanding. He draws me into the excitement as his tongue sweeps into my mouth, filling me with a hit of that yearning I felt the first time.

He withdraws his fingers and a moment later I feel the head of his dick push against me. I suck in a breath and let it out, too distracted to keep kissing. I grasp his shoulders as he comes down on top of me, easing inside of me. I shift, already uncomfortable, and he pauses.

"You okay?" he asks, low and husky.

"Mmhmm," I murmur, but I'm tense as hell.

"Relax," he whispers, not moving any deeper. "I don't want to hurt you."

I try to relax, but it's not an easy thing to do. A few steady breaths later and he pushes a little more of himself inside me. Experimentally, I wrap my legs around him, opening up my hips a little more. He slides an inch deeper and there's pain, but I bury my face in his shoulder so he won't see if he pulls back to look at me. "It's okay," I murmur, despite the noises I can't stop making. Instead of pushing any harder, he pulls back. I think he's going to stop, but then he pushes back in, that time pushing all the way inside of me.

"Ouch, goddamn it," I say through clenched teeth, making truly ugly faces against his shoulder. I'm really glad he can't see them.

"Are you okay?" he asks again.

"Yeah, I'm fine," I tell him, despite my body's insistence otherwise.

He tries to go easy on me, moving slowly for a few minutes, but it's still uncomfortably tight when he pushes inside me. Eventually my body adjusts to the invasion, and I realize it's starting to feel better. Noticing, he picks up the pace, and then it starts to feel even better than before.

When he really gets going, my breath hitches. I try to find a perfect rhythm with him, but I'm a little off. It's okay, it still feels great, and I can tell he agrees. I love the look on his face, the pleasure, knowing he's getting it from me. From my body.

I feel that pressure starting to build, promising me a pleasurable payout, but I don't quite make it, because he gets there first. A guttural groan escapes him and his body goes rigid. I try to clench him with my feminine muscles and he groans again before collapsing against me.

I wrap my arms around him and let him settle into the crook of my neck, sated. I don't even mind the weight of his body crushing mine. I feel like I swallowed sunshine, all warm and toasty and… lovey. I know it's just afterglow, but I don't care; I'm going to enjoy it.

Eventually, he rolls off me, reaching for the box of tissues on my nightstand. Once he's cleaned up, he rolls back over and pulls me into his arms. It feels like heaven.

Lying in his arms, watching the rise and fall of his chest, I've never felt so at peace.

"You okay?" he asks me.

Smiling up at him, I assure him, "I'm great."

"Good," he says, leaning in to give me a soft little kiss.

I wish we could stay like this forever. I know we can't, but looking into his eyes, I vow to enjoy every second I can. Maybe it won't last forever, maybe it won't be normal, but whatever it is, it'll be ours. Right now, that seems like enough.

# CHAPTER TEN

MOST MONDAYS aren't much to look forward to, but as I stand in the hall crowded with parents waiting for their kids, I wish Allan would hurry the hell up so I can drop him off and hustle over to the bakery for my first day of work.

I can't help smiling, wondering what it will be like. Aside from babysitting—which I've seldom been paid for—this will be my first job ever. And I'll get a chance to develop at least a working relationship with one of Vince's family members.

As I rock forward on my toes, I somehow bump into the man next to me.

"Oh, sorry," he says.

I flash a wordless smile, unconcerned. I glance down the hall again. I know class hasn't let out yet, but it will any minute.

I feel the man's eyes still on me, and I glance back at him. I cut my eyes away quickly, since he catches me looking, but out of the corner of my eyes, I see him *still* watching me.

I frown at him that time.

He glances to his left, then his right, casually, but I notice. Then he leans slightly closer to me. "Mia?"

My heart about stops. I've picked the kids up many times before and I recognize many of the parents here—but not him. He's tall with nice blue eyes, a Clark Kent jawline, and dark hair. He has a trustworthy face, but he shouldn't know my name, so I don't trust it.

I decide to move away from him.

Shouldering past people with the occasional 'excuse me,' I make way to a less crowded part of the hall.

Only, Clark Kent follows me.

He doesn't look Italian, but Vince's words about them having associates they aren't related to flash across my mind and I'm about three seconds from fleeing the school without my brother.

I back up, fixing to turn and run down the hall, but the stranger anticipates my move and reaches a strong hand out, grasping me by the wrist.

"I'm not here to hurt you," he states firmly, his gaze serious.

My heart hammers inside my chest and I yank my arm. He doesn't immediately release me, but then he does, glancing around to make sure no one noticed. Apparently satisfied that no soccer mom is quietly calling the police, he comes to stand beside me again.

"I'm a friend, not a foe," he says.

"Who are you?" I ask, trying to still my shaky hands.

"My name's Ethan. I'm a private investigator."

I frown at that, confused. "A private investigator?"

"The Morellis didn't send me," he reiterates. "I suspect if they sent someone for you, there would be less talking and more bleeding."

Well, that's reassuring. "What do you want?" I ask him.

"To warn you. I took this assignment because it was supposed to be on the up and up, but you won't see me again after today. I'm not getting tangled up in this mob bullshit again," he says, with enough derision that I can finally accept he's *not* here on behalf of Mateo Morelli.

"Warn me about what?"

"I've been on your case for two days, and I already understand how Vince met you." He pauses, letting that land. "If Mateo takes an interest in looking into you, how long do you think it will take before he figures out where you live?"

I look at him, suspecting I know where he's going with this, but looking for verification.

Looking regretful, he says, "And how long after *that* do you think it will take before he sends someone to tie up this loose end?"

"But I'm not…. I wouldn't…I'm not a loose end."

"He won't believe that."

"But it's true!"

## Accidental Witness

"It doesn't matter." Shoving his hands into his pocket with a neutral expression, he looks like we're discussing the weather. "This is the only warning you're going to get, and if you're smart, you'll heed it. End it with Vince immediately. He's not like the older ones; he won't punish you for leaving him—at this point, at least. Walk away, don't look back. Don't go to the bakery after you leave here, don't get entangled with them at all. Give Mateo Morelli no reason to look twice at you, because if he does…" He trails off, shaking his head. "It won't end well for you."

He glances at me one last time, then he makes like he's walking to a different part of the hall, but slips out the exit doors instead.

What the *fuck* just happened?

I pull out my phone, hands still shaking. Vince *finally* gave me his phone number after we had sex, and as I dial the number for the first time, I can't believe this is why.

"Hey, you," he greets, almost brightly.

"Vince? I need to talk to you. Can you meet me somewhere?"

"Right now?" he asks, understandably surprised.

"I have to drop Allan off at my house first, but could you meet me right after that?"

"I'm kind of in the middle of something. Can it wait?"

I hesitate, glancing at the doors the man left through. "I don't think it can."

My heart feels pulled in a hundred different directions when I see Vince emerge from his car, slamming the door shut. He spots me immediately and heads my way, a look of concern on his handsome face.

Hands shoved into his pockets, he asks, "What's going on?"

I told him nothing on the phone, paranoid that somehow someone would hear. Logically, I realize it's usually the feds who would listen in on a tap, not the bad guys, but I'm too nervous to take even a single chance at this point.

"There was a man at Allan's school today."

Vince scowls. "What do you mean, a man?"

"A man. A private investigator. He was looking into me."

Vince's face goes white, and my fear morphs into something darker.

I'm quick to assure him, "He wasn't—your cousin didn't send him. He wasn't from your family."

"How do you know?" he asks, still pale.

"He—I don't know for sure who sent him, but he said he was a friend, not a foe, and—and he warned me. From what I've heard, I don't think Mateo would warn me away." I pause, glancing down at my feet, then back to him. "Especially because he figured out what I know. Based on where I live, and...."

"He knows you saw me," he reiterates, but more to himself than me.

"Not Mateo—this guy. But he pointed out that if he could make that connection in two days... so could Mateo, if it occurred to him to look."

"Son of a bitch. Who would sic a PI on you? That doesn't make sense."

Obviously, I've thought about that pretty thoroughly since that moment happened. I duck my head, unsure how this is going to go over. "There's only one, maybe two things I can think of. The other day after school, your friend Cherie approached me. And she took me for cupcakes."

Vince's eyes close, a look of fury passing over his features.

I go on, anyway. "I didn't see any guys, but I met Francesca. And she asked for my name, and... the timeline would make sense. If he's been looking into me for two days...that was three days ago."

"Francesca wouldn't sell me out to Mateo," he says, shaking his head.

"I don't think she did," I say quickly. "But I don't know what you've told her about me. I know she referred to me as 'Vince's Mia' when Cherie introduced me, and she seemed about as paranoid regarding Mateo as you, so maybe she just wanted to see what would turn up?"

Eyes closed, Vince turns away from me, cursing at the wind. I know it's a crazy thing to absorb, so I try to give him time. I still feel like I'm going a little crazy with worry, and the paranoia is already wearing on me. I can't imagine having to live like this, the way Vince seems to.

He doesn't turn back around though, and after a few minutes, I approach him, resting a hand on his shoulder. He still doesn't turn, so I lean my face against his back.

"What do we do?" I ask, quietly.

His silence stretches on, seemingly forever, before he finally turns back to face me. When he does, the look on his face makes me sick to my stomach.

"We can't see each other anymore."

Shaking my head in denial, I say, "No. No, that can't… that can't be the only way."

"It is. I never should've gotten involved with you to begin with. I put you at risk, and I wouldn't be able to live with myself if something happened to you because of me."

Clutching the front of his shirt, I shake my head again. "Nothing's going to happen to me. Listen, what if we got ahead of this? It seems like right now the worst part is the waiting game—will he somehow notice me, or won't he? If he does, sure, we're probably screwed, so why don't we take that possibility off the table? What if we take it to him? What if we stop waiting?"

"No," Vince says, looking at me like I just suggested we summon the devil to offer him a cup of tea. "No, Mia. Trust me… That is not an option."

"But why? Isn't it more suspicious if we try to cover it up? Isn't honesty the best policy? I want to *be* with you, I'm not going to *tell*. I'd be hurting myself as much as you at this point, and if we just explained that to him—"

"He won't believe it, Mia."

"Why does everyone keep saying that?" I demand, stomping my foot in frustration.

"Because *we know him*. You don't. You can't fix this, Mia. Mateo doesn't believe in loyalty, he doesn't *trust* people—he doesn't trust people he's *related* to, he sure as fuck isn't going to trust some random high school girl!"

I balk at being labeled so dismissively, but I don't bother mentioning it. "But we have to try!"

"No, we don't," he says, defeated. "There is no trying. There are no second chances. I take this to him, I tell him you were a witness, that's it. There's no taking that back."

"But maybe he would surprise you. Maybe he would—"

"He wouldn't."

Frustrated by his obstinacy, I argue, "You can't *know* what he'll do."

He shakes his head. "I know the odds, and I won't take that chance. I won't gamble with your life."

I shake my head, refusing to accept that. "This can't be... This isn't fair."

He sighs, wrapping an arm around me and pulling me close. I throw both arms around him, clinging to him like I can change his mind through sheer force. "I'm so sorry, Mia," he whispers, pressing a kiss against my forehead.

I don't want him to be sorry. I want him to be braver. Nobody wants to believe me, but I just can't imagine someone being so unbending, so unreasonable. What if he's wrong about how his cousin would react? What if it would be okay?

So many thoughts are swirling through my head, stitched together with sadness. It seemed like just a minute ago I was wrapped in his arms in my bed, my skin against his, our bodies entwined. I knew it probably wouldn't last forever, but I thought it would last longer than this.

Vince pulls back, but it takes a few minutes. The look on his face hurts my heart and infuriates the part of me that wants to keep fighting, confident this is a fight we could win. We'll never know if it would've worked, because he's too damn afraid.

"So this is it?" I ask, wrapping my arms around myself. "I don't get to see you again?"

"We'll pass each other in the halls," he says, with a sad attempt at a smile.

Despondency wallops me and I shake my head. "I don't want this."

He nods. "I know." After a brief pause that I hope he's going to follow up with a flicker of doubt, something I can work with, he leans in and brushes his lips against mine in a soft, chaste kiss. Ironic, considering I just threw my virginity at him a couple nights ago.

"Goodbye, Mia."

I don't move as he heads to his car, still hanging onto a flimsy hope he'll change his mind. I wait, each second, for his steps to slow, for him to stop. I wait for him to look back at me over his shoulder, realize he'll do anything to hold onto me, and head back. Slow at first, then he'll jog. I'll meet him halfway and he'll wrap his arms around me, pulling me close. He'll assure me we'll figure this out, but he's not ready to give up on me, not yet.

## Accidental Witness

But it doesn't happen. Everything feels heavier as he opens the car door and slides in, and the last of my hopes fall away when he fires up the engine and drives off, leaving me standing in the middle of some random sidewalk, all by myself.

## CHAPTER ELEVEN

NOW THAT it's over, I know I should go home. Crawl into my bed, listen to sad songs, and spend the rest of the day mourning the relationship we never even got to have.

Instead, I go to the bakery.

Francesca starts to smile when she hears the jingle of the door bells, but her pleasure stalls when she spots me—probably especially because it's clear from the state of my face that I've pretty much cried the whole way here.

"Mia," she says, in that trailing off way like she's not sure what to say.

"Why did you have to do that?" I ask, figuring she can piece together what I'm talking about. "If you didn't want to risk it, you didn't have to hire me."

Francesca sighs, glancing over her shoulder, but no one else is around. "I wasn't trying to hurt you, Mia. I just… I know my brother, and I wanted to see if there were any skeletons in your closet, anything he might take issue with. I didn't expect to find anything."

"I didn't do anything to wrong your family in any way. I did the opposite of that—I kept quiet, despite human *decency*. I kept my mouth shut; I could've hurt Vince anytime I wanted to, for literally any number of infractions. Do you know how many times he broke into my house? Twice. I couldn't have been *better*, and still I lose?"

She truly does look sympathetic, but inexplicably, her sympathy makes me feel worse. If she'd only been trying to come between us, if I had someone to blame, someone's bad intentions… but she shouldn't look so sympathetic. She *broke us up*.

"I know it seems so unfair," she says, coming around the counter so she can stand closer to me. "I know it's hard, and you're so young, and you shouldn't have to deal with any of this. I truly didn't mean to hurt you."

The helplessness is the worst of it. I feel like a puppet on a dark stage, dancing for an invisible audience. "Why won't anybody consider that maybe your brother would *see* how good I've been, and he would be okay with me and Vince?"

Concern flickers through her sympathy, not the sad kind, but the kind laced with fear. "Because he wouldn't, Mia. You're not wrong—you *did* do everything right. But I promise you, even in the best of scenarios, this is *not* your happily ever after. Even if Mateo saw how good you've been, even if he didn't…. hurt you… You're *too young* to get trapped in this life."

"But it wouldn't be trapped if I chose it."

"It wouldn't be worth it," she states, implacable. "Take it from a woman born to this family, Mia. I would sell my soul to get away from it—and it would be far worse for you."

Chills move over me, not just at her words, but at how sincere she seems as she says them. I swallow, not sure how to respond to that.

Patting me on the shoulder, she offers me a sad grimace. "You want to take a cupcake?"

I shake my head no, certain I couldn't eat right now if I tried.

Francesca walks back around the counter and pulls out a small handbag. A moment later she holds out a fifty dollar bill. "Take what I would've paid you today, for your trouble."

I want to leave it there, on principle, but I'm too damn poor. I feel nothing as she hands it to me, but I push out a wooden, "Thanks."

"I wish you the best," she tells me. "I know Vince really liked you."

That only makes it worse. If I could at least blame him, maybe I'd feel better. Maybe I would be angrier, bitter instead of sad. He took my virginity and then ditched me—what a bastard.

But no.

We both have to be sad, because everyone thinks his cousin is the big, bad fucking wolf.

Tuesday drags by in a depressing crawl. Vince gets to our class together early enough to reclaim his old seat, and when a confused Cody drops into the seat next to me instead, I have to fight back tears.

It's like we never even happened.

I have to pick up both kids after school, so I'm holding onto Casey's hand as we wait in the hallway at Allan's school. My tired eyes scan the parents for the investigator again, but of course he isn't there.

Once I have them both and we're on our way home, I realize I'm too exhausted to cook. I know it's unwise, but I put a dent in my $50, ordering a sausage pizza from the place Vince took me to.

I have to pick all the meat off and still listen to Allan complain about any potential sausage residue, but the worst part is, I can't even eat it. I pick at the sausage with a lump in my throat, thinking of Vince, already missing him.

Bedtime brings the relief of silence, the cover of night, but I can only lie there, wishing Vince would sneak into my room again. I'd welcome him, even now, even after dumping me, even if it didn't mean anything. Even if it was just one more night.

Those fantasies lead to more tears and no more sleep, so come Wednesday morning, I'm a puffy eyed zombie.

I take a long shower and try to mask my sadness with makeup, but I'm so tired that I feel nauseated. I *have* to get some sleep tonight. I can't go three days with only a few interrupted hours to keep me going.

The whole morning, I debate skipping the class I have with Vince, but the part of me that still wants to see him overrules it. I was too sad to deal yesterday, but today I want to see how he looks. Of course I don't want to be forgettable, but I hope he doesn't feel as hopelessly sad as I still do.

It seems like he has enough sadness without me adding to it.

I approach our mutual class with the same tired anticipation as a reluctant junkie approaching my dealer. I'm disappointed when he's not there yet, but he arrives before Cody and sits away from me again. I understand he wanted to end things between us, but I don't see why he can't even sit next to me anymore.

When class ends, he's out the door before I am, and he doesn't even look at me.

Maybe it *is* easier for him.

After that class, I completely bomb my French test. Studying in the courtyard during lunch didn't do any good, because I haven't done the reading for the past two nights. I have an A in that class anyway, so I guess I can afford it, but I'm still not looking forward to getting that grade back.

The school day finally ends. I don't have to pick up my siblings today, and I'm so glad. My body feels like it weighs 800 pounds, which is really not helping me bounce back from this break-up. I need sleep so my stupid brain can start to function again. I might actually try to take a nap, since the house should be quiet and empty when I get there.

I wish I had the car today. I'm too tired to walk all the way home. Technically, I could probably ask Lena for a ride, but things have been so weird between us lately that I don't.

I nearly make it to the end of the school's sidewalk when a blue car slows to a stop beside me. I don't even look, figuring they're slowing down for the stop sign, until the window rolls down and I hear, "Get in."

Frowning, I look over to see Cherie in the driver's seat.

"What?" I ask, not sure I'm understanding.

"I'll give you a ride home."

I want to tell her no thanks, but I'm too tired. Sliding into the passenger seat, I give her my address and sag against the door. "Thanks," I murmur.

"Vince wanted to get you a car, but he didn't have time," she tells me.

Pain twists in my gut, but I don't respond.

I expect her to say something on the short drive to my house, to address our break-up, since she obviously knows about it. But she doesn't. She leaves me alone, turning the radio on at a low volume and humming along as she drives.

She pulls into my driveway, looking at the charred house beside it. I can't tell if she knows anything about how it happened.

Flashing me an almost smile, she says, "If you ever need a ride, just let me know. I know we don't have to be friends now, but…"

That's honestly so nice of her, and I've been *such* a bitch to this poor girl. I realize if Vince does end up with her, I can't even pissed about it. She's kind, and he deserves that.

Impulsively, and more because I need one than because she does, I lean over and hug her. "Thanks, Cherie."

She's understandably surprised, but she offers a smile as I open the door and climb out.

Fishing my keys out of my bag, I climb the porch steps.

A car door flies open behind me. "Mia," Cherie calls out.

I turn back to see what she wants, but when my eyes land on her, her face is a mask of fear as she runs for me, a phone to her ear.

"What?" I ask, perplexed.

She knocks into me, grabbing me, standing way too close—for a second, I get the very confused feeling she's going to kiss me. "Get back in my car, Mia."

I can't grasp what's happening, but I look back at her car.

Into the phone, she says gravely, "You need to get here *right now*."

Fear surges through me and I consider bolting, running into my house. "Who is that?" I ask.

I try to pull away from her but she grabs me, hustling me back to her car. She's small, but surprisingly strong.

"Cherie, what are you *doing*?" I demand as she throws open the car door.

"Adrian's here," she says, like that's supposed to mean something to me.

"What?" I ask, confused. She shoves me into the car, but doesn't leave my side to get back in the driver's side. "Cherie, what the hell?"

She isn't looking at me. I realize then she wasn't talking to me, either, but to the person on the phone.

"Who's Adrian?" I ask, wishing I knew what the hell was going on. Is Cherie a good guy or a bad guy?

"I'll do what I can," she says into the phone. "Hurry, Vince."

Relief pours through me when she says his name, and a spike of exhilaration hits when I realize he must be coming here.

It drains immediately when I realize there's only one reason he would have to.

"Mateo?"

Cherie meets my gaze, with far more trepidation than I'm comfortable with.

## Accidental Witness

Then she nods. "Mateo's here."

## CHAPTER TWELVE

IT FEELS surreal.

I've heard the monster's name so many times, those closest to him trying to drive home the threat he presents, that I can't imagine the legend of Mateo Morelli having a physical presence. He's more myth than man to me, and as many times as they've expressed their paranoid fears about him, I've never experienced it.

Not until I watch Cherie shrink as the soft clap of footsteps along my driveway moves closer. I don't know what happens when he gets to me, and I'm terrified to find out.

Cherie clutches her phone, backing up against the open car door, but staying by me, like a momma bear with her cub.

The man comes to a stop beside the car, and for several seconds, I don't think anyone dares even breathe.

"Go home, Cherie."

His voice sends fear slicing through me—smooth and deep, possessing the seamless confidence exclusive to a man no one says no to.

Cherie swallows audibly. I want to turn and see what he looks like, but I'm too afraid to move.

"I can't do that, Mateo," she says, but if I can hear the fear in her voice, I know he can.

She's going to abandon me here with him. She won't have a choice. Maybe she's a good friend to Vince, maybe she even knows his family better than I do, but she's not going to stand up to this intimidating man to save my neck—not for long.

My breath hitches as he steps closer and I feel glued to my seat, like my legs couldn't move if they wanted to. The testaments I've heard about him come rushing back and no amount of optimism can deny the reality that Mateo Morelli is standing in my driveway, knowing it's my driveway, mere feet away from the house where Vince killed two people.

Oh, God.

They're going to kill me.

I want to get out of the car. Not to run, there would be no point, but to appeal to him. He's here, he's caught me—throwing myself at his mercy is my only remaining option.

"Vince is blowing up my phone." That's a different voice, quieter, not Mateo's. Again, I want to look, but I feel safer if he knows I haven't seen his face. I know that logic doesn't hold here—he's not some mystery assailant; he won't let me go because I can't identify him—but I'm in survival mode here, just trying to find a way out of this exchange that doesn't end with my dismembered body being dumped in a large body of water.

"He's on his way," Cherie says, not moving. "He… Just, please, wait for him to get here. I can't leave until he gets here."

"Sure you can," Mateo replies, smoothly.

"I won't leave her with you," she tells him.

"How heroic," he says, not trying to hide his amusement.

There's more movement but I still don't look. My head may as well be glued to the headrest, for all the movement I'm capable of.

Someone walks in front of my car. It's a man, but it's not Mateo. I recognize his shaggy hair as he turns to look in at me, and it takes me a moment to realize it's because he was the other man who came out of the house with Vince that night.

It feels like my chest is going to cave in as he stares at me through the windshield. He doesn't move, and he's calm enough that it scares the shit out of me.

You're only that calm if you know you have nothing to worry about.

I try to find my voice, knowing I need to start speaking for myself while I can.

"Cherie, let me out," I say, my voice unsteady.

Her eyes widen and she glances at me like I'm experiencing a psychotic break. "No."

The door is open, but she's standing right in my way. To protect me, but also to keep me inside. I glance over at the unlocked driver's side door, aware that either one of them could just slide into that one if they really wanted to. Her human barrier thing is sweet, but I'm not stupid; she's not in their way any longer than they allow her to be.

"See, she wants to meet me," Mateo says lightly.

Dread runs through me and I realize for the first time, no, I really *don't* want to meet him.

His amusement at the scariest moment of my whole entire life has finally convinced me. Vince and Francesca were right, and I am a fucking idiot.

He ducks his head to glance in at me, but I can't look. Can't move. Before I see more than a vague blur of him, he's straightening again.

"Move aside, Cherie."

His amusement is fading, impatience moving in.

"Please," she says softly, not moving. "Vince will never forgive me."

"He'll be here in a few minutes," Mateo says reasonably. "I won't do anything that can't be undone until he gets here and has a chance to explain himself."

My stomach sinks, hearing him word it like that, and that does it—that breaks my phantom paralysis. I turn, pushing one leg out of the car, then the other. Cherie doesn't move, so I can't stand, but I finally get my first glimpse of Mateo Morelli in real life.

I've seen pictures, but they don't do him justice. I guess his age to be somewhere around 30, but I'm not sure. He *feels* much older than me. Towering over me in my driveway, the dark-haired, dark-eyed Morelli can easily be identified as a relative of Vince's, and yet, they feel nothing alike. A mantle of power hangs from the broad shoulders of this man, worn with the comfortable familiarity only attained by never having known anything else. This isn't a man who had to climb to power—it's his birthright, and if you want even a shred of it for yourself, you'd better be prepared to fight.

My blue eyes tentatively meet his gaze. I wish I felt confident, as I had all the times I insisted to other people he would probably be more understanding than they thought. "What do you mean, explain himself?" I question. "Vince didn't do anything wrong."

Instead of answering me, he smiles a slow, predatory smile. "She speaks."

In a flash, he's reaching into the car and grabbing me by the arm. A fearful cry slips out of me as he yanks me from the car, and Cherie gasps, skittering out of the way. Once I've cleared the door, he slams me against the closed door of the backseat.

"Hello, Mia," he says calmly.

My breath hitches, staring into a pair of brown eyes so unlike Vince's. Where Vince's have that attractive spark of warmth, the emptiness in this man's eyes chills me to the bone.

That's the scene when Vince's car flies around the corner, coming to a sudden, squealing stop in the middle of the road. He launches out of the car and heads toward us.

"Get away from her," he calls out.

Mateo moves his body closer to mine. I try to lean away, but with my back against the car, there's nowhere to go. Vince's footsteps slow and he looks at me, more fearfully than I've ever seen him look.

I realize then, he might not be able to control this situation any better than Cherie.

Mateo's still grasping my arm, and it's definitely going to bruise. I look away from Vince, at Mateo, trying to come up with a plan, fast.

We all stand there for a wordless moment; opponents, not friends. Vince moves closer, but stops when he realizes Mateo advances on me more with each step he takes. His warm, hard body presses against mine, so close I'm certain he can feel my heart thundering inside my chest cavity. Vince stops, so consumed with dread that I can't even imagine what he's thinking.

And then Mateo's free hand moves slowly, threateningly down my side to my hip. My blood turns to ice in my veins and I can't breathe. Confusion and terror band together and render me completely useless, a glorified hood ornament. He doesn't pay any attention to me while he does it—his eyes are on Vince. My horror grows when he smiles, as if he likes what he sees.

Oh, God. What is this?

Practically vibrating with resentment, Vince takes a step back.

Mateo's smile doesn't change, but something sparks in his eyes, something… deceptively pleasant. "That's better."

I get the feeling this is all a game to him. A parlor game, a way to pass the time. He comes out the victor in every tournament, so this… this goes on as long as it amuses him.

He obviously likes submission, so I let my arm go slack in his grip. It gets his attention, since up until then, I've been straining to pull away.

"Now that the gang's all here, why don't we take this somewhere more private?" he suggests, as if I have any say in the matter.

I nod, meeting his gaze. He doesn't need my permission, but I give it anyway, preferring at least the pretense that I'm in some kind of control here.

He drops my arm, taking a step back. My hand automatically rises to give it a little rub, which Vince notices but doesn't remark upon.

The other man approaches me, and I look at him, wondering what happened to his face. He has burn scars along the left side and down his neck, disappearing into his shirt. They wouldn't have healed like that if they were from the fire next door; not to mention, he hadn't seemed injured.

"Give Adrian your car keys," Mateo says as he passes Vince. "You're riding with me."

Vince finally gets close to me, and as soon as he does, I throw myself into his arms.

"I'm so sorry," he tells me again, holding me tight. "I'm so sorry, Mia."

"Please don't let them hurt me," I murmur against him, trying to hold back tears.

"I'm gonna do everything I can," he promises, placing a kiss on my forehead.

"Are you sure they're gonna take us to the same place?" I ask, not at all trusting this Adrian guy.

"Yeah, we're just gonna go home so we can sort this out. Adrian won't act unless Mateo tells him to. Isn't that right, Adrian?"

"Sure is," Adrian says, easily.

Vince lets me go, but I want to hold on. I wish I could ride with him, but I know they'd never allow that.

Once Adrian gets Vince's car keys, Vince gives me one more hug, promising he'll see me soon, and heads toward the black Escalade Mateo already climbed inside. Adrian takes hold of my arm lightly.

"Don't try anything stupid," he warns, tugging me toward Vince's car. "Mateo wants to hear what Vince has to say first, but you draw attention, I'll drop you right here."

I feel like we probably already drew whatever attention we were going to, but I don't say that. I nod and climb in the passenger side seat of Vince's car.

Adrian drops into Vince's seat, shoving the key in the ignition and firing it up. Before he puts it in drive, he holds out his hand, saying simply, "Phone."

It takes me a second to remember I have mine in my pocket, but I take it out and hand it over without question.

Adrian pops something into the side and slides out a tiny chip, then he dismantles it completely, removing the battery and throwing all the pieces into the back seat.

As if this is his every day, he turns on the radio, pushes a button a few times to change songs, and puts the car in drive.

I look out the window as we pass my house, and I'm sick at the thought that this could be the last time I ever see it.

## CHAPTER THIRTEEN

THE RIDE to Vince's house is silent and brief. I guess I expected Adrian to probe—ask questions I didn't know how to answer, try to trip me up before I have a chance to talk to Vince. He doesn't. He just listens to classic rock and drives like he isn't escorting me to my own doom.

When we pull up outside the black wrought iron gates, I am floored. Obviously I knew Vince didn't worry about money, but the sprawling edifice behind the gates is more Parisian opera hall than house. Two stories of white stone sit back off the road, pretty as a picture with a royal blue roof. Three stone steps lead to the front door, thick white columns holding up a beautiful balcony overhead. In front of the enormous house there's a circular driveway of gray-white brick, and a large fountain at the center. Mateo's Escalade has stopped at the front of the fountain, and Adrian pulls up behind it.

"Vince lives here?" I can't help asking.

"Yep," Adrian verifies.

"It's like a castle," I say, still in awe.

"Might as well be," he mutters, shoving open the door and climbing out.

I don't ask what that means, too awestruck to care.

Up ahead, Vince and Mateo ascend the three steps, while I linger in the driveway, gaping at everything. Off the right is a covered patio, and I see a pool through the columns.

"Come on," Adrian says, a hand on my back nudging me forward.

I can't believe this is a house—people actually *live* here. Not even just people, but *Vince*.

## Accidental Witness

As soon as we enter the house, I'm blown away again. The biggest chandelier I've ever seen hangs from the second story, with twin curved staircases. The tan and white tile floor gleams, and I feel like I've stepped into a luxury real estate pamphlet.

"This way," Adrian tells me, heading left past the staircase.

We don't make it far, as Adrian leads me to the first gleaming oak door on the right side of the wide hall.

"This place is bananas," I tell him, in case he missed it.

He cracks a smile, but it quickly dissipates as we enter the room where Mateo and Vince are waiting.

Another huge, beautiful room, this one clearly the study. Floor to ceiling wood, with built-in shelves full of leather-bound books. There are four puffy red leather chairs that look like they belong in a gentleman's club flanking an area rug in front of the fire place, and to the far right, an imposing desk, presumably Mateo's.

"How was the ride?" Mateo asks Adrian.

"Quiet. Until she saw your house," he adds, his tone lightly mocking. "Apparently it's like a castle."

Both Morelli men look at me, but I just shrug. "I could fit my whole house in your foyer."

Mateo's gaze lingers on mine, reminding me I'm not here for the tour. I can't imagine anyone being barbaric enough to commit a murder in such a beautiful room, but my nerves jolt when he speaks to me. "Come here."

My gaze jumps fleetingly to Vince, but I don't take long obeying. He points to the ground when I don't come close enough, but I frown in confusion, looking down at the red area rug.

"On your knees. On the rug, just in case."

"What—what do you mean?"

"Get. On. Your. Knees," he says slowly, staring at me. "Were those directions easier to follow?"

I look to Vince again, but he doesn't speak. His face is a mask of dread, which doesn't give me much hope.

Swallowing, I drop to my knees at the center of the area rug and look up at Mateo.

Mateo nods once, then takes a menacing step toward me. "All right, Mia. I don't have a lot of time to figure out what to do with you. You live with your mother, you're in high school—people will notice you missing. For the sake of expedience, I'm going to lay out the rules for you. Once. No sobbing, no complaining or questioning—just listen and obey. I don't like repeating myself, and I rarely do things I don't like to do."

I wait for further instructions, but I somehow don't expect him to pull a Glock out of his jacket and point it directly at my forehead.

"Oh, please, no," I whimper, dropping back on my heels.

"The first thing we're going to do is see how honest you are. Vince assures me you're a goddamn saint, so let's find out, hm? Sit forward. You don't have to be afraid if you're honest."

I can hardly manage breathing, but somehow I get back up to my knees.

"You're going to tell me your story," Mateo states, bringing the cold, hard barrel of the gun to rest against my forehead. "The first time I hear a lie, I pull the trigger."

Blood surges through me, and for a split second, everything feels faint, and I fear I'll pass out. "But… how will you know if it's a lie?"

"Well, see, Vince told me his version of events in the car. So this really works both ways—if you lie to me, you die. If he lied to me and you tell the truth, you die. Either way, we all learn not to lie to me."

"Oh, my God," I whisper, bile rising up my throat.

"Start at the beginning."

Mind racing, horrified tears gathering in my eyes, I hope to God Vince was honest. "I… I was outside my house to make a phone call to a guy from school. I noticed something strange next door, and realized it was fire. I didn't have time to call for help, because I saw someone coming out of the house." Raising a shaky hand, I indicate Adrian. "Him." I swallow, my eyes moving up to the gun, struggling to focus. "Um… and then a second person came out, and I recognized Vince from school. I… I…" I stop, not wanting to admit the next part. Closing my eyes, swallowing convulsively, I force myself to go on. "I crouched in the bushes so he wouldn't see me, and I tried to take a video on my phone. I fell, and he saw me, and I ran."

"A video of him leaving the house?" Mateo asks, to verify.

"Yes. It was stupid, I didn't… It was a stupid thing to do."

"Yes. Go on."

## Accidental Witness

"I dropped my phone and... I had heard rumors about Vince's family, so I was afraid. I didn't go back for the phone until the next day, and it was gone. Vince took it. He erased the video, and broke into my house. He threatened me and gave back my phone. My mom came home so I hid him in my bedroom until I could leave. I assured him he could trust me, that I wouldn't tell, and I meant it."

Mateo is unmoved by the last line, but he hasn't shot me yet, so I continue to summarize my time with Vince up to this point. Occasionally he asks questions. I don't know how detailed I'm supposed to be about things unrelated to what I saw, but I figure it's no time to hold back.

"You had sex?" Mateo questions, when we get to that part.

My face already had to be red from the stress of the situation, but I imagine the color somehow deepens. "Yes. After that is when he broke up with me." I'm sweating bullets, having skipped the part about being warned away by some random dude Francesca must have hired.

"And why did he break up with you?"

I'm not looking forward to this one either, but I stare at his hand, wrapped around the grip, and say, "Because he was afraid if we stayed together, you would notice me. He was afraid if you noticed me, you might look into me, and if you did... you would realize what I must have witnessed."

Glancing back at Vince, he says, "See, she even calls herself a witness."

"But I would never tell anyone," I add. "I didn't and I wouldn't. Vince was *right* to trust me. It doesn't matter what I saw, no one will ever know. I even... I didn't believe Vince, I didn't think we should hide what I saw."

Mateo's head cocks to the side, but he seems interested enough that I go on.

"Vince was afraid you would...well, do this, I guess. But I wanted to bring it to you. I thought the crime was in the cover-up. I wanted to tell you what I saw, so there was nothing to hide. I wanted you to know I wouldn't say anything."

"Why would you care?" he asks, frowning slightly.

"I just... I just wanted to be with Vince. I thought if I showed you I was trustworthy, maybe you would be okay with that. Vince didn't seem to agree. I guess... he was probably right on this one."

"No," Mateo says, shaking his head. "You were. This would have gone differently if you were telling me something I didn't know. As it is, I had to find out about you myself. Confessing once you're already caught doesn't mean much."

"I understand that," I say quietly.

He draws the gun away from my head, but doesn't put it away. I sag with relief, drawing in a shuddering breath and bracing my hands on the floor, sending up a silent prayer of thanks.

"I like your instincts, though," he adds. Turning his attention to the scarred man, he asks, "What's your opinion on this, Adrian?"

My gaze flashes to him, but Adrian isn't looking at me. "I haven't really talked to her enough to form a firm one, but my instinct is we trust Vince's judgment on this one. He dumped her and she still didn't talk."

Mateo nods. "And kind of pushed her into the relationship to begin with, sounds like."

I open my mouth to voice my objection to that, but, realizing immediately this isn't a battle I want to pick, I settle on a scowl that no one sees anyway, since they're too busy deciding my fate amongst themselves.

Now Mateo turns to Vince. "Are you committed to her?"

I expect an enthusiastic yes, seeing as my life's on the line, but Vince's guards are up even higher than that first night he accosted me in my kitchen. He gives Mateo a measured, wordless nod that does little to reassure me.

"All right," Mateo says, surprisingly amiable as he tucks his gun away in his jacket again. "Never say I didn't do anything for you. As long as you want her and she doesn't give me reason to change my mind, I'll let the girl live."

Relief washes over me like a tidal wave, but I'm confused by Vince's lack of response. Lack of positive response, anyway. He's still holding Mateo's gaze, still not speaking, and there's this bitter little smile on his face that I can't figure out.

Mateo turns his back on Vince, addressing Adrian. "Do you have her phone?"

The other man nods. "I took it apart. It's in Vince's car."

"Can you fix it?" he asks, following Adrian out of the study.

"Of course."

# Accidental Witness

As their voices fade with distance, I push myself up off the floor. My legs still feel a little weak, and my nerves are absolutely fried, but I'm alive and no longer in any danger. Vince still hasn't moved. I'm a little disappointed he's not happier that I'm not going to die.

"It's good news," I tell him, smiling tentatively. "He's not going to hurt me."

"He didn't say that," Vince says easily, speaking for the first time since we arrived here.

I frown, replaying the moment that just happened over again. "He said he wouldn't kill me unless I gave him reason, which obviously I won't. He said we could be together—he's fine with it."

Nodding again, with something that looks like a smile but isn't, he corrects me. "He said as long as I want you, he'll let you live. He just tied your life to our relationship, Mia. I'm 18, and I may as well have just married you."

My stomach feels all weird at that, and not the good weird. I like Vince, I like Vince a lot, but I've known him for less than a month. "What?"

He shakes his head, still visibly aggravated, but he finally reaches out and pulls me in for a hug. "I'm sorry I got you mixed up in this shit. I knew better. This is my fault."

I hug him, but not as tight as I thought I would. Struggling to wrap my head around our different interpretations of the same scene, I say, "Maybe we should ask for clarification. I think maybe he didn't mean it the way you think he did."

"I know Mateo, Mia," he tells me evenly. "That was a performance. There was no chance he'd let us off the hook and let you go; he just chose a different method of punishment for both of us and wrapped it up in a nice package. He doesn't want you to live, but you don't pose an immediate threat, so he made keeping you alive my responsibility. He's punishing me, and he's using you to do it."

"I know I'm usually the one overthinking things, but… I think it's you this time. You're 18, why would he want to saddle you with me already?"

"Because I tried to keep a goddamn secret from him."

Adrian's back a second later, fiddling with my phone. He brings it over to me, and as it transfers into my hand, he looks at Vince. "Sorry, man."

Vince shrugs one shoulder. "Could've gone worse, I guess."

Frowning, I say, "It's *good* news."

Adrian spares me a sympathetic glance before walking out of the study, just as Mateo's coming back in. My relief is starting to fade. Vince could be paranoid, but it seems like Adrian doesn't view this as a victory either.

Mateo comes closer to us, his eyes moving over my body. Without meeting my gaze, he says, "Call your mother. Tell her you're staying the night at a friend's house. I'm going to call someone to take you to Francesca's room; you should be about the same size, so you can borrow something of hers to wear for dinner."

"I'm staying for dinner?" I ask, pleasantly surprised.

"You'll stay the night. I have a lot of arrangements to make. I prefer to keep you under my roof while I get it all sorted. You can stay with Vince, or I can put you in a guarded room. Extra precaution, you understand. You're free to roam the house, as long as you have an escort."

I blink, trying to keep pace with what the hell he's talking about. "A guarded…?"

"She'll stay with me," Vince states.

"Perfect. Cherie brought your backpack in, so if you have any homework to attend to, it's in the foyer."

Frowning in confusion, I say, "Cherie's here?"

"Of course. Someone will show you around."

The way he's delivering all this information like I'm supposed to understand it, I feel a little stupid that I don't. "Um, what if my mom doesn't want me to stay over at a friend's house tonight?"

Shrugging like he's never been asked a dumber question in his life, Mateo says, "Handle it."

That doesn't answer my question, exactly, but I nod anyway. "Okay."

Flashing me a smile, Mateo holds my gaze. "Welcome to my home, Mia."

His words are friendly, but I pick up a weird vibe. Doing my best to ignore it, I muster a smile in return. "Thank you, Mr. Morelli."

## CHAPTER FOURTEEN

CHERIE ESCORTS me to Francesca's room. She asks Vince what happened, and since I don't feel like listening to his grim retelling of events, I go out to retrieve my backpack.

My mom didn't answer her phone, but I left a message that I was over at Lena's and she wanted me to spend the night, so she'd give me a ride to school in the morning.

Sitting in the floor of Vince's palatial home, I think about how having dinner with his family was something I desperately wanted a few days earlier. But in my daydreams of that event, Vince was happy I was there. Right now, I don't think he's happy I'm here at all.

*Burden.*

The word rises unbidden to my mind, but I push it away. I'm not a burden. Vince *likes* me. He wanted to be able to date me, he just didn't want... well, this.

Everyone is just worked up right now. It's been a crazy hour, but today will pass, the dust will settle, and everything will be okay.

Confident, I rise, slinging my backpack over my shoulder. I hesitate outside the door of the study, seeing Cherie comforting Vince with a sympathetic expression and a reassuring shoulder squeeze.

I need to figure out what her deal is. I decide to ask, once I'm alone with her.

Eventually, I'm spotted hovering outside, so Cherie flashes Vince one last smile and comes out to see me.

"I guess I'm supposed to help you find something to wear for dinner."

"I guess so," I say, looking down at my T-shirt and jeans. "Is there something wrong with what I'm wearing?"

"No, of course not. It's just, the Morellis don't wear jeans to dinner."

I frown, but she's already walking, so I follow along.

"I can show you Vince's room, too, if you want to drop off your bag. Vince said you're going to be staying with him."

"Tonight, yeah. Which is weird, isn't it? I mean, we're teenagers, and they're just okay with us sleeping in the same bed?"

"Mateo doesn't care," she says, simply. "He's not Vince's dad, and… he wouldn't care anyway."

"Seems weird."

"It won't, eventually."

It's so weird how everyone seems to accept without question there was some mandate, locking me into this family, and apparently I missed it?

By the time we make it to the wing housing Francesca, I decide that I could have a sufficient workout routine if I just walked through this whole house twice a day. At the end of the long hall, there's another hallway to the left, and a hallway to the right. Directly ahead, an enormous painting hangs on the wall. Apparently Francesca is on the left hall, because that's where Cherie turns.

"The room across the hall is empty," Cherie tells me. "If they don't keep you with Vince permanently, you may get that one. Then you and Francesca will be neighbors," she says brightly.

Neighbors is a good way to put it. This house really is more like an apartment complex, judging by the size of it. "I don't think I need my own bedroom," I say, glancing over my shoulder as I follow Cherie. "Do all the family members live here?" I ask.

"Not all of them. Francesca, Adrian, Mateo, Vince, Alec—Mateo's dad, too, but he's sickly…" She's walking ahead of me, but she slows down until we're side by side so she can say lowly, "and an old bastard. You probably won't even meet him. Mateo pretty much has him tucked away, just waiting for him to die."

My eyes widen, but she goes on, still quiet. "There are cameras throughout the house, by the way. You won't always be able to tell where they are. Some are obvious, some aren't. They do record audio."

"Cameras? Like, surveillance?"

She nods, then speaks at a normal tone. "And here's Francesca's room."

When she opens the door, I see an opulent room of whites and pinks. Like every other room I've seen so far, it's huge. It doesn't even look like a bedroom when we first walk in—there's a sofa in front of a fireplace with bookcases flanking it and a side table, like a living room. A television is mounted on the wall. Beyond that, though, is a wall with an open arch, and that leads into Francesca's sleeping area. There's another door at the back of the room. It's only cracked open, but it looks like a bathroom.

"And over here," Cherie says, walking around the bed, opening a door I didn't notice between the bed and the bathroom, "is the closet."

I should expect it at this point, but it's a walk-in. A huge walk-in, larger than my bedroom at home, with a floor-to-ceiling mirror as soon as you walk in, and a fancy upholstered bench—pale pink, of course—right in the center. Racks and racks of clothing, handbags and shoes fill the room, and I can't even deal.

"What *is* this place? How rich is this family?"

"Super rich," she tells me. "Mateo's actually a really good business man, and he's been systematically buying up his side of the city. Most of his money now is actually legit, from what I hear."

"Why not get out of the crime stuff then?"

She shrugs. "No idea. Anyway, sit, I'll pick you a dress."

I sit there awestruck, looking around at all of Francesca's possessions, remembering her telling me she would sell her soul not to be a part of this family. Maybe she has an inaccurate idea of what the rest of the world is like, because from the cushy fucking seat I'm sitting in, being born to this family seems more like a blessing than a curse.

I mean, crime boss head of the family or not. Look at all these shoes!

Cherie plucks a dress off the rack and brings it over to me. "High neck. Try this one."

I feel a little weird undressing right in front of her, but she doesn't leave, and she doesn't seem fazed in the slightest as she waits to zip me up.

Once it's fastened, I admire my reflection for a moment while

Cherie pops over to the shoes. She picked out a black lace sheath dress, and while the neckline *is* high, it's super pretty.

"What's your shoe size?" she asks, picking up a pair of suede turquoise heels.

"Usually 8."

"Perfect," she says, bringing them over. "Do you need pantyhose?"

"I think I'm okay," I tell her, stepping into the heels.

"Do you have makeup with you? You could use some lipstick."

I don't, so our next stop is Francesca's vanity in the bathroom. Cherie navigates the drawers like a pro, and before long she picks a shade and applies it before I can argue.

Flashing me a smile as she puts it away, she says, "Perfect. You look very pretty."

"Are we going out somewhere to dinner?" I ask.

"Nope. This is just how Mateo likes things."

I frown a little at that, but I don't say anything.

Cherie starts to head back to the walk-in closet, but she slows to a stop near the door, and instead, she closes us both inside and turns back to me. "Can I give you some advice?"

"Of course," I say, open to anything that might help me.

"It's going to be an enormous adjustment, becoming a part of this family. I can see right now you don't realize that, and there's no reason you would, but as someone who's grown up here, let me tell you… Everything you think you know about the world is wrong inside of these walls. This is Mateo's kingdom. He rules it, and the men in this family rule over the women."

I must look horrified, because her expression grows firmer.

"Balk all you want internally, but you're better off if you don't. Play nice with Mateo, and keep Vince happy. Survival is your new motivator. If you have to dress up for dinner so Mateo can admire his collection of dolls, just do it. If you possess any strong feminist values, let them go. You'll be much happier if you submit. The world outside, the world you're used to, is not your world anymore. Vince is your man, Mateo is your boss, and this is your home—but it's their home, first. The more you fight, the less comfortable you'll be. You will not always be treated with respect, you will damn sure not be treated like an equal, and on Sundays? The women of this house make dinner. Don't make any other plans, because it's mandatory. Vince is a good guy, probably the best in this family, but he was raised here, so he won't be perfect. Right now, he's feeling a bit burdened. If I were you, I'd try to make him more comfortable with the fact that he's sort of stuck with you now. This life will be whatever you make it, and if you go in realistic, you'll be able to make more out of it. If you fight at every turn, you'll be miserable. I can't imagine coming into this life from the outside, and if you ever need someone to talk to, you can talk to me. Preferably at school, or in a bathroom, because that's the only place there are no cameras. Be very careful, because Mateo's paranoia is not exaggerated."

Opening the bathroom door without giving me a chance to respond, she says, "You look very pretty. Now I'll show you to Vince's room, so you can drop off your things."

Vince is in his bedroom when we get there. Like Francesca's, there's a sitting area when you first walk in, but there's no wall between that and the rest of the room. Vince's bed is enormous—I guess a king, but it looks even bigger. His room is decorated in reds and blacks with pops of silver. Beyond the bed, he has a desk with a laptop and various items scattered across the top. In the far left corner, a black upholstered chair that faces the bed. Where Francesca's walk-in closet was, Vince has a bathroom.

Cherie leaves right away to give us some privacy. Vince was lying back on his bed, staring at the ceiling when we came in, but now he's sitting on the edge of the bed.

"These bedrooms are like apartments," I tell him, managing a smile.

He still looks down in the dumps. With Cherie's words fresh in my mind, I walk over to the bed, kick off my shoes and climb up behind him. Leaning in, I wrap my arms around his shoulders.

"Yeah, they're not small," he agrees, lightly touching my wrist.

"I'm sorry it's been a rough day," I tell him.

Laughing lightly, he looks at me over his shoulder. "It's been far rougher for you."

"Yeah, but I think we're gonna be okay," I say, wanting to stay positive. "I think the worst is over."

"I think that's inaccurate, but I'll let you believe it as long as you're able."

I duck my head around his shoulder, kissing him on the cheek. "We get to sleep in the same bed tonight, and you don't even have to break into my house to accomplish it," I tease him.

"Look at you with the silver linings," he says lightly. Then, reaching behind him, he topples me over his shoulder until I fall into his lap. He cradles me with his arm, winks, and leans in to kiss me. I wrap a hand around his neck to draw nearer, and at the same time, I feel his hand slide up my thigh. Wasting no time with teasing, he slides his fingers inside the fabric of my panties and pushes a finger inside me.

"Vince," I say on a gasp. I spread my legs for him, but not as wide as I'd like, because of the dress.

"At least now," He leans down, capturing my lips as his fingers tease the bundle of nerves between my legs. "I can do this anytime I want."

"You sure can," I agree, back arching as he sends a spike of pleasure right through me.

## CHAPTER FIFTEEN

DINNER IS, in fact, a whole thing.

A long, gleaming table seats five on each side, with one chair on each end. Place settings have already been put at each one, with two tall candelabras and a round flower arrangement at the center. This room also has a fireplace and a huge, sparkling chandelier.

We seem to be the last to get there. Mateo, unsurprisingly, sits at the head of the table. On the opposite end is Adrian, who glances up at me as we enter, but quickly becomes distracted by a young blond woman leaning over to fill his water glass. A man I don't recognize sits at the first chair on Adrian's left beside Francesca. There are three empty seats next to her, but the other side of the table is completely empty. Vince heads for the seats on the empty side, closest to Adrian, but Mateo speaks up.

Indicating the two seats to his left, he says, "These two are your seats."

"No one else is coming?" Vince asks.

"Not tonight." Then, to me, Mateo explains, "On Sundays there are more people. During the week, it varies."

Vince goes to take the seat nearest Mateo, but Mateo shakes his head. Vince's jaw locks, but he pulls the chair out and gestures for me to sit anyway, then he takes the seat to my left so I'm essentially sandwiched between them. Fun.

The blonde girl makes it to Mateo's glass, and I notice when he glances up at her and smiles, she begins to glow, smiling more than I can imagine Mateo's attention ever making a person smile.

At the other end of the table, Adrian slams his seat back and stands, startling everyone.

"Bathroom," he says shortly, before storming out.

I glance over at Vince for explanation, but he just gives a subtle head-shake.

Unconcerned, Mateo addresses the two at the other end of the table. "Francesca, Alec, this is Vince's girlfriend, Mia."

"Hi, Mia," Francesca says, offering a faint smile.

The man just acknowledges me with a nod, looking up at the blonde as she fills my water glass, then Vince's. "Can you bring me a beer when you get done with that?"

"Of course," she says, taking her water pitcher and disappearing through a doorway.

"That's Elise," Vince tells me. "She's a maid here."

"You have a maid," I remark, not sure why I'm surprised. Someone would have to keep such an enormous house clean.

"Two, actually. Maria's in the kitchen, but once the food comes out I'm sure you'll meet her, too."

Mateo takes a sip of his water, his eyes on me. "You look very nice in Francesca's dress, Mia. I think you should keep it."

I feel my cheeks flush. "Oh, thank you. I couldn't—"

"Francesca doesn't mind. Do you, Francesca?" he asks, without looking her way.

"No, I have plenty," she tells me.

I have to look away from Mateo, because he won't stop looking at me and I'm afraid my face is going to catch on fire. I look at the intricate blue lace design on the runner at the center of the table instead.

"There," Mateo says easily. "Now you have something to wear to dinner."

An edge to his voice, Vince says, "I will get her a couple of dresses for dinners."

Mateo merely smiles.

Vince is still agitated, though, and I don't know why he's letting something so minor get to him. Out of all the bullshit that's happened today, a relaxing dinner seems better than one fraught with little fights I don't even understand.

"Were you able to reach your mother?" Mateo asks me.

"I didn't talk to her, but I left a message about staying at Lena's. It shouldn't be an issue. Normally I'd have to babysit my siblings, but as luck would have it, I didn't tonight or in the morning. I do have to watch them after school tomorrow though."

"Until when?"

"Um… I—four, I think."

"Good. You can make it back for dinner."

A little uncomfortable, I say, "For just dinner, sure. I don't think she'd let me stay the night again. I really very rarely spend the night at my friend's house, so… she won't accept that excuse indefinitely."

Elise is back with a large bottle of wine. She starts pouring at Mateo's seat, then pours some for me and Vince, despite neither of us being old enough to drink.

"I want you to set up a dinner with your mother," he tells me, grabbing the wine glass and taking a sip.

"With…you?"

He nods. "Me, you, Vince. I want to meet her. I'll tell you the place, we'll work out a time this week."

"This week?" I ask, eyes widening. "She's only even met Vince one time, and barely."

"Does she know who he is?"

I pause, awkwardness creeping up over me as I shake my head. No, weirdly enough, I did not tell my mother that the guy I was sort of seeing was from a mob family.

I can't tell whether or not that news pleases him. "Friday night works best for me."

I know she works until two this Friday, but I don't know if she's doing anything after. I guess she might be willing to cancel her plans for a dinner with Mateo Morelli. "I'll ask."

Adrian comes back and settles in at the side of the table opposite Mateo, I wonder about the order of things here. Vince said the core people were all Morellis, so I assume Adrian is, but he doesn't resemble Mateo. Alec does—a watered down, less attractive version with a slightly bigger nose, but you can tell he's a Morelli. Francesca has the same coloring, the pitch-black hair and chocolate brown eyes. She's really very pretty, and like me, she's wearing a black dress tonight.

Adrian, though, has smaller eyes, a different nose, hair a little lighter than chestnut—none of the same coloring. Only half his face is scarred, and I wonder if he'd look as intense without it.

Until Elise approaches him again to deliver his salad, then his whole demeanor softens.

I make a note to ask Vince about that whole situation later.

I'm surprised when Cherie comes through the doors next, holding two baskets of bread. She places one at each end of the table, then leaves again, coming back with two little dishes of dipping oil.

I frown, confused. Once she slips away again, I turn to Vince. "Is Cherie a maid?"

"Uh, sort of," he says. "Her mom's a maid. Maria. Cherie helps out."

"So, she *lives* here?"

"In the servants' quarters," he says with a nod, reaching for his wine to take a sip.

"There are servants' quarters?" I question, watching him with wide eyes. Now that he's had a drink, I think I might, too. I thought maybe Elise poured it by mistake, but Mateo doesn't seem to care.

Biting back a smile, Vince says, "I'll take you on a tour after dinner."

"I have so much to learn," I say, under my breath.

"That's an understatement," Adrian murmurs.

After dinner, Vince gives me the tour, as promised. There's an indoor pool for when it's too cold to swim in the one outside, a gym, an obscene number of suites for family members to live in, a *library*, a movie theater room, and so many other rooms that many of them are practically empty. When we get to the servants' quarters, it gets homier. I wasn't sure what to expect of a servants' quarter, but it's basically a house within a house. There's a separate hallway behind the kitchen leading to it, and like a house, it has a living room, dining room, and kitchen all in an open space. Down a hall there are four bedrooms and two bathrooms, all occupied.

"Who all lives here?" I ask him.

"Marie, Cherie, Elise, and Mateo's nanny, Ju."

"Mateo's nanny?"

Nodding, he tells me, "He has a daughter, Isabella."

"She wasn't at dinner," I say with a frown.

"She takes dinner with the nanny."

"Well, I didn't even realize he was married. His wife wasn't at dinner?"

"He's not. They were never married, but Beth isn't around anymore."

I wonder why, but I don't ask. He goes to lead me out, but I glance back, noticing a staircase. "What's upstairs?"

"Mateo's dad."

My eyes widen in surprise. "He keeps his dad with the servants? Isn't he the actual boss of the family?"

"Until he dies," Vince verifies. "There's no love lost there. Mateo's… Mateo, but his dad was a real lunatic. He didn't even want anything to do with this life when he was younger, but he ended up married to a woman who didn't love him and she eventually cheated on him, got pregnant, no one knew who the dad was—I guess the whole situation sort of made him… cruel. I could tell you horror stories about what he did to her and Mateo's mom, but I'll spare you. Suffice it to say, they're both dead, and Mateo's mom killed herself just to get away from him."

"Jesus," I whisper, feeling an unexpected swell of sympathy for Mateo. "How old was he?"

"Five. And he found her."

My stomach starts to feel ill just trying to picture what that must have been like for such a young child. Sadness washes over me, sort of ruining me for the tour.

"Why don't we do the grounds outside tomorrow after dinner?" I suggest, knowing that's next. "I actually do have some homework before bed, and I'd kind of just like to chill out for a little bit. It's been a long day."

He tucks me into his side, dropping a kiss on top of my head. "Yeah, it has."

Funnily enough, Vince and I spend our first full night together *not* having sex. After I finish my homework, we cuddle on the couch and watch some TV. When he loses interest, he starts pestering me until we're kissing and touching, but it's less sexual and more comforting just to be with each other.

I obviously didn't bring anything to sleep in, so he gives me one of his T-shirts for tonight.

When we turn off the lights and climb into bed, I curl up in his arms and we talk until I drift to sleep.

Waking up the next morning is a little jarring, because I'm not used to waking up in strange places. Vince is already in the shower, and when he gets out, he tells me there'll be breakfast waiting downstairs.

Breakfast is usually a Pop-Tart, a bowl of cereal, or a cup of yogurt, depending on how much time I have. Breakfast at Vince's house is eggs with bacon, home fries, toast, and little bowls of fruit. Also orange juice poured from a crystal decanter. It's a hard life.

Mateo's not around, but Cherie is at the table this time, studying some handwritten notes while she eats. She doesn't even look up when I come in.

"Vince didn't leave already, did he?" I ask, since I expected him at the table.

Finally looking up, she says, "Oh, no, not yet. He's in with Mateo." After another minute of studying her notes, she finally stuffs them back inside a folder. "How was your first night as a mob wife?" she asks, lightly.

I laugh shortly, caught off guard. "I wouldn't call myself a mob wife, but last night was nice. Much nicer than the early parts of the day," I add, derisively.

"Yeah. I'm glad it more or less worked out for you, though. I don't know all the details, but I know Vince was really worried about Mateo ever finding out about you."

I stab a quartered strawberry, not offering anything more on that since my life sort of depends on my discretion.

## CHAPTER SIXTEEN

"WAIT, YOU want me to have dinner with who?"

It's been weird trying to explain this to my mother, but since I have to leave soon for dinner at Vince's (and I assume Mateo is expecting a response), it has to be done.

"It's Vince's cousin. He's Vince's guardian, I guess. Vince doesn't live with his parents."

"Who raises him?" she asks, frowning.

That's a good question, actually. Though, thinking back over the wine and the lack of weirdness about him having his girlfriend sleep over in his bed, it doesn't seem like they treat him like a kid.

Shaking my head slightly, I say, "Anyway, can you go or not? He wanted me to invite you, and I'll have to let him know tonight so he can make arrangements."

"That place is expensive," she tells me, clearly wondering if I've lost my mind.

"He's paying. They have money."

"Well, yeah," she says, since that much is obvious. "Gee, I don't know, Mia. Is this safe? I always heard that family was bad news."

Safe was too strong a word to use, considering I'd spent much of the night before lying in bed, remembering how it felt to have Mateo's gun resting on my forehead. Instead of that, I say, "It's safe. It's fine. You'll like him."

I expected her to agree, and she doesn't disappoint. She did have plans with Brax, but the prospect of dolling up to go entertain a mob boss at a restaurant she can't afford is more excitement than she can resist. Once she agrees, I tell her I need to borrow a dress for dinner tonight, and go to raid her closet.

As soon as I get out of the shower, however, Mom is outside the door, practically bouncing with excitement.

Tucking my towel, I frown at her. "What is wrong with you?"

"I don't think you need to borrow a dress," she says, sing-song.

"What?"

Flashing me an exuberant grin, she takes off down the hall. I follow, warily. On the couch, there's a Nordstrom shopping bag and two garment bags draped across the back. A note is tied around the handle of the bags, a rich, creamy business card with gold edges. In bold black, it says simply:

> Mia—
>
> For dinner.

"Open it, open it," my mom says, more excited than I am.

I roll my eyes at her, but I can't stifle a smile myself. It's not often I get presents, and I have a good feeling about these ones. Peeking inside, I find two shoe boxes. I pull out the one on top, labeled Jimmy Choo. My mom is already losing her shit, and I haven't even taken the lid off to see what they look like.

"Do you know how much those cost?" she demands.

They're beautiful—a burgundy-purple suede pair of heels.

My mom grabs them, inspecting them like they might be fake. I move on to the second box, but I don't need to read the name to know what kind they are—the bold red soles of the shiny black pointy toe pumps tells me right away they're Louboutins. They're also instantly my favorite, with a fancy criss-cross strap on the front

"I'm wearing these," I tell her.

"Tonight or tomorrow?"

"Both. To school. To buy groceries. When I die. Forever. I'm never going to take them off."

Grinning, she takes them and admires them with a series of little gasps as she rotates them, admiring them from every angle.

There's a dress in each garment bag, one a short, dark blue sequined dress I'll have to pour myself into, the other a nude fit and flare dress with black lace overlay and a plunging neckline.

"He done good," my mom announces solemnly.

"Oh yeah," I say, nodding in agreement.

"You've only been dating a month, right? I think he spent more on you right here than Brax's spent on me *ever*. Marry this boy."

I roll my eyes at her, but I can't hold back a smile, holding up my very own pretty dress.

For some reason, instead of sending Vince, they send a town car to pick me up. I can only imagine it's to impress my mom, and boy, does it work. She stands on the front porch with her eyes popping out of her head, practically salivating as I climb into the backseat in my pretty new dress and sky-high Louboutins.

I allow myself to get excited on the drive over, and by the time I get there, I feel like Cinderella at the ball. The driver even opens my door for me.

Adrian answers the door, Elise trailing behind him. "I was coming!"

Smiling at her affectionately, he says, "You do enough."

She smiles warmly, lightly touching his arm before she turns to head back to whatever she was doing.

"She's pretty," I remark, none too innocently.

For some reason, I don't expect him to remain soft, and say, "Yeah, she is." Missing a beat, he asks, "Looking for Vince?"

"I am." On impulse, because I feel like he's more human right now, I do a little twirl and point to my shoes. "Like my new outfit?"

"Very pretty," he says gruffly, with an obligatory nod.

I beam and follow him, but I slow down when he heads for the study.

"Is he with Mateo? I should probably wait."

"Nah, come on in. We're not doing anything important."

There are more of them tonight—Mateo perched on the edge of his desk with a glass of amber liquid, Alec from the night before in one of the arm chairs around the area rug, a third guy I haven't met—but clearly a Morelli, by the look of him—pouring himself a drink from a crystal decanter. Vince is in an arm chair across from Alec, and without more than a moment's hesitation, I run over and hop in his lap, wrapping my arms around his neck and showering his face with a bunch of little kisses.

The guy I don't recognize laughs, saying, "Vince's girlfriend, I presume?"

"That's her," Mateo confirms, voice laced with amusement.

Vince grins at me as I finally pull back, shifting the drink I didn't notice in his hand. Thankfully he didn't spill any of it on me. "Not that I'm complaining, but what's that for?"

"You're the best," I tell him, simply. "You deserve a million face kisses."

"For?"

Eyes widening, I lean back and indicate my whole body. "The dresses. And the shoes—oh my God, I'm going to *marry* these shoes. Thank you so much."

He hasn't stopped smiling, but it's certainly dimmed, and there's a crease of confusion in his brow. "What are you talking about? What dress? This dress?"

My enthusiasm stops short. The room has gone quiet. Adrian passes behind Vince and I glance at him, scratching the back of his neck awkwardly. I glance at the next man I can see, the newcomer, clearly in the dark, but paying attention as the scene unfolds. Then I look at Mateo, and he's the only one still amused.

Stomach sinking, my smile finally falls.

Raising his glass in my direction, Mateo winks. "You're welcome."

The silent tension in the room grows, and I slowly look back at Vince, pasting on a more apologetic smile. "I guess I should've asked," I murmur quietly.

Shaking his head very slightly, he says, "Natural to assume the person you're sleeping with is the one buying you gifts."

Instead of having the decency to feel bad for Vince's discomfort, Mateo tells me, "I'll take an I.O.U. on the million face kisses, by the way. Seems like we'd be late to dinner otherwise."

He doesn't shove me off his lap, like he probably wants to, but Vince does throw back the rest of the liquid in his glass.

I wish I didn't feel trapped in his lap now. Getting up feels like a rebuff, but sitting here while this awkwardness lingers is pure torture.

Adrian takes Vince's glass and refills it, bringing it right back.

"Good man," Vince says, putting a good dent in that one, too.

Another tense minute passes before I give up. Leaning in to give him one last kiss on the cheek, I say, "I'm gonna go see if they need help in the kitchen."

"The maids have it under control," Mateo says.

"Then I'm going to pee," I reply, promptly.

"Bathroom's broken."

"Then I'm going to drown myself in the pool."

Smirking, Mateo says, "Have Elise grab you a towel."

Vince is in a pissy mood for the first part of the night, and he's a little drunk for the second half. I'm still tense through dinner because of it, while Mateo seems quite content. The newcomer's name is Joey, and apparently he is another of Mateo's brothers. Elise comes around, but Mateo ignores her tonight, so Adrian doesn't join Vince in being pissy.

I feel like I'm going to need a notepad in order to keep track of the politics in this family.

Francesca makes things worse, innocently remarking, "I like your dress, Mia."

"Yeah, it's great," says drunk Vince.

Mateo just grins, taking a sip of his wine.

It's not like I ever doubted he was an asshole, but... yeah. The worst part is, it was a *nice* thing to do, buying me the dresses, but now that I've inadvertently humiliated Vince in front of half his family, I can't even bring myself to thank Mateo. He couldn't have known I would make such a spectacle, but he did know Vince said he would buy me new dresses when it came up the night before.

I'm a little embarrassed I didn't know my own boyfriend's handwriting from Mateo's though. He's never written me anything, and

I've never even peeked at his notes in class. Mateo could have also signed his name to the card so I *knew* who they were from, so it's hard to imagine there wasn't a certain calculated edge there.

I won't let him trick me so easily again.

Mateo sends another car to drive me and my mom to the restaurant in the city.

Brax is watching the kids for the first time, and I imagine them all bro-ing out on the couch, watching football and drinking beers. Mom assured me she whipped up some mac and cheese for dinner before she left, so there was no chance the kids would starve.

"This is so exciting," she tells me, conspiratorially, once we get to the restaurant. It's a nice evening, so we didn't bring coats, but there is a bite to the wind. Since we didn't drive though, we're dropped off right by the door.

All the way here, she's drilled me. What are they like? Do they seem like a crime family? How rich *are* they, anyway?

I don't know how to describe the strange culture of the Morelli family, so she has to yank even brief responses out of me.

Vince and Mateo are already waiting when we get there. Since I wore the other dress already, I'm in the sequined minidress. It's sexier than I realized at first sight, and it makes my legs appear to go on for days.

I'm still wearing the Louboutins; I don't care if they caused trouble, nothing can come between our love.

"Oh, *wow*," she murmurs, when she spots them at the table. "That is a handsome man."

I know she's talking about Mateo, since she already knew what Vince looked like. I don't burst her bubble, telling her that he's also a dick.

"Hi!" she says, approaching the table with way too much excitement. She's already embarrassing me, and we haven't even sat down yet.

Mateo stands, offering her a warm smile and shaking her hand as he introduces himself. Vince offers me a tepid smile, his gaze lingering on my dress a little too long. I can't tell if he's thinking I look good in it, or thinking about where it came from.

I don't roll my eyes as Mateo pulls out my mom's chair for her, but considering she's already as smitten as a school girl, it's difficult.

Turns out I didn't have to spend all that time wracking my brain, trying to figure out what any of us would talk about at this dinner, because Mateo carries us completely. It feels like he and my mom are on a date, with Vince and me awkwardly chaperoning.

Once she's drained her second martini—and he's already ordered her a third—Mateo offers my mother the dessert menu and steeples his hands on the table.

"Shelly, I'm so glad we could get together tonight. It's been a real pleasure meeting you."

"I know! It has been. You're nothing like I imagined. I'm *so* glad we came, too," she gushes, mooning at him.

"There is one more thing I'd like to discuss with you, though. I wanted to wait until you had a pretty good feel for me, but I think you're pretty comfortable with me," he says, with a coaxing, in-joke smile.

My mother laughs, delighted. "Oh yes, I'd say so."

"That's good," he says, finally glancing over at me. "The main reason I wanted us to get together here tonight is because I have a wonderful opportunity for Mia, but I wanted to run it by you first, make sure you're on board."

"Oh?" Attempting a more serious tone to match his, she leans on the table. "Okay, I'm all ears."

"I mentioned my daughter, Isabella?" To illustrate, he has his phone at the ready, and a couple swipes later he's showing off her picture like an adoring father.

"Oh, she's just so darling," my mom says, clutching her heart like she just may die from the cuteness.

"She is," he says warmly.

I make a note that I've *still* never seen him with said daughter. I'm not convinced she even exists.

"My problem is, she needs a nanny. She has a nanny during the day, when everyone's in school, but I need someone for the evenings. I need someone live-in. I want Mia."

Understandably shocked, she says, "You want Mia… to be a live-in nanny?"

"Yes. I pay well, and since I'll take care of her room and board, I'm sure Mia could send some of it home for you. You're a single mom, I'm sure it would be nice to have the load lightened a bit." Reaching into his jacket pocket, he extracts a thick white envelope. He places it on the table and slides it across to my mom.

Her eyes widen and she cracks it open, inhaling and exhaling slowly when she sees it's thick with cash.

"Think of it as a sign-on bonus," Mateo tells her.

I'm glad my mom is distracted with the money, because I think that's the only reason she hasn't noticed my jaw hanging open. Not only has Mateo not asked me about being a nanny to this child I'm not convinced exists, but he actually wants me to *live* at his house? *Full-time*?

"Mia will have her own room, of course. Really it's like a little apartment, just with more supervision. She'll stay in my sister's wing."

"Wing?" my mom echoes, lost.

Flashing one of his charming smiles, Mateo tells her, "We have a very large home."

"Wow," she says, frowning as she visibly tries to process. "So she would... *live* with you? For how long?"

"As long as she wants to work for me. Until she goes off to college? If she goes to a local school, she can stay; we'll work her schedule around the other nanny."

"Where's your daughter's mother?" she asks, confused.

His lips press firmly together and he leans back in his seat, distraught. "Unfortunately... she abandoned us, a couple of years ago."

Hand to her heart once more, my mother laments, "Oh, how terrible."

He nods, accepting her sympathy. "Mia's very good with her, so I think it'll be good for Isabella to have her around. And Mia's nearly finished with high school anyway, so she probably would've moved out soon—I believe she mentioned you might be moving in with... Brax?"

Still haven't met Isabella. Never once mentioned Brax.

Less enthused at the prospect while sitting across from a wealthy single father, she says, "Oh, yeah, well, maybe. I don't know, we'll see." She looks at the envelope again like it's dessert. It's gotta be killing her not to count it and see how much is there.

"Well… I think… if it's okay with Mia, we could probably try that out. I'll have to pay a sitter to take her place, so I think it would definitely be a good idea for her to send half her pay home," she says, glancing over at me. "But yeah. I mean, it sounds like a great job. We were talking about her trying to find something to help out—this wasn't what I had in mind, exactly, but when opportunity knocks…"

Mateo's grin isn't even victorious. He knew he'd win, because he came armed with money and bullshit.

And just like that, I'm for all intents and purposes sold to the Morelli family.

## CHAPTER SEVENTEEN

VINCE'S HAND moves along the curve of my bare back, his touch light, almost absent-minded.

I'm tummy down on the bed, my head resting on my arms on top of my soft, fluffy pillow. I like him touching me. I like sharing a bed.

"You're gonna put me to sleep," I tell him with a relaxed smile.

Cracking a smile, he says, "It's after midnight; that's probably a good thing."

I sigh as his hand settles along the small of my back, and turn my face to look at him. It reminds me of the night he snuck in to hold me. It's so strange, at our age, to know he won't have to sneak anymore.

It's been two weeks, and the transition hasn't been as hard as I expected.

Mateo seems to have backed off Vince now, letting us get settled. I'm staying in Vince's bedroom, not my own, like he told my mother, but that's proving to be really nice. I've still only seen Isabella once in passing, when her actual nanny was hauling her out of the room. Vince got me a few more dresses so I have a variety to choose from for our nightly dinners, and the one on Sundays is actually kind of nice, not as obnoxious as it initially sounded.

It's bizarre, but I really *do* feel like I'm becoming part of this family.

"Shouldn't *you* be asleep," I point out. In the time I've been here, I've noticed Vince generally rises even before I do, and I take a lot more time to get ready for school. I thought sharing a bathroom on the same schedule might prove difficult, but Vince is usually at the gym first thing—the *in-house* gym—and apparently he showers there.

It does explain the physique I so enjoy, I guess.

"Maybe. I like looking at you in my bed," he tells me, eyes twinkling. "Seems like a better use of my time than sleeping."

I grin, stretching my arms out. "Well, when you put it that way…"

His hand doesn't leave my back but he scoots closer, bringing my body against his. "I know I shouldn't, but I like having you here."

At that, I roll my eyes. "Gee, thanks."

"You know what I mean," he says, easily enough. "I didn't want it under these circumstances, but I rest easier with you next to me."

Snuggling my face into his chest, I murmur, "Well, I'm happy to be of service."

For a few minutes, he just holds me. I find myself getting a little tranquil, ready to drift off, when his quiet words hit me like a bucket of ice water. "I didn't want to do it, you know."

I'm quiet, not sure what to say, but I think I know what he's talking about. I'm tempted to cut him off, to tell him we don't have to talk about it, but it's a selfish impulse. We've never actually addressed what happened the night of the fire, and to be honest, I never really wanted to. If he needs to talk, though, I don't want to shut him down.

"Do what?" I finally ask, when he doesn't go on.

"Your neighbors."

*Damn.* I take a breath, searching my brain for what to say in this scenario. "I figured as much."

"When you saw me outside that night, I didn't even know what to feel. Part of me was almost relieved. If you would've told on me, if I would've been caught, at least it would've been over."

I pull back, frowning. "Well, it wouldn't have been over. You would've been in jail, but probably not forever. Even if you were, don't they… I don't know, again, my knowledge comes from movies, but you wouldn't really be 'out' of your family, right?"

"Mateo wouldn't have let me go to jail. He doesn't trust me."

I don't get it at first. I think he's saying Mateo has enough influence to have kept him *out* of jail, but then how would he be out of anything?

Then it hits me, and I can practically feel the color drain out of my face. "He… he would've killed you?"

"Would've had to. I know way too much."

"But you wouldn't have talked," I say, though I don't know why I believe that. I guess I figure if *I* wouldn't talk, surely someone born to this family wouldn't.

"He wouldn't have believed that though. They would've thrown the book at me, to try to get me to talk about him. He knows that. Wouldn't have taken the risk."

"But you're family," I point out, baffled.

Meeting my gaze, Vince tells me, "We have to be loyal to him, Mia. He doesn't have to be loyal to us."

Scowling, I tell him, "That's not right. It should go both ways."

"As long as it doesn't inconvenience him, it does. But he doesn't let anyone get in his way."

I lean back into him, hugging him tightly. I was too afraid to report them anyway, but it scares me to know that if I wouldn't have been, I might've gotten Vince killed.

"I try not to think about it," he goes on, my head tucked beneath his chin. "But it's harder at night, when I'm alone. I don't know how Adrian does this without feeling it."

I'm still not altogether clear on Adrian's role in this family, but he seems to be Mateo's right hand man, and he was there with Vince that night, so he seems pivotal. I want to ask, but it doesn't seem like the right time.

"Maybe he doesn't," I suggest. I don't know how either, but I try to come up with something comforting. "It's not supposed to be easy to take a life," I add, though I'm not sure if that's helpful. It sounds more like a lecture, now that I think about it. "But what was the alternative? If you wouldn't have done it, I assume it still would've happened, right?"

"Yeah."

"So… really, it wouldn't have made a difference. I assume things would've been worse for you, there would've been some penalty for disobedience. You only did what you had to do."

"But I still did it. Me, not someone else. It doesn't help to know it would've happened anyway; I don't *care* about those people, I just…."

I want to tell him I understand, but I don't. I can't fathom doing what he did, even if I didn't have a choice.

"Sometimes we have to do things we don't want to, just to make it," I tell him, even though it sounds generic to my ears. "It's okay to feel badly about it—that's healthy. But… it's done now. Don't let the guilt crush you. Learn something from it if you can, but let it go. You're young, you still have your whole life ahead of you. If you start carrying that kind of baggage already, what hope do you have of a happy life?"

"I don't think I have a chance at that regardless, Mia."

"Well, I disagree. Maybe Mateo would be more understanding than you think. Maybe you could tell him you don't want to do stuff like that anymore—or, if you don't want to talk to him about it, just… make yourself more useful in a different division."

"Division?" he asks, amusement finally breaking through his gloom.

"Yeah, department, whatever. I don't know how this crap works, but another *area*. Whatever you want to call it. If Mateo's interested in utility, be more useful doing something else. He won't waste you on something literally anyone could do if it benefits him to have you doing something else."

He doesn't immediately respond, and I wonder if that wasn't good advice in this scenario. In a company I think it would be, but I guess it could be different in a criminal empire. When he does speak, however, he says, "That's a good point."

"See," I say, a little proud of myself. "Plus, you have this wonderful live-in girlfriend to come home to now. If that's not a recipe for a happy life, I don't know what is."

He pulls back just enough to kiss me, and the look he gives me after looses a swarm of butterflies in my stomach. "You are pretty wonderful," he agrees.

"You have your moments, too," I tease.

"We should just stay in this bed and never leave," he decides.

"Oh, that we could," I say, wrapping my arms around his neck as his body comes down on top of mine. He grabs a condom, moving easily between my legs, and I sigh happily as he pushes inside me for the second time tonight.

"Who are you marrying?"

Francesca looks up, startled, as I drop into the seat across from her.

Seeing it's just me, she gives a little laugh, flipping the next page of her *Bridal Guide* magazine. "No one. Ever. I'm going to die childless and alone."

"Sounds like fun," I say, spearing a strawberry and popping it into my mouth.

"All fun, all the time, that's my life," she agrees easily, tilting her head as she gazes down at a beautiful white ball gown.

After a few minutes, she flips her magazine closed and passes it across the table in my direction. "You can have it if you want."

I blink at the magazine in surprise. "Me?"

"You'll get married before I do," she says wryly, standing and collecting her breakfast dishes.

"Does everyone in this house know I'm only 18?" I ask, partially in jest, but also legitimately baffled. "Who gets married this young? Also, while Vince and I are... you know, great, I've only been *officially* his girlfriend for two weeks. I think we all need to pump the brakes on our expectations of this relationship."

With a look verging on haughty, Francesca shakes her head as she heads for the kitchen. "I tried to tell you."

When she returns, Francesca pauses beside me at the table. "I know you don't really need the money anymore, but if you wanted something to do, you could help me out at the bakery."

There are plenty of leisurely activities to do at the house, but it might be nice to actually be around other people once in a while. Not to mention, Francesca and Vince seem to get along, and I should probably nurture relationships with the Morellis he actually likes.

"Sure, I'd like that," I tell her, nodding my head.

Flashing me a smile, she says, "Great. You can have Vince drop you off after school," and then she's off, leaving me to finish my breakfast by myself.

## CHAPTER EIGHTEEN

ALTHOUGH THE girls assure me I'm totally-definitely-for-sure not a prisoner of any kind, Mateo is still not enthusiastic about the idea of me going out unattended. Vince usually gives me rides to and from school, but now that I'll have a job, I don't know if he'll always be around to escort me. I don't know how that'll end up working, but for my first day, Vince gives me a ride.

When we enter the bakery and see a fairly attractive guy behind the front counter, I notice Vince's arm possessively moves around my waist.

The guy behind the counter smiles at me. "You must be Mia. Francesca said you'd be in."

"Is she not here?" I ask, confused.

"She had to step out. She'll be back soon. I'll be training you today anyway, so if you wanna come on back, we can get started."

I go to pull away from Vince, but he pulls me into him, kissing me. "I'll pick you up when I'm done."

He's being silly, but I just smile, catching his hand for a squeeze, then dropping it. "Be safe."

Once Vince leaves, my trainer introduces himself as Mark. "I take it you're Vince's old lady," he says lightly.

"Oh yeah. Heavy emphasis on the old," I say, nodding.

"So, Mia, you do a lot of baking?"

"If fish sticks count," I tell him.

Smiling, he heads to the back and grabs a plastic-wrapped package. "All right then, we'll start you off with assembly. I need to wrap and tie 250 cookies for a wedding—you can speed it up by helping me. These cookies are already dry, but I have a batch I'll have to decorate tonight. I'll show you how to flood and decorate them. I assume you're not going to be here on your own?"

"Oh no, I am firmly an assistant. The cakes I do make come from Betty Crocker."

"Gotcha."

After showing me around the bakery, we get to work on the cookies. "Have you been a baker long?" I ask him, tying the cookie bag.

"A few months," he says. "What about you? Been an old lady long?"

Cracking a smile, I shake my head. "Not at all."

He messes up a cookie and sets it aside. "Gotta be kind of a rough gig, huh?"

"Rough? Uh, not really, not so far. The food's good."

Mark sets a tray aside. "Oh, yeah, I bet. What's your favorite?"

"That's hard. We have, like, legit family dinners *every night*. It's basically like living in the 50's, but with iPhones." I pause to consider. "I guess… Francesca's chicken and pesto pasta. I've never been able to make a batch of pesto that's good enough to make a second time, but Francesca's was delicious."

Nodding like I just earned street cred, he says, "Great pick. I have a pretty good pesto recipe myself. One of these days when you're working a long enough shift for lunch, we'll have to have a pesto cook-off, see whose is better."

"That may be the best idea anyone has ever had," I state.

Time flies by as we pack up the cookies. Mark's really easy-going and friendly, which is a nice change of pace from the intense, gun-wielding men I now live with. It's refreshing, and by the end of my shift, I'm really pleased I took the job.

Adrian is pacing.

I'm coming back from the pool when I see him outside Mateo's study, trying his best to wear a hole in the floor.

"Hey, Adrian," I greet.

I didn't expect to, given our bumpy start and his position within the

## Accidental Witness

Morelli family, but I quite like Adrian.

Glancing up, he offers a gruff nod and resumes his pacing. "Everything okay?" I ask.

He nods again, not looking up or interrupting his pace.

I'm just about to shrug this off as him being an oddball and go to the kitchen to grab some lunch when the study door opens. Mateo is standing there, and he pushes it open for Elise to walk out. I peer in to see they were alone together. Elise flashes Adrian and me a wordless smile before she slides past us and down the hall.

Adrian stops short, standing in front of Mateo with all the eagerness of a kid on Christmas morning. "Did you talk to her?"

"I did," Mateo replies, but he's distracted. Instead of looking at Adrian, or having the conversation he's obviously eager to start, Mateo's eyes are wandering over my body.

I remember I'm in a bikini then, and promptly flush. There's a towel wrinkled up and draped over my arm, but I can't exactly whip it off and wrap it around myself now without being pretty obvious.

Amusement at my discomfort is written all over his face as he smiles at me. "Enjoying the amenities?"

"I was," I say, doing my best not to look as awkward as I feel.

"I wanted to ask you how your first week at the bakery was. I have some business to attend to with Adrian first, but we'll catch up at dinner." His eyes rake over me one last time, then he turns and ushers Adrian into his office.

Drooping as I roll my eyes at myself, I make a note to order a cover-up before I go to the pool again.

"You can take out the bread."

I grab both bread baskets and make my way for the dining room. It's Sunday, so the table is at capacity tonight with family members I've met, but still don't know. At least half the time I'm not involved with the conversation anyway, so it doesn't matter. As Cherie told it to me, I was concerned the family would be more chauvinistic, but as it is, Sunday night dinners just seem like a nostalgic callback to old traditions. I won't begrudge them that.

When I get back to the kitchen, I grab Vince's salad. Before I make it out the door, Cherie calls, "Take Mateo's, too."

With an "oh" of surprise, I turn back. "I haven't the last two weeks," I point out.

She's stirring with impressive focus, but her gaze flits to mine, wary. "His request."

Frowning slightly, I ask, "Am I bringing him dinner, too?"

"Yep."

That's odd, but I don't argue. While the women do the cooking and serving, the "married" women only serve their own husbands. At least, that's how it's been the last two weeks. The unmarried women deliver the food to the unattached men, usually Francesca since she's quickest. While I'm obviously not married to Vince, for the past two weeks, I *have* been considered his spouse in that respect.

It probably doesn't matter. Less work for Francesca if I pitch in—I thought that at the beginning anyway. I guess I get the logic of only serving one "master," but... oh, who am I kidding? It's stupid.

I give up the thought, sprinkling some croutons over a second plate and resuming my path to the dining room. Once I get there and see both men assembled at the table, flanking me, since I'm still in the same seat I sat in that first night, I wonder if order matters. I guess since Vince is mine he should get served first? But Mateo is the head of the family.... I need an informational pamphlet on the etiquette of this shit if they're going to complicate things.

I go to Vince first, placing his salad down and dropping a little kiss on his cheek. He smiles up at me, until he sees the second plate. A little crease forms between his eyebrows as I step over to drop off Mateo's.

"Thank you, Mia," Mateo says.

"Yep."

Before I can move away, he catches me by the wrist, just a light grasp to get my attention. "Can you bring out dried cranberries for mine?"

"Oh. Yeah, of course. Sorry," I say, off-handedly.

"It's okay," he says easily, dropping my wrist and picking up his fork. "Now you'll know for next time."

I blink, at a loss. I glance at Vince, seeing all the light has drained from his face. "She's serving *you* now?"

"And you," Mateo says, like it's a favor.

"Good thing I have two hands," I say lightly, not wanting this to be a whole thing.

Mateo smirks, but doesn't comment.

Skittering back to the kitchen, I enter with a pronounced, "Ugh." I have to locate the cranberries for Mateo's salad, and I'm not looking forward to Vince being in a pissy mood.

Deciding to get confirmation, I say to Francesca, "It doesn't matter that I'm serving both of them, right?"

Appearing not to know what I'm talking about, she murmurs, "Huh?"

"The stupid dinner thing," I say, rolling my eyes. "They've only had me serve Vince before, but now Mateo's requested I serve him, too. Vince seems annoyed, but it doesn't matter, right?"

Looking tired, she sighs. "Mateo's stirring the pot. Just stay focused on Vince. Quietly reassure him, you'll be fine."

I'd been hoping for simple agreement, so that's annoying. "I mean, you serve half the table; what's the difference?"

"The difference is I'm not spoken for."

I roll my eyes, in this instance inconvenienced by their eccentricities. Cherie comes up beside me, handing me a little dish of dried cranberries.

"You forgot these for Mateo's salad," she informs me.

"I had no idea he wanted them," I point out, taking the cranberries.

"Francesca took out the last batch, so you can take out your salad and have a seat now."

When I make it back to the table, Vince still seems surly and Mateo, as usual, is utterly unconcerned. He does make a point to catch up with me, as he said he would, asking how I'm liking the bakery, if I get along with the other employees. I assure him everything is fine, but by the time the salads are finished, I realize Mateo and I have been talking to each other exclusively, and Vince has moved on from wine to something stronger. I was supposed to be the one getting his drink, and I realize I didn't even notice he'd gotten up.

Shit.

Before I get up to clear our plates away, I offer Vince a private little smile and lightly squeeze his thigh.

He ignores me completely.

Unsettled, I stand and collect the plates from my place, Vince's and Mateo's, making a point not to actually interact with Mateo. I'm the first woman back in the kitchen, aside from Cherie, who doesn't eat dinner with the family.

"Don't make me go back out there," I whine, turning on the faucet to rinse off the dishes before setting them in the sink.

"Vince mad?" she guesses.

I nod, rolling my eyes. "Like it's worth getting mad over."

Instead of agreeing with me, she shrugs. "Mateo doesn't have a reputation for keeping his hands to himself."

That's a little insulting, and I can't help my response being a little short. "Well, *I* do. I've never given Vince a reason not to trust me. He shouldn't let Mateo get to him like that. He makes it *so* easy. All the man has to do is *smile* at me, and Vince goes cold."

Still not taking my side, Cherie shakes her head. "You don't *know* Mateo, Mia. Vince does. I understand that you think it's annoying, but you're not the one he doesn't trust."

"Sure seems that way. It takes two to tango, Cherie."

Looking at me more seriously than I expect, she responds, "No, it doesn't."

I don't understand that logic and I feel a little hollow inside in regards to this conversation—it's pointless and insulting. Serving the man dinner—and not even because I want to—is not a legitimate reason for anyone to think Mateo is… what, interested in me? Or that I would even be open to his attentions, if he offered them. Sure, from a physical standpoint he's an attractive man, and his unchecked power is… interesting. But he's far too old for me, and Vince's cousin. And also? I have Vince.

Since Cherie isn't the ally I expected, I drop it and start dishing out three plates of food. "Does Mateo have any main dish special requests?" I ask, a touch sarcastically.

"Just make sure he has parmesan," she says, her back to me.

## CHAPTER NINETEEN

VINCE IS peeling off his dress shirt from dinner when I come in.

My first instinct is to duck back out of the bedroom to give him privacy, but I guess that's dumb. We're having sex, we're living in the same space—we're past that.

I subtly clear my throat anyway, just so he knows I'm here.

He glances back over his shoulder just long enough to acknowledge me, then goes to his closet and moves a few hangers before settling on a T-shirt.

"We should watch a movie," I tell him. "I'm too stuffed for popcorn, but I think a movie night could be just what the doctor ordered."

His stony silence stretches on, indicating he isn't going to answer me.

I slip my shoes off, using my foot to scoot them over beside the bedside table. "Or we could do something else, if you want."

"You can do whatever you want," he finally says, brushing invisible lint off his sleeve. "I'm going to Joey's."

Taking a seat on the edge of the bed, I consider for a moment before I say, "You know I didn't do anything wrong, right? He told Cherie he wanted me to bring him his food. It's not like I could say no to him."

Spinning on his heel to point at me, he says, "Exactly."

Shrugging helplessly, I say, "That's what you're mad about? That I had no choice so I did this stupid little thing that doesn't matter to anyone? It's crazy. This is an *insane* thing to care about."

My logic does nothing to calm him. "It's not about the dinner.

You're not *that* naïve, Mia, come on."

Scowling, I push up off the bed and walk around the bed so I'm closer to him. "What the hell is that supposed to mean?"

"I'm not here all the time," he says, eyebrows rising. "How do I know what's going on when I'm not here?"

My mouth opens and closes four different times, but I'm fucking flabbergasted, and nothing will come out.

Finally I throw my hands up in the air. "You're being crazy!"

"I'm being realistic," he mutters. "He'll come between us, just watch."

"That's so *stupid*," I state. "And even if he wanted to, which, I want to reiterate, *is insane*, he can't come between us if we don't let him. Period. It's impossible. He's not *God*, he can't make us stop caring about each other."

With a bitter, knowing nod, he says, "No?"

I take a breath, telling myself to simmer down. Yes, Vince is being unreasonable, but escalating the situation won't make it any better. After a moment, I manage calmly, "There is *nothing* going on when you're not here. It's insulting that you would even wonder."

"Then why are you giving him his dinner?"

Throwing my arms in the air again, I walk past him to the dresser. Grabbing a hair clip, I yank the fancy pins out and toss my hair up instead. "Okay. We're back to this. Your cousin is not interested in me, Vince. And I'm damn sure not interested in him."

"You see the way he looks at you," Vince counters.

"Like he wants to piss you off? Yeah, I see those looks. I think he likes to piss everyone off."

"Adrian asked me about it," Vince states, like he's caught me.

I consider the moment earlier when I was in my bikini and Mateo was looking me over in front of him. I wouldn't have thought that was worth reporting back to Vince—any man would've looked, it didn't *mean* anything. Maybe I like Adrian a little less.

All I can do is shake my head. "Whatever. I'm not going to keep defending myself. I think this is stupid, I don't know why you're being so weird about all this, but I wish you'd stop. Stop giving him so much power over you. If he didn't get such a rise out of you every time, he'd probably stop doing stupid little shit to piss you off."

"It'd be nice if you were on my side about this," he states.

"If your side and mine were the same, I would be, but it kind of feels like I'm being blamed for something, and I haven't done anything wrong. If you're accusing me of any sort of impropriety with Mateo, you're *completely* mistaken. I've barely *spoken* to the man. Yes, I try to play nice, when he was friendly at dinner, I talked to him—I have this weird feeling that pissing him off for no reason *isn't* the best idea."

Shaking his head, Vince says, "Mateo isn't *friendly*, Mia. He's manipulative. I still don't think you get it."

"I'm really tired of being warned about him."

"And I'm really tired of you not getting it," Vince states.

"I must be impossibly naïve," I return, fed up with this conversation. "Since he said he wouldn't hurt me and you and I could be together, he *hasn't* hurt me and we *have* been together. He gave my mother thousands of dollars and moved me into a mansion with my boyfriend. He's been so atrocious to me that he bought me some things to help me fit in, and has conversations with me sometimes at the dinner table. Holy shit, what a monster."

Making a face somewhere between anger and disgust, he says, "Whatever, I'm out of here."

I sigh, turning toward him as he heads for the door. "Are you coming home tonight?"

"Why do you care?" he tosses back.

"I don't *want* to fight with you," I say, but he's already slamming the door shut behind him.

Since I'm on my own with no homework and no company, I make my way to the library. It's still kind of crazy to me that there's an actual library in this house, but there is, it's huge, and there's this comfy couch that really tops off the whole experience.

I can't find anything to read though. You wouldn't think more choices would be a bad thing, but there are too many and I can't decide.

The door creaks open as I peruse a shelf, so I glance back to see who's there.

Mateo ducks his head in, not seeing me. "Anyone in here?"

Clearing my throat, I take a step toward him. "Yeah, I am."

"Oh, okay. I was just going to shut the light off, thought someone left it on."

"Nope," I say, offering a slight smile. "Just looking for something to read."

He nods, stepping inside. "Vince go to bed already?"

I shake my head, glancing at the floor. "He left. Went with Joey or something."

Gesturing to the area near me, he says, "Mind if I come in for a minute?"

"Not at all," I say, stepping back to make room, which is absurd, since there's nothing *but* room. I just feel a little awkward after everything with Vince, and I've never actually been alone with Mateo, but I think I've been warned against it 850 times.

Nodding toward the book in my hand as he approaches, he asks, "What are you reading?"

"Oh, nothing yet," I say, glancing down at the old, illustrated copy of Pinocchio. "I was just looking. You have some really cool books in here."

"Yeah, I think there's a little bit of everything," he agrees, glancing around at the walls of bookshelves.

"Well, not everything, but pretty much."

"What's missing?" he asks, frowning slightly.

I blush, feeling a bit stupid. "Uh, I was looking to see if you had any graphic novels. There aren't any."

Now amusement dances in his eyes. "Graphic novels? Like, comic books? Heroes and villains? Good winning out over evil?"

I shrug. "They're fun. Maybe not great literature, but I got sort of hooked on them last summer. The air wasn't working at our house and we didn't have any money to do anything, so I'd take the kids to the library. They could pick out books to read, there was a little play area, and I just sort of stumbled upon the graphic novels. They're quicker to read than a book, less wordy, so it was a nice way to pass a little time. Some of them are really interesting. You shouldn't knock them until you try them," I advise him.

"My apologies to the graphic novel community," he says solemnly. "Which one's your favorite?"

"Oh, I couldn't choose," I say, shaking my head.

"Well, why don't you make me a list. I'll order some for you—you know, to rectify this gross oversight in my library."

I can't help smiling. "I will. Then you can read them, and decide for yourself whether or not they're stupid."

"I do enjoy a good hero versus villain showdown," he says, winking.

"So do I," I admit. "In books, not so much… life, but…"

"Hey, now you've got firsthand experience, maybe you can write your own graphic novel," he jokes.

"Oh, no, I'm not a writer. It takes me like 23 years to write a 3 page paper, double spaced. Also, I'm not sure dressing up for dinners and lounging by the pool in a 28,000 square foot mansion necessarily qualifies me to…you know, show the ugly underbelly of humanity."

His eyes dance with amusement, and I wonder how I ever thought them cold. There's definitely warmth there. "Give it time; you're still new to the family."

"Oh, I know, I'm always being warned about the horrors that await me," I say unthinkingly, rolling my eyes. "What next, will I be forced to go on a cruise to the Bahamas?"

He maintains his smile, but glances down. "By whom?"

I look back at him, raising my eyebrows questioningly. "By whom will I be forced to go on the cruise?"

"By whom are you warned?" he specifies.

"Oh." I pause, flushing, realizing that had been a dumb thing to say, given all the warnings have been about him. "Uh, I mean… I didn't mean specifically, just…" I trail off awkwardly, hoping he'll save me here, but he just watches me scramble. "Cherie was telling me how you guys—this family—the—how, like, you're pretty traditional, and not, you know, feminist-friendly."

I'm already feeling like an assbag for offering up her name, but I didn't know what to say. I didn't want to throw Vince under the bus, and I couldn't really say, "Well, everybody. Everybody says that."

Nodding his head, he said, "Cherie's not a big fan of my family. I don't *blame* her, her father certainly isn't the best example, and given that, I'm sure her mother feels the same way, but I wouldn't take her opinion to heart. We *are* traditional, but tradition isn't always a bad thing."

"Her father?" I ask, interest piqued. As long as I've wondered about Cherie, I still don't know much about her. "I haven't met him. Does he live here, too?"

"Ben?" he asks, eyebrows rising. "No. No, he moved to Vegas years ago, when Vince's mom died."

"Vince's mom?"

"His wife?"

I give up and frown. "What? Sorry, I'm not following. I don't know anything about Vince's dad either."

"Oh, Vince and Cherie have the same father," he explains.

My jaw drops open. "They're… siblings?"

"Half, yeah."

All the times I've felt catty and jealous over her suddenly come flying back to me, and I feel so incredibly stupid. "Oh, my God," I say, slapping my palm to my forehead with a little smile. "Wow, I wish someone would've told me that a long time ago."

"You had no idea," he realizes.

"I was *such* a bitch to her when she first tried to befriend me. Legendarily bitchy."

He has the nerve to laugh. "Why?"

"I thought she was trying to… you know, horn in on my man," I say, giving up and laughing at how stupid I sound. "Oh my God, I'm an asshole."

"I'm surprised Vince didn't tell you," he remarks.

"Yeah, me too. We never even talked about it—he knew I had siblings, of course, but… he didn't want to talk too much about his family."

Mateo nods, understanding. "We try not to. You can't trust people."

Dimming a bit, that makes me think of the fight Vince and I just had. "I think you can trust people more than you guys do. Give people a little credit, they might surprise you."

He looks amused. "I'm rarely surprised."

Raising a finger to point at him, I say, "But rarely isn't never, now is it?"

"I guess not," he says. I know I haven't cured him of his paranoia, but at least he gave me that.

## Accidental Witness

"You all need to just relax. You guys have this awesome life, and you're too busy watching over your shoulders to enjoy it. A month ago I had to find ways to make dinner for $2. If I got sick, I had to drink orange juice from the school cafeteria and hope the vitamin C helped because we couldn't afford to buy medicine. You guys have a *country club* at your *house* and you're all wearier than I've ever been."

"You're young," he reminds me. "You're correct that I've never experienced poverty, but you've never experienced a man you've grown up with for 20 years, more brother than friend, try to assassinate you because another man wanted what was yours. You've never had your older sister gouge you in the leg with a throwing star and try to end your life. You've never had to live every day knowing the only thing between you and a body bag is a good bodyguard and the people who would kill you being too afraid of what you'd do if they failed."

My eyes are wide by the end. Being tucked away here, it's easy to forget the ugly life that makes all the extravagance possible. "Wow, that... sucks. I'm sorry."

He shrugs, like it's business as usual. "I *have* trusted people close to me. I learned not to."

I can't help the wave of sympathy that comes over me. I can't imagine being betrayed in such grand fashion by the people closest to me. He's different here, alone, without everyone around to posture for. "That sounds really lonely," I tell him.

"That's life," he says simply.

"It doesn't have to be," I say, softly, since I don't really know how to argue that. I'm sure in my convictions though, so I attempt to come up with evidence to base that claim on. "There are people here you *can* trust. I mean, Adrian seems like a good friend."

"Adrian despises me," Mateo states, smiling.

I rear back a little at that. "I thought he was your bodyguard?"

"He is," he says, simply.

That... doesn't make sense, but I move along. "Francesca—your sister is great."

"So was my other sister—the throwing star one," he reminds me.

Grimacing slightly, I say, "Damn, two for two. Well, you can trust me," I decide. "I mean, I know I'm not powerful or connected and I couldn't protect you from a bullet or a throwing star, but if you ever feel lonely, you can count on me as a friend."

He's looking at me in a way I can't quite pin down, but I see traces of amusement there. "You always try to befriend people who've threatened to kill you?"

"Exclusively," I say, not missing a beat. "How else will I know they care?"

Shaking his head, he states, "I'm not sure if you're terribly idealistic or a little bit dim."

Lightly whacking him in the arm, I say, "Hey, that's not friendly!"

"I'm not a friendly guy," he states.

"Oh," I say, with a dismissive wave. "I think you're friendlier than you want to admit. You don't have to intimidate me into not wanting to kill you, so you don't have to keep up the front."

"Front, huh?" he repeats, still amused.

I nod. "There's good in you. There's good in everyone, and you're no exception."

With a disbelieving headshake, he says, "I think I'm starting to see why Vince is so fond of you."

That draws a frown out of me. "Eh, he's not so fond of me tonight."

His eyebrows rise, like he's surprised. "No? Well, his loss."

My frown turns to a slight smile at that. A second passes, then Mateo takes a step away. "Well, I'll leave you to your books. Turn the light off on your way out, would you?"

"Of course. Thanks for keeping me company."

"Anytime," he says, offering a slow smile before departing the room.

## CHAPTER TWENTY

AFTER I left the library, I retired to my room for the night to wait for Vince. My pleasant exchange with Mateo got me thinking, and I realized I need to be kinder to Vince. Maybe he is being paranoid and crazy, but fighting will make that worse, not better. Regardless, Mateo isn't an actual threat outside of Vince's mind, and I don't want to harm our relationship by letting things get out of hand.

I sent him a text to ask him when he was coming home, but he didn't answer me. Before I got in the shower, I sent him one more text, telling him I was sorry for snapping and that I didn't want to fight with him.

The shower I took was too hot, but it felt so good to stand under the hot spray, I lost all track of time.

Tucking the edge of the towel into the front near my breasts, I step out of the bathroom. The coolness of the bedroom by comparison feels nice.

Approaching the desk, I check my phone to see if he's responded. Nothing. I was in the shower forever, so he had to have read the message by now.

I sigh and flip open my history book. I probably could study tonight and get it out of the way, but right now I'm too tired. I decide to lie down in bed for a few minutes first and just rest my eyes.

Only I fall asleep. I don't realize it until the bed dips beside me, Vince crawling in and wrapping an arm around me in the dark. I stir, but I'm not ready to wake up. I'm relieved he's home safe. I know he had been drinking at dinner, and I wasn't sure if he was driving to Joey's or not. I would've asked, but he slammed the door in my face.

"Hey, you," I murmur, reaching back to caress whatever my hand lands on. It's his hip, and he's still wearing dress pants, not pajamas.

His arm snakes around my waist, finding the edge of the towel and tugging.

Without opening my eyes, I smile. I don't have the physical stamina to have sex right now, but that he wants to makes me think he doesn't want to fight anymore either. "I'm really sleepy. Can I get a rain check?"

His hand touches my bare stomach, then skates down between my legs.

Despite my meager objection, I let my legs fall open for him. Arousal stirs at his touch, and I guess it won't kill me to wait 20 more minutes for sleep.

My head falls back as his fingers move inside me, first just one, but he promptly pushes a second inside. His thumb massages my clit as the other two explore, but to my disappointment, he stops after only a few seconds.

"Tease," I murmur, when he withdraws.

He chuckles quietly. Then his hands are on my hips and he's guiding me to roll over on my stomach. I do, not totally sure where we're going with this, but then he does the most amazing thing—he starts rubbing my back. If this is how he's going to make up after fights, I think they might be easier to get through in the future. Everything tingles as his strong hands work my muscles, and while I feel positively blissful, there's a good chance he's going to put me back to sleep.

Until he stops, nudging my legs apart. His hand passes over my bare ass and I feel the bed shift as he changes positions. I push up to my hands and knees, assuming he's going to enter me doggie style, but he doesn't unbutton or unzip. Instead he invades me with two fingers again and begins pumping. This feels different, he's not just toying with my clit, but plunging deeper, quicker.

"Oh God, that feels good," I tell him, shifting my ass.

His free hand moves from my hip to my ass, and he gives it a light smack, startling me, but also exciting me. Anchoring his hand on my hip, his thrusts pick up even more speed, and I feel the telltale build of an orgasm. When it hits, it's like no orgasm I've had before. I cry out far too loudly, trembling as my orgasm shudders through me.

I feel like a limp spaghetti noodle as I fall down on my stomach, panting. "Holy shit."

Then the kisses start. He kisses a trail down my spine, straddling the backs of my thighs. I've never been so satisfied in my life, but I won't object to more kisses. He can do just about whatever he wants to my body right now, I won't mind.

He moves off me and I hear the covers rustling as he pulls them up. I don't know what he's doing until he rolls me over onto my back again. He's under the covers. Before I can object, he starts dropping kisses along my inner thigh.

Oh, God.

"Vince, I can't," I say, laughing lightly. "There's no way."

But then his hot breath hits me, his fingers spreading me open, and his tongue delves into me.

I was wrong, I realize, as a breath rushes out of me. I'm so wet that it's embarrassing, but he's positively devouring me, and the arousal I thought was exhausted is roaring back to life.

He pulls his tongue back out, wringing a tortured cry from me, and runs his mouth over me, nibbling on me with his lips.

"Jesus Christ," I mutter, digging my hands into the soft black sheets. "Don't stop, please."

He obliges, tonguing my clit until I think I'm going to die from the building pressure. My whole body tenses as I approach another climax, terrified he'll stop or move or breathe differently—anything that might interrupt me. "Yes, yes, don't stop. Oh, God."

Pleasure explodes within me for a second time. Actually, pleasure is too slight a word for the incapacitating satisfaction that claims me as I arch up, then fall against the bed.

Now I really *can't* move. Holy shit.

"That was incredible," I say slowly. "Holy fuck."

His laughter rumbles against my belly and I reach down, tenderly threading his hair through my fingers. "You're amazing. Thank you."

He lays his head down on my belly and I continue to absently play with his hair. I know I should return the favor, but moving my body is a legitimate impossibility at the moment. I vow to myself I will do it tomorrow. Right now, all I want to do is bask in the afterglow of that awesome pair of orgasms and run my fingers through Vince's hair.

Ordinarily Monday mornings aren't my favorite, what with the early rising after a weekend of sleeping in, but as I make my way downstairs for breakfast, I'm feeling pretty damn good.

Vince was up before me and already out of the room by the time I got up to shower, but I smile, seeing him with Mateo at the breakfast table.

Wrapping my arms around his neck from behind, I lean down to give him a good morning kiss. "Hey, you."

"Hey," he returns, sounding mildly surprised to see me. "Sleep good?"

"Oh yes." I give him another kiss for good measure, lips lingering, before I finally stand back.

Mateo glances up at me, and I want to be friendly and say hi, but I also don't want to make Vince sulk. I settle for a warm smile at him behind Vince's head, then make my way to the kitchen.

When I return to the table, I take my usual spot at Vince's right, with Mateo on my right, at the head of the table. I wonder why we never switched spots, since Vince obviously doesn't enjoy sitting so near him. It's not like he ever said we couldn't.

I guess if I'm going to keep being his Sunday server though, it makes sense to keep us all together.

"I made that list," I tell Mateo, because it just popped into my head. "Started it, anyway. It's not done, but I expect it will be by the time I get home from school."

He gives a nod of approval, picking up his coffee cup. "Good, I'll order them right away."

"What list?" Vince inquires.

"Oh, books for the library," I say, placing a hand on his thigh and smiling. "I had some recommendations."

This time, my leg squeeze move seems to appease him, because he accepts this explanation without getting irritable. Score.

Newly confident I can make this work and get along with everyone, I start chowing down on my oatmeal with strawberries.

"Do you work tonight?" Vince asks.

"I do."

"I'll give you a ride. That guy there again today?"

"I have no idea," I state calmly.

This catches Mateo's interest. "What guy?"

"Nobody. Mark—the baker. He was training me last week."

"Ah," he says with a nod. "Nice?"

"Yes, he's very nice. A good trainer, too."

Vince finishes his food first, since he started before me. After he drops it off in the kitchen, he comes back, playing with his key. "I'll be in the car."

"I'm almost done," I tell him, shoveling a bigger bite on my spoon.

I finish the rest in record time and hustle to clean off the dishes. Since Vince isn't here, I offer Mateo a smile a little more freely. "Have a good day."

He's reading the newspaper at this point, but he folds it aside to offer back a smile. "You too, Mia."

"Now *that* is a perfect cookie. I can just resign, they don't need me here anymore."

Laughing as I inspect the smudgey mess of a cookie, I say, "Shut up."

Holding his hands up in defense, he says, "No, I'm serious! Watch." Grabbing the cookie, he takes a bite, then rolls his eyes back in exaggerated ecstasy. "Oh, my God," he says, mouth full of cookie.

I snort, wadding up the paper towel by my hand and throwing it at his stomach. "I quit. You can design the cookies by yourself, I'm not helping you anymore."

Grinning as he drops the cookie into the nearby trash can, he says, "I think that's probably for the best. You just sit there and look pretty; I'm gonna do all the manly work."

I roll my eyes and make a gagging face.

He still smiles, outlining and then flooding his cookie in a way I just can't manage. "Sorry, am I giving you flashbacks of your home life?"

I take a seat on the stool next to his work table. "What home life?"

"Your whole mob wife deal," he says, flashing a playful look my way. "From what I hear, they're very..."

"Traditional?" I offer.

"I was gonna say sexist, but sure, we'll go with that." He switches icing bags. "Do you at least get to hear any juicy tidbits?"

"Juicy tidbits? No, I'm not in on any of that. Whatever they do outside of the home, I don't know. My job is to serve the guys at dinner and wear a pretty dress."

"Aw, come on. I'm sure you get something more than that. I love

*The Godfather*. We should meet for coffee one day and you can dish."

"There's really nothing to dish. And I'm 100% sure Vince wouldn't let me get coffee with you."

His eyebrows rise, but he at least keeps watching the cookie instead of me. "*Let* you? Is he your boyfriend or your master?"

"There's not as big a difference as you might think," I say lightly.

"Ew," he says.

I don't disagree, but like Cherie said, it doesn't really serve me to think about that. "It is what it is. What about you, do you have a lucky lady to call your own?"

That time he cuts me a smirk. "Nope, no one around to forbid me from getting coffee with a friend."

I roll my eyes. "It's not like that. He wasn't… controlling when we dated, but I'm starting to notice it a lot more now that we're living together."

"I'm pretty sure that's how it always works," he says, levelly. "How long did you even date the guy before you moved in with him?"

"I reserve the right to avoid answering that question," I state.

"Not long enough, I take it?"

"It wasn't my choice."

Mark frowns, grabbing a new tray of empty cookies. "Moving in with your boyfriend wasn't your choice?"

Glancing at the table, I realize, "We should probably talk about something else."

"But I'm interested in this. I like hearing about your life—it's far more exciting than mine. I'm not above a little girl talk," he jokes. Then, a little more seriously, he said, "Plus, it sounds like things get a little intense at home. Just want you to know you have someone to talk to, if you need it."

"Well, thanks. But honestly, it's not how it sounds. Vince isn't a bad guy, he just has a really weird family. I don't think he would be so…whatever, it's just, he reacts and certain family members think it's amusing or something, so they prod him, and…"

"He Hulks out," Mark surmises.

"He doesn't Hulk out. He's not violent," I assure him, seriously. "He's just paranoid. They all are. Crazy levels of paranoia in that family."

With a nod-and-shrug he says, "I guess I'd probably be paranoid too though, you know?"

"Not *that* paranoid."

"What's the craziest paranoid thing you've seen since you moved in? They have, like, spy cams set up," he says, indicating around the room dramatically.

My eyebrows rise. "You joke, but they do have surveillance. Apparently that you can see, and that you can't. I haven't spent too much time thinking about that Big Brother aspect though. I assume it's more for outside threats than monitoring my trek to the pool."

"Yeah, mob beefs and all. I know, I know, that's how I roll, too."

I shake my head at him, because he's crazy. Hopping off the chair, I tell him, "Well, since I'm completely useless back here, I'm going to see if Francesca needs any help up front."

"No," he drawls. "Stay and keep me company!"

I shake my head at him, but I ignore his request and go up front.

# CHAPTER TWENTY ONE

"WHAT ARE you thinking about?"

I lift my head, pushing down the pillow as I roll over on my side to get a better look at my beautiful boyfriend. We've been cuddling for the better part of an hour, still naked from an impulsive after-school quickie.

Right now, he's lying next to me, arms crossed behind him under his head, staring up at the ceiling. "Lots of things," he tells me.

"Like? Share some of the things," I say, gently prodding him in the side with my index finger.

"Like… I hope you're happy with me."

Melting a bit, I give him a little hug. "I'm *very* happy with you."

"I don't mean just now," he says, pensive. "We didn't get a chance to cover a lot of things that normal people should talk about before they get serious."

"Well, let's talk about them now."

"I don't want kids," he states, readily enough that I think that might've been on his mind already.

I frown a little, since I never imagined *not* having kids. "Well, we always use protection; I don't think we have to worry about that right now."

"No, I mean… ever. I never want kids."

"Never?"

He meets my gaze, shaking his head no.

"You've thought about this," I realize.

"A lot. It's not fair to bring kids into this family. Boys, girls—they're fucked either way. I don't want to do it."

"Well... I mean, they'd be *our* kids. We would decide how to raise them..."

He's already shaking his head. His gaze returns to the ceiling. "No, that's not how it works."

"Well, what about—Cherie was saying how a lot of your family's business interests are legitimate now. By the time we would even have kids, by the time they would be old enough for this to be an issue, maybe your family would have withdrawn from the whole crime scene. Things could change."

But Vince shakes his head. "We're not moving in that direction. The opposite, actually. The other big family in Chicago has played nice with us, but they're starting to get greedy. Things are going to get *worse*. Mateo's considering eliminating them, and then our territory will actually expand. If anything, they'd want me to breed more goddamn pawns for the next generation."

I stare at his profile, surprised by his calm as he talks about what sounds to my ears like a mob war. "That sounds... really dangerous."

"Will be."

Swallowing, I ask, "What's your role in all that? Will you be in danger?"

"I don't know," he mutters. "Most likely."

Curling up close to him, I say, "Well, I don't like that at all."

"Neither do I. Me and Joey... we're thinking about trying something on our own, but... I don't know. Mateo wouldn't allow that, and if we tried to keep it from him, he'd probably find out. I don't think I'll survive keeping another secret from him."

"Then don't do it," I say immediately.

"I want something of my own, something to... get me out from under his thumb."

"It doesn't sound like that's what this is. It sounds... suicidal."

Vince sighs heavily. "All-knowing fucking Mateo Morelli."

It also reminds me of what Mateo had talked about with me that night in the library, how every time he trusts someone, they make him regret it.

"Promise me you won't do whatever you were thinking of doing," I tell him. "It's a bad idea. I get why you're tempted, but I don't think it's worth it, and I don't want anything to happen to you."

I rest my head on his chest, but all of a sudden, all I can think about is… what would happen to *me* if something *did* happen to Vince?

This time when Vince says he's going to Joey's, it makes me nervous. Knowing that Joey's trying to convince him to do some stupid fucking thing behind Mateo's back, I'm losing my enthusiasm about him. If he wants to get himself killed, that's his problem, but I don't want him dragging Vince into it.

Kissing me goodbye at the front door, he promises me, "Everything's fine, don't worry."

I want to tell him again not to do it, but Mateo's study is open and I don't know if he's inside. It's far enough away that it's unlikely he would hear me, but one never knows.

Once Vince is gone, as I'm about to walk past his office, Mateo calls out, "Mia."

I brace a hand on the door frame, leaning inside. "Yes?"

Indicating a rectangular box in the corner, he tells me, "Your books came."

"Ooh," I said, rubbing my hands together in anticipation as I step inside. "Mind if I dig in?"

"Be my guest."

I kneel down in the floor by his desk and attempt to get all the tape off, but I end up needing scissors. Once inside, I pull them all out, flipping through them one by one, fanning out the colorful pages.

"New books are so exciting," I tell him, sighing happily.

For nearly an hour, I stay in Mateo's study, flipping through books, reading when I get sucked into a panel, and telling him about each one. I'm sure he doesn't care, but to his credit, he lets me yammer on anyway.

Adrian comes in while I'm still there. Understandably confused to find me in Mateo's floor, surrounded by graphic novels, he stares at me for a moment before asking with a confused frown, "Should I come back?"

"No," Mateo says, looking up from whatever he's writing. "What is it?"

He glances at me again, then says, "I should probably come back."

"It's fine," Mateo says again.

"But…" Adrian indicates me in the floor, like Mateo may have forgotten.

Mateo merely nods.

Still Adrian hesitates, but ultimately he says, "There's a shipment coming in this weekend. I have dates and times I was going to share with you. A location. *Sensitive* information."

Unmoved, Mateo steeples his hands on the desk and meets Adrian's gaze. "So share them."

More stunned than Adrian, I can only sit there frozen in shock, staring at the same page of the graphic novel in my lap, terrified to move, to breathe, to do anything that might remind Mateo of my presence. There's no way he *forgot* I'm sitting here, right? It would be impossible. I haven't shut up since I peeked my head in the door.

Of course, nothing Adrian says *matters* to me, but I feel like it matters that Mateo's letting him say it in *front* of me. I feel… well, epically flattered, until I think about it a little longer. What if, somehow, this information leaked? Through some channel that obviously *isn't* me, but Mateo's mind would go straight to me in the floor of his office when Adrian spilled all the details. As mistrustful as he is, and with his record of having been screwed over before, I really don't *want* the responsibility of knowing this kind of information.

Suddenly it hits me—is this the kind of pressure that weighs on Vince every day? Knowing these things and knowing what a mistrustful person Mateo is, is actually really terrifying.

It also occurs to me that since Adrian told on me to Vince for having the audacity to wear a bikini to the pool and be spotted by Mateo wearing it, he's probably going to run and tell Vince that Mateo did this, too.

My stomach is in knots when Adrian finally leaves the room. I think I'm going to throw up, but I don't know how to leave the room after that without seeming really suspicious.

Mateo glances over at me, but he doesn't say a word before returning to his work.

I force myself to flip through the books for a few minutes, but there's no more joy in the task. I'm a ball of anxiety, and I don't know what to do about it. I guess I could tell Vince myself? Then if Adrian tries to tell on me, he'll already know.

Of course, I'm not sure that would be sufficient. If he was convinced something was going on because Mateo made me serve him dinner, even *I* won't be able to blame him for thinking something must be going on for Suspicion Incarnate to share with me sensitive information that could legitimately put them all behind bars if I told.

Mateo was only trying to extend a gesture of trust, and now he's completely screwed me.

"Why does Adrian hate you?" I suddenly ask.

Mateo glances over at me, but returns his attention to some paper he's filling out before answering. "He's in love with Elise."

Well, okay, that makes sense. "Why would that make him hate you?"

Smiling slightly, he says, "Elise is in love with *me*."

My stomach sinks, and I'm not sure for whom. "You and Elise are…?"

"Nope. Girlhood crush she hasn't outgrown yet, I think." Then, with a little smile, he informs me, "I'm quite irresistible, you know."

I crack a smile, but roll my eyes at him. "You're something."


After agonizing all evening about what to tell Vince, I give up waiting for him. It being a school night, I doubt he'll wake me up once he gets home, so I'll have to talk to him in the morning on the way to school. *If* I talk to him. I still haven't figured my way out of this mess.

Turns out he *does* wake me when he gets home though. I'm dead asleep, drooling on my pillow, and all of a sudden I wake up to his hands roaming all over me.

I'm a little relieved, figuring if he still wants to fuck me, Adrian probably hasn't ratted me out yet.

And fuck me, he does. I get another earth-shattering, building from the deepest part of me orgasm that knocks me out of my senses for several minutes, but then I feel more wetness between my legs than I expect to. A lot more. I'm tummy down on the bed after doggie style, Vince's arm thrown across my back as he catches his breath. Reaching down between my legs, I realize something's wrong.

"Vince... can you check the condom?" Patting the sheets, also wet and sticky, I start to lose my cool a little. "Oh my God, I think the condom broke."

Before he can check, I launch out of bed and dart into the bathroom. I've already been lying there for several minutes, but I jump in the shower anyway, desperately scrubbing between my legs.

This can't be happening. He literally *just* told me how much he didn't want kids, and now the condom breaks. He's going to be paranoid about having sex now.

I need to get on the pill.

When I emerge from the bathroom, Vince and the soiled bedding are gone. The bed has been made up to perfection, indicating one of the maids has been here. That's kind of embarrassing, since they can probably guess why we needed a change of sheets in the middle of the night, but that's literally the least of my worries right now.

Climbing into bed alone, I sigh and pull the covers up to my neck. I'm still a little tired, but now the adrenaline has me wide awake. I guess when Vince comes back, I could talk to him, but somehow nothing seems sufficient. "Hey, so, I know you don't want kids and we just had our first broken condom incident, but I also wanted to tell you that your mistrustful cousin, the one you've been worried wants to get in my pants? He's now comfortable talking about top secret criminal activity shit in front of me for some crazy reason! So... that was my day. How was Joey's?"

Yeah, no.

## CHAPTER TWENTY TWO

I'M SICK with worry the next morning—over all my own shit, and the fact that from what I can tell, Vince never came back to bed last night.

I don't know where his head's at, but it can't be good. I do what I can to check my cycle, seeing if there's any chance I could've even been ovulating, but I forgot to mark my last period and I can't remember when it was looking at a calendar. I'm sure there's nothing to worry about from one slip-up, but I would feel better if I could offer him something solid.

"You look pensive," Mateo remarks.

I glance up at him, biting my bottom lip uncertainly. I suppose I *could* ask him for help. He's the head of the family, after all.

"Kinda. Um, do you guys have, like… a family doctor, or…?"

Smirking at me, he asks, "A mob doctor?"

"No, just… I mean, maybe, if they can get the same stuff."

"What is it you need?"

Squirming, I say, "I would rather tell a girl. I can go to my mom, but it'll take longer and we don't have good insurance—I don't know."

Frowning slightly, he asks, "What's wrong?"

"I just… I need—God, I don't want to ask you. Please don't make me ask you. Is Francesca here? Cherie? Literally anyone with a vagina?"

"I've seen my fair share of them, if that helps."

Grimacing, I say, "Ah, gross! It doesn't. No. God."

"We're all adults here," he states, firmly.

Well, not *all* of us, but I don't argue. "I need birth control. And possibly the morning after pill."

Dead silence.

## Accidental Witness

My face might combust in *actual* flames, and I can't look at him. Why, oh why, oh why did I start this conversation with him? I mean, I don't really have anyone else to ask... Lena could probably get me the morning after pill, but we haven't really been talking and that would be a humiliating way to suddenly start talking to her again.

After a moment, picking up his paper, he says simply, "No."

Swallowing down the feeling of hollowness, I say, "No, you don't have someone who can help me with that?"

"No, you may not have birth control or the morning after pill," he amends.

Eyes widening, I ask, "Why?"

Opening his paper, he meets my gaze and says without apology, "Because I said so."

I sit there for a moment, horrified, waiting for him to be joking, but apparently he isn't. I don't know how to respond to that. I don't understand why he would deny me something so basic—at least the birth control part. Given their heritage, they may be lazy Catholics—I know they murder and don't go to church, but maybe they still cherry pick the traditions they want to keep. Vince did mention all Morelli women tend to have lots of babies, but... I didn't realize that was because they had no choice.

Jesus Christ.

Well, I'll have to double down on my fervent hopes that the broken condom incident didn't ruin my life, because apparently if I'm pregnant, Vince is just going to hate me forever.

Oh, and that's before he even finds out about my being in the study.

Great.

Just fucking fabulous.

Without another word, and certainly without the usual goodbye and have a good day niceties, I get up from the table and leave.

I make it outside before I realize I have no ride.

I won't go back in though. I'm calculating how long it would take me to walk and how late I'll be when I spot Adrian in the driveway.

"Hey," I call out, impulsively.

He turns to me, but doesn't speak.

"Could you give me a ride to school?"

"Have you talked to Vince?" he calls back.

I shake my head, brushing a stray lock of hair behind my ear. "No, not since last night."

Adrian nods, glancing toward the road, then back at me. "He's still at Joey's. I don't think he's going. Why don't you stay home today, Mia."

I frown, shaking my head as I walk over to him. "I have a quiz—wait. What do you mean, he's still at Joey's? He came home last night."

Adrian's lips press together into a firm line, but his face doesn't betray his thoughts. "No, he didn't."

"Yes, he did," I reply, eyebrows rising.

Adrian takes a step closer, getting right in my face. "No. He didn't."

I'm frozen again, unable to move. Even in the terrifying moments after meeting Mateo, when he had me on the ground in front of him with a gun pressed to my forehead, I've never experienced time standing still until right this moment. My life could have ended then, and still seconds ticked by, then minutes, then hours.

But now, the world no longer spins.

My brain has shut down. Information is flying in, confusing information, nothing I can make sense of. Nothing.

Until one certainty cements itself.

If Vince never came home last night, I couldn't have had sex with him.

But I had sex with somebody.

I feel at once like I weigh 1,000 pounds and like I'm weightless, falling through time and space, waiting to crash into solid ground.

My knees turn to jelly, but I somehow stay upright. Everything trembles—or it feels like it does. I can't tell, I can't *feel* physical things right now—not the wind whipping my face, not Adrian's hand on my arm. I think I could take Mateo's sister's throwing star and gouge myself in the chest with it right now, and I wouldn't feel a thing.

Gasping, coming back to life, I turn on my heel and head back into the house. I don't run. I walk, slowly, impressed with my ability even to do that.

I go back to the dining room, but by the time I get there, he's gone. I know he isn't in his study, because I would've seen him.

Elise stands at the table, cleaning up the mess I left, and Mateo's coffee cup.

"Where is he?" I hear myself ask her.

Elise spins around, surprised to see me. "Who, Vince?"

"Mateo."

"Oh, I don't know. He was here a few minutes ago, you just missed him."

For the first time, the enormity of this goddamn house is a hindrance. My blood is pumping through my veins with such violence I can hear my heart beating in my whole body. I don't know how long the adrenaline will keep me up. But I want to find him and scratch his fucking face off before I crash.

After he fucking admits what he did. I want to hear that, first.

I have no idea where to look, though. I don't want to go to his bedroom, and I don't know why he would go back there anyway; he was already up for the day and dressed in his perfect goddamn suit and tie.

Maria is the next person I see, and I stop her. "Do you know where Mateo is?"

I've rarely interacted with her outside of the kitchen, but Maria studies my face, then advises, "Why don't you go to your room for a bit, have a rest."

"Do you *know* where Mateo is?"

"You seem angry. Best to go to your room."

"Oh, my God," I say, giving up and walking away from her.

After storming through half the house, I come to the largest wing—the master suite. I stand at the center of three separate halls, all leading to rooms of his.

Common sense leaps out at me, telling me to turn back. He's not up here, and even if he is... I don't want to go in.

But I'm too fucking angry to listen.

I want to set him on fire.

I *need* to know he did it. It had to be him, but I need to *know*.

This wasn't part of Vince's tour though, so I don't even know which hall to walk down. One is the bedroom, one is probably a sitting room... maybe the third is an enormous bathroom? I don't know.

I go left.

It's a sitting room, and there's no one inside. My heart beats faster—I'm not sure if with relief at not finding him, or if it's because one door down means only two to go.

I go with the middle door next, since I approach it first.

It's a bedroom, but clearly not used, and possibly for children? There are a few boxes scattered around, one of them with a pink sparkly sweater on top.

Frowning, I back out of that one.

I'm just about to try the third door when I *feel* him. Not physically, not touching me, but he's near enough I can feel his presence.

Then he speaks, his voice husky with expectation. "Looking for me?"

Suddenly my body trembles and I feel it all down my spine. My stomach pitches as I slowly turn around and see him standing there at the opening of the hall, where I was just a couple of minutes ago.

My words suddenly dry up and to my absolute horror, tears well in my eyes.

Mateo walks toward me, a predatory glint in his eyes.

I'm supposed to be the one confronting him, but it suddenly hits me as he moves closer, faster, not apologetic, not retreating, not remorseful, but… stalking me.

I chased my rapist to his bedroom.

Launching away from the wall, I go to move past him but he catches me by the arm, his grip rough, not light like it normally is.

"Get your hands off me," I say, my voice shaking through every syllable.

"Oh, but you like my hands on you," he says, a wicked smile grazing his lips.

"No, I don't," I say, feeling as if he just slapped me.

"Sure you do," he says, using his body to move me backward. "You liked my hands when they were playing your pussy like a fiddle, making you scream with pleasure. You liked my mouth, when I was devouring you like my favorite dessert. You certainly seemed to enjoy my cock, when I was fucking you in Vince's bed."

A noiseless sob escapes me as my back hits the wall, and he presses his body against mine.

"You like me a lot more than you let on, don't you, Mia?"

I struggle to get my arm away from him, but he's holding it too tight. I raise my other hand to hit him, but his reflexes are too fast and he catches me, pushing both arms over my head and pinning me against the wall.

I can only shake my head, trying for words that won't come, gasping for breath when my chest feels like it's about to cave in.

He doesn't even have the decency to be ashamed. He looks straight into my eyes with no trouble—and they're dancing with something. Amusement?

"You're a monster," I whisper.

He tilts his head as if considering it, then shrugs.

My words are finally coming back. "You *raped* me."

"You were pretty willing," he tells me.

"I thought you were someone else!"

"Yeah." Making a face that would seem to indicate 'this is awkward' he inhales through his teeth. "I probably wouldn't go with that. I feel like Vince wouldn't be terribly pleased that you couldn't tell when you were having sex with him, and when you were having sex with me."

"I didn't have *sex* with you," I say, jerking my arms, rabid at his wording. "That wasn't sex. You manipulated me. You tricked me. You snuck into my *boyfriend's bed* in the dead of night when I was asleep, for fuck's sake. Why would I think it was anyone but him?"

"Well, he did warn you," Mateo points out.

It's like another slap to the face, and I physically rear back from the force of it.

"And… Cherie. And… well, everybody, isn't that right?"

He lets that land, giving me enough time to fully process the truth of that statement. To relive myself fighting with Vince, telling him how sick I was of being warned about Mateo. Telling him he was being paranoid.

"Even *I* told you I wasn't a good guy," he adds, that time looking a little apologetic. "I mean, you just didn't want to believe any of it. I have this nice house, I bought you pretty dresses and fucking stories about how good triumphs over evil—it doesn't, I could've told you that, but… you were warned, Mia. And still here you stand, a few feet from my bedroom."

I feel like the biggest fool in the whole entire world. Humiliation swallows me whole as I recall feeling sympathetic toward him, feeling sad because he seemed to lead an ultimately lonely existence.

But he deserves to be lonely. He deserves to have no one.

And me, maybe I fucking deserved this, because he's right, every single person who knows him tried to warn me, but I wouldn't listen.

With no pride left, I break down in tears, right there in front of him. Between sobs, I ask, "Why? I was *nice* to you."

Sighing heavily, he says, "You're right, you were. It's not your fault. You just saw something you shouldn't have. It was just rotten luck, and I'm truly sorry for it. I don't know if I admire or pity your ability to see good in people where none actually exists, but I don't want to snuff that out of you. I didn't even want to know you—really, this is Vince's fault. I could've finished it quick, it would've been painless, we could have all moved on with our lives."

"You said you wouldn't hurt me," I remind him, even while realizing how foolish it is to remind him of anything he said like it holds any weight.

"I said as long as Vince wanted you," he responds, correcting me. "If he doesn't anymore... well, your fate's left to me then, isn't it?"

It's profoundly embarrassing to have been this wrong about someone, but it's worse that Vince was so *right,* and I've been so goddamn sure of myself.

"You planned to kill me all along, didn't you? This was just a game to you."

"I'm not going to kill you," he replies. "Not yet, even if Vince comes home today wanting to kill you himself."

"Why would he...?"

"He knows. A little birdie told him some things, so... well, that's not going to be a fun time for you."

I can't stand up anymore. My legs wobble and I try to sink down the wall, but he's still holding my arms, so I can't.

"Why don't you just do it now and get it over with," I whisper, tears flowing freely down my face now.

He rearranges his grip on me, pinning my arms at the wrist to free up a hand. Then he runs it along my jawline in a gesture that would be tender, except it's coming from him. "Because I'm not done with you yet."

I can only stare at him, empty, broken, alone.

Then he adds, "Not to mention, you could be carrying my child."

## CHAPTER TWENTY THREE

I FEEL nothing as Mateo takes me into his bedroom. I try to break away, I use my body weight, but he's too strong and I'm too depleted. When he throws me down on his bed, I try to crawl away, but he's on me too fast, slamming my arms down against the soft pillow top and straddling my body. His eyes gleam like a lion about to consume a gazelle, like he's won. I wonder if it's a relief not to have to pretend to be nice anymore.

"Get off me," I cry, angrily throwing my useless body.

"Oh, no. This is the fun part," he tells me, leaning in to kiss my neck. "Do you know how hard it was not to speak when I fucked you, Mia? It was torture."

"Stop saying that—it wasn't sex."

Rolling his eyes, he says, "Fine, when I *raped* you. Is that better? Do you like that word? Does it turn you on?"

"You're sick," I hiss, glaring up at him.

"Well, if you like that word, you're going to love what happens next. What we did before, whatever you want to call it, that was sex. You wanted it. Now? Now I'm going to take your sweet little pussy while you beg me not to. *Now* I'll give you rape."

It's not fair that he's cheating me out of the anger I have every right to feel, but speaking so plainly about his intentions, he's pushing me over into fear.

Even though it kills me to ask him for anything, especially something I should never have to ask for, I say, "Please don't."

"It can be a game," he tells me, taunting. "You can pretend you have a choice, if it makes you feel better. Would you like a safe word?"

It's obviously a trick, so I don't speak.

"Go ahead, pick one," he says, leaning down on my arms with more force as he kisses my neck again.

I hate this game and I don't want to play, but I throw out, "Red light."

"Okay, your safe word is red light."

"Red light," I say, immediately.

His hands shift again, holding my arms with just the one, and the second snakes up under my shirt. He lifts my bra, shoving his hand inside and squeezing my breast, ignoring my utterance completely.

"That was fun, wasn't it? We should do that again sometime," he states, his hand moving around to the clasp of my bra.

"Mateo, please," I say uselessly, as he gets it unclasped. "Please."

Squeezing my nipple until it hurts, he says, "Beg all you want; I like it."

Eventually, he has to let go of my arms to get my jeans off, so I wait until he does to attack. Throwing myself at him with everything I've got, I growl, I scratch, I hit—and I end up wrapped in his arms, wrestled until I'm belly-down on the bed, my jeans around my knees.

Growling at the injustice of my defeat, I try again, rearing back against him, attempting to curl into a position where, even if he can get my clothes off, he won't be able to rape me. Not easily, at least.

Finally seeming agitated, he gives me one more violent toss to the bed and sits up on his knees. I scurry, about to climb off, when I hear the metallic click.

One foot touches the floor, the other leg still bearing the brunt of my weight on the bed, and I come face to face with Mateo's gun—again.

"Let's try this a different way," he says, finger on the trigger.

I'm not terribly confident, but I say shakily, "You're not going to shoot me. I could be…" I pause, the words too horrible to come out.

"Eight hours pregnant?" he questions. "Become a big enough pain in my ass and I think I'll survive without ever knowing."

I won't accept defeat—I won't. That's not what this feeling of a thousand bricks resting atop my lungs is—it's not defeat. It's not.

But I don't move the rest of the way off the bed. I'm too afraid.

Using the gun to gesture, he says, "Back on the bed."

I swallow, slowly easing back onto the bed, my eyes glued to the barrel of the gun. "You wanna hear something stupid?" I ask him, shakily, as I sit down.

"Sure," he says.

"After we talked in the library that night…." I shake my head, seeing now how foolish I must have looked to him. "I thought you never would have done it. I thought you never would have actually shot me before, in your study. I thought it was…"

"A front?" he finishes, almost sympathetic.

I nod, choking on the acidic taste of my own foolishness.

"Sadly, no. I don't make threats I'm not prepared to follow through with." Nodding toward my lower half, he says, "Take off your panties."

Lips turned down in a helpless pout, I steel myself, pushing down my panties.

Trying one more time, I say, "You don't have to do this."

"I've already been inside you, Mia. It doesn't have to be so dramatic."

*Bastard.*

Swallowing convulsively, I will away the nausea gripping me, threatening to make me sick. Mateo moves over me, the gun falling to the side for a moment. With his free hand, he jerks my chin until I'm looking into his eyes, then he leans down and kisses me.

I try to turn my face away, refusing to take part in this. When he gets nothing back, he lets the gun trail up my arm, bringing the barrel to a hard rest at my neck, just below my ear. A fearful sob escapes me but I open my mouth, letting him have access.

"Kiss me," he growls, before his tongue pushes into my mouth, catching mine and overpowering it, just like he's overpowering the rest of me. The gun is still pressed firmly against me, digging into my skin uncomfortably, so I do. I kiss the bastard back, just like he demanded.

The worst of it is, my blood races, my heart pounds, and even though I tell myself there's only fear here, I feel a sudden tingle between my legs that fills me to the brim with self-loathing.

Willing it away, I remind myself he's a monster. He tricked me and now he's forcing himself on me—he's threatening my life, for fuck's sake.

Withdrawing from my mouth, he leans back. He holds my gaze as he unbuttons and unzips his black slacks, and I feel a throb of fear and arousal confused and mashed together. Befuddlement and resistance sweep through me, but there's no time—free of his pants, he's now running his hands over my legs, up over my knees and trailing up my thighs.

"Do you remember how it felt when I was eating your pussy, Mia? When you were clutching the bed sheets, crying out in pleasure, writhing as I fucked you with nothing more than my mouth?"

Another awful throb of arousal. "Stop talking like that," I say.

"Why?" he asks, smiling as he enters me with a single finger. "Because you like it?"

I do my best to hold my body still while he touches me, first with one finger, then with two. I close my eyes, afraid of what he'll see if he looks into them, knowing he will taunt me if he sees anything but loathing, and I can't take that. Not when I'm feeling so uncertain about it myself.

Maybe *I'm* sick.

He brings the gun up my bare torso, and in a sickening twist, I feel relieved. Relieved at the reminder that I have no choice, that this terrible, terrible man is going to do what he wants to me no matter what I say, and that my body is just… experiencing physiological confusion. He *has* turned me on before, he *has* brought me to orgasm before, and he has been inside me, pounding into me until I cried out — even though I didn't know it was him, it still happened. My body still knows he's capable of bringing me physical pleasure.

I open my eyes and see him watching me. He withdraws his fingers from my body, bringing the gun down slowly, trailing lightly down my abdomen, and along the inside of my thigh. I hold my body still as goose bumps rise up, but I can't keep from gasping when I feel the cool tip of the gun being pushed inside me.

"Mateo," I say, gasping. Fear floods me, trying to remember if it's still cocked. What if he accidentally fires it? "Please…"

"Mm, ask again."

I hate that he's enjoying this, but I can hardly breathe with the barrel of his gun pressing against my clit.

"Please. Please, Mateo. *Please.*"

Instead of removing it, he moves it in and out, in and out, mocking me.

"Please," I say again, my breath hitching. "You're scaring me."

The gun is finally pulled out of me, and better, he deposits it on his night stand. I can't help staring as he sets it down, wondering if I could get to it….

"Don't even think about it," he says coldly.

My gaze jerks to his.

"You'll miss, for one thing. You don't know how to fire a gun, and you damn sure won't be able to fire it when I'm wresting it away from you. And when you miss, or even if your finger never makes it to the trigger, I will finish raping you, and then I'll kill you and your entire family. Trust me, it's not worth it."

I think he's probably right, but I sure would like to try.

I'm not fighting now like I was when he first got me in his bed, but he still pins my arms over my head before climbing between my legs. I think he just likes it.

"If you stop now… we can pretend this didn't happen," I say, even knowing it's useless. There's no consequence for him. He isn't afraid to do this to me—he knows he'll be fine.

Smiling, he drops a little kiss on my lips, as if I've amused him.

Then he thrusts his hips forward and his cock moves into my unwilling body, sealing the deal.

Caught somewhere between a gasp and a sob, I try to rear up, forgetting I'm pinned. Uselessly I plead, "Stop!"

But he doesn't.

I watch him close his eyes, experiencing pleasure as he moves, thrusting deep inside my body, then pulling back, thrusting deep, then pulling back. It doesn't hurt like I expect it to—there's a fair amount of discomfort as he stretches me, but not outright pain. I give up fighting altogether. I turn my head to the side so I don't have to watch, but I can feel him everywhere—his breath when he leans in to kiss my neck, his cock battering its way inside me, his hands, still nailing me to the bed. The weight on my arms hurts more than the actual act, but I don't bother complaining.

He finally releases my arms, hiking my legs up and fucking me from a different angle. The friction starts to feel less awful and I close my eyes, praying he'll finish before he notices my body reacting to him.

Remembering what started this whole mess, I do murmur, "Please don't finish inside me."

Then, out of spite, I guess, he groans against my mouth as he buries himself deep, coming as deep inside me as he possibly can.

He remains inside me afterward, but he's spent, so he relaxes against me. I lay motionless, blessedly empty on an emotional level, but so aware of him still filling me physically.

*It takes two to tango*, I remember saying.

But Cherie was right.

It doesn't.

## CHAPTER TWENTY FOUR

I DON'T know where to go when Mateo's done with me.

He climbs off the bed, retrieving his gun from the night stand, and gets himself cleaned up and dressed. I don't move. Dread has swallowed me up. I don't know where I go from here. What happens to me.

Does he send me back to Vince's room?

Does Vince really know? *What* does Vince know?

Oh, God. Vince.

Swallowing down the lump in my throat, I try to turn my feelings back off. I can't process them right now, I just need… nothingness.

Once he's finished, Mateo looks as good as he did at the breakfast table, all decked out in his sharp suit. You can't tell there's a monster inside him. His hair's a little more tousled than it was prior to our struggle, but wouldn't you know, it looks good on him.

Tears form in my eyes again, but I'm not even sure what they're from.

"You can stay in here if you want," he offers. "Vince won't come in here."

"What did you tell him?" I ask quietly.

"*I* didn't tell him anything."

I sigh tiredly. "What does he know?"

"Enough," he says simply.

I hesitate, hating the question so much I don't want to ask, but I ask anyway, because I have to. "What is he… what is he going to do to me?"

"I'm not sure," he says honestly.

My last vestige of safety, gone.

"I won't let him kill you," he says.

I guess I'm supposed to be grateful.

I'm not.

It looks like he's about to move away from the bed, but he stops, leaning over to look at me. "I know you're angry right now, hurt, scared, but you should know this doesn't change anything. Like me or hate me, you *will* remain loyal to me. You speak a word about anything you shouldn't, and I will end you."

I can't believe he's making me declare my goddamn allegiance to him moments after raping me, but I give a brief nod. "I know."

"Good," he says, taking a step back. "Take all the time you need."

And with that, Mateo Morelli leaves me, a broken mess, in his goddamn bed.

I don't know how long I remain hidden in his room, but it feels like an eternity.

Eventually, I drag my body from his bed and into his bathroom—his huge, ridiculous fucking bathroom. There's *furniture* inside. Who needs furniture in their bathroom? A chaise is angled in front of the tub, like he sits there, watching people bathe. Who would ever even use it? And if for some reason you needed to? There's a goddamn cushioned window seat along the wall.

I'm disgusted instead of impressed by the excess now. His fucking bathroom is bigger than my mother's living room—and it's not even close.

The shower stall is huge, too, and impeccably clean. I'm relieved, because I wind up sitting in the corner under the spray, sobbing.

When all the hot water is gone, I finally pull myself up and get out. I don't have any clean clothes and I'm too afraid to go to Vince's room to get any, but none of the maids have come to check on me, so I can't even ask them to bring me a change.

Finally, I emerge from Mateo's master suite in the clothes I dressed in this morning, an eternity ago. Terror keeps my steps slow, wondering if Vince is home, if anyone will pass me in the hallway and know where I'm coming from. I can't help but assume everyone knows, and everyone hates me now.

They all tried to warn me, after all.

Even Mateo knew that.

I find one of the sitting rooms without coming into contact with anyone, so I stop there, thinking maybe I'll stay. It's sparsely furnished and not exactly cozy since it's one of the aggressively untouched, secondary sitting areas, but I don't know what awaits me where the people are.

I assume Vince is home by now. I don't know what time it is, but it seems like enough time has passed. Unless he isn't coming home at all. Maybe he's abandoning me here with Mateo; maybe he's too disappointed even to confront me.

I wish I knew what he'd been told. At least then I could try to prepare for it.

Nobody finds me, and after a while I leave the sitting room. The huge house suddenly seems very lonely, and I wonder if it feels this way to everyone else. I've been so dazzled by it up until now, but ultimately it's too big. Even for so many people.

Maria comes down the hall as I meander off to nowhere, pausing when she sees me. It looked like she was in a hurry, so I'm surprised when she stops.

We just stand there, staring at each other.

"There's an empty room in Francesca's wing," she finally says. "I can't put you there or promise they'll let you stay, but if you're looking for somewhere to…"

*Hide.* She doesn't say it, but she doesn't need to. The fact that she knows I should worries me.

"Is… anyone here?" I ask.

"Vince just got home. Not happy."

My stomach sinks. I realize I was *hoping* he would stay away, at least for today.

"He's looking for you," she adds. "If I were you, I wouldn't be easy to find."

I nod woodenly, but I continue toward the main hall instead of changing directions and heading for Francesca's. "He'll find me eventually."

She crosses herself before walking away. I don't take it as a good sign.

I'm not sure if it's a low point, exactly, but I'm legitimately terrified Vince is going to hurt me. I don't want to believe he ever would, but given how angry he got over far less, it seems a likely outcome.

What I'm hoping is he'll surprise me. Instead of angry at me, he'll be hurt with me. He'll hold me, comfort me, take me back to our bedroom.

"I don't need you fucking following me, Adrian."

The sound of Vince's voice freezes me in my tracks. He's just around the next corner. I'm tempted to turn back and change my mind, but I don't, because there's no time.

Adrian's voice is low, gravelly as he tells him, "I just want to make sure you don't do anything you'll regret."

If he was going to respond to Adrian, he doesn't. His eyes land on me and he stops short. I hold his gaze for a few seconds, neither of us moving. Adrian still takes a couple steps forward, eyeing me warily.

Then Vince is in motion, eyes narrowed and more or less vibrating with rage.

"You're fucking him?"

I shake my head, unmoving, tears welling up in my eyes. "No."

"Don't fucking lie to me, Mia," he snaps.

"I'm not. I'm not. I didn't know, Vince. I didn't—"

"How the *fuck* do you not know?" he demands, grabbing me by the wrists and pushing me up against the wall.

I cry out, not because he hurt me, but because I'm afraid he's going to. "I'm sorry," I say, not even struggling against his hold. "You were right about everything and I should've listened… I should've listened, but I believed him," I say, choking on a sob. "I didn't think he was… but he is, and I'm so sorry."

"Now that you've fucked him you're sorry? Isn't that convenient!"

"I didn't," I cry, face crumbling. "Stop saying that, I didn't…"

"In my bed, Mia. *In my fucking bed.*"

"I thought he was you!" I cry. Whether he likes it or not, it's the truth. "I was *asleep*, it was the middle of the night in *our* room and I thought you came home—why would I ever think it could be anyone else?"

"You have *eyes*, don't you?" he demands, his own eyes widening with belligerence.

I shake my head, looking away from him. "I wasn't facing him. I didn't think anything of it at the time. I didn't know, Vince. I didn't do it to hurt you, I didn't even know. He manipulated me, just like you said."

"How many times, Mia?"

At first I think he's asking how many times I was with Mateo, but before I can answer, he continues.

"How many times did I try to tell you? I tried *so fucking hard* to protect you."

Adrian hasn't moved to interfere, but at this, he takes a step forward. "Vince, come on."

"What?" he practically roars, glaring at Adrian.

"It wouldn't have mattered," Adrian states.

I'm a sobbing mess, but I look up, surprised Adrian would say anything in my defense.

"You know that," Adrian states, shaking his head. "This was always going to happen; it was just a matter of how and when. You knew that."

"And I tried to stop it," he states.

"But nothing could have," he points out. "You know who he is. Maybe Mia didn't, but you did. If he couldn't have tricked her into docility, he would have hurt her. The end result would have been the same."

"Stay out of this," Vince says lowly.

Nodding once, Adrian eyes up Vince's hands on me. "Why don't you let go of her and I will."

"This isn't your fucking business," he states, eyes narrowing.

"I'm okay," I tell Adrian, nodding. "Really. I understand why he's…angry."

"Don't sink to his level," Adrian says to Vince.

At that Vince laughs. He drops my arms and takes a step back, spinning around a little wildly. "Maybe I'm just fighting the inevitable, Adrian. Ever think of that? They're all like this. Every fucking one of them. And you know what, shit like this doesn't happen to them. They *do* shit like this, but it's never done to them." Spinning back around to me, he glares with such anger, such hatred, that it nearly knocks the breath right out of me. "How am I supposed to look at you now, Mia?"

Lip trembling, I shake my head. "I don't know," I whisper.

"How many times did you fuck him?"

"Never," I say. "I never—"

"Just..." He holds a hand up, stopping me. "Once? Twice? More?"

I bow my head, wishing I could disappear. I refuse to answer, I don't care how many times he asks. Instead I repeat, "I'm sorry. I wish I would've listened to you. Trust me, I can't feel worse than I already do. Nothing you say to me could make this worse—he's humiliated me enough for both of you."

He's still shaking his head, still practically shaking with fury, but his voice is low and unsteady when he says, "I loved you."

I was wrong.

There *was* something he could say to make it hurt worse.

A sob bursts out of me, followed by a cluster of hitching breaths, and I sink to the floor, overcome with a feeling of immense loss. Whatever we could have been, whatever we could have had, it was gone. He didn't want me anymore.

Pushing out an unsteady breath, Vince clears his throat. I look up through my tears, seeing his eyes look a little red, too.

Shaking his head one last time, he turns around and disappears down the hall the way he came.

The rest of the day melts away.

With nowhere else to go, Adrian takes me back to Mateo's room. I would be cynically amused at having to return to the bed where I was raped, but that would require feeling something, and I'm dead empty at this point.

I don't even flinch when Mateo comes into the room at the end of the day, flicking a glance at me before beginning to undress for the night.

I'm unresponsive when he climbs into bed with me, reminding me of those stupid fucking nights he came to Vince's room.

"That was a long day, wasn't it?" he murmurs.

His arm curls around me, like we're lovers. I don't attempt to move it, not even when he begins touching me, palming my breasts through my clothing, slipping the button of my jeans through the hole and tugging them down.

I don't fight when he takes them off, or when he climbs between my legs. I don't even respond when he enters me dry, painfully, forcing his way even more than he had to this morning, when there was at least some lubrication.

I don't cry when he comes inside me again.

I don't object when he gets back into bed afterward and pulls me against him, like we're fucking snuggling.

I don't care.

What's the point?

"Have I broken you already?" he asks lowly, sounding almost disappointed. Not at having possibly damaged me, but that his fun is over, I think.

I don't know the answer to that question, and even if I did, I probably wouldn't dignify it with a response.

---

He takes my body again the following morning before he gets up and goes to shower. I wonder numbly what Vince would think of how quickly the number is climbing, but thinking Vince's name pierces the veil of numbness and causes pain, so I stop.

Once Mateo leaves, the door opens and Adrian steps inside. "Are you okay?"

I offer a weak nod.

"Do you want some breakfast? Do you need…anything?"

I shake my head again, but then I pause. "Actually, yes. Get me Elise."

Surprise flashes across his features briefly, his gaze moving from me to the bed, then back. "Elise?"

I nod.

"Okay," he finally says, backing out of the room.

It takes a little while, but eventually there's a light knock at the door and Elise's blonde head pops in. "Hello," she greets, smiling until she sees me. "Oh, Mia. Hi."

"Hi."

Her gaze rakes over me, over the bed, confused. I guess her confusion at my being in Mateo's bed indicates everyone *doesn't* know, but it's hard to feel any relief. They will soon enough.

"What can I do for you?" she asks, a little haltingly.

I sit up, wrapping the top bed sheet around my body and dragging the comforter onto the floor as I push up off the bed. Elise gasps at the streaks of blood on the sheets, her cheeks turning pink.

"Oh, dear. Do you need me to get you something for your monthly?"

"That's not from my monthly," I say simply.

She stares at the sheets for a moment, then at me, at my bedraggled, dead-eyed appearance. Dread clouds over her clear blue eyes, but I don't torture her further.

"I need to get in the shower. Could you please see that they've been changed before I get out?"

Nodding with her eyes locked on the bed, she murmurs, "Of course."

# CHAPTER TWENTY FIVE

I DON'T get out of bed to do more than shower or pee until Sunday. Mateo makes me eat breakfast, even though it makes me feel ill, and I would stay here in my dead little shell for much longer, only he doesn't let me.

Draping a new garment bag across the foot of the bed, he says, "Time to get up."

"Why?"

"It's family dinner day. Mandatory."

"Still?"

He merely smiles.

I'm not prepared for this hell, but I force myself to shower and get dressed. The new dress is white and sleeveless, high necked, but tightly fitted. Gazing at myself in Mateo's bathroom mirror, I consider the irony that he's dressing me in white now that I'm sullied beyond redemption.

For shoes, he had my Louboutins brought in. I didn't think anything could make me stop loving those damn shoes, but boy, he managed to find a way.

It's the first I've really seen anybody in four days, so I guess it's not surprising that everyone I come across stares before awkwardly saying hello. Despite my dark mood, I managed to pull it together physically, and I don't *look* as horrible as I feel.

I expect Cherie to hate me, since she's Vince's sister, so I'm surprised when she wraps an arm around me in the kitchen and asks, "You okay?"

I shrug. "I guess so."

Francesca avoids my gaze, and when it's time to serve the food, I understand why.

I grab two plates, dropping Mateo's cranberries on his, and none on the salad for Vince.

As gently as I think she can, Francesca takes Vince's plate. "I got this one."

I close my eyes, bracing myself on the edge of the counter. I get it now, why Vince was so pissed about it before. Not only have I been stripped of my relationship, now I'm going to walk out there and his entire family is going to see the evidence.

Worse, they're going to see me only serving Mateo now.

Steeling myself for whatever's about to come, I grab Mateo's salad and head for the dining room. My eyes find Vince immediately, expecting him to have moved, but he's in the same spot as always, my seat open next to him. My heart skips a beat, realizing they didn't move *my* spot, so I'll still be stuck between them.

Perfect.

Vince looks up when I walk in, hurt transforming his features at the sight of me. His gaze moves over my body, unfortunately prominently displayed in this tight-ass dress, and comes to settle on the single salad plate in my hand.

I feel like I'm stepping on his heart with the heel of my stiletto when I stop by Mateo, putting it down in front of him.

Vince's hands are clenched into fists on the table, and I see him squeeze, his jaw locked so tightly it looks painful.

I go back and get my salad, even though there's no chance I'll be able to eat.

I slide into the seat next to Vince, scooting forward, willing myself just to push the food around as long as I have to.

I don't expect Vince to speak to me, so I'm more than a little surprised when he says, "You look pretty."

I dare a glance in his direction, but his eyes are glued on the glass of alcohol on the table in front of him.

"Thank you," I say, quietly.

My stomach pitches and turns like a ship caught in a storm. After a few bites, I give up on the salad and turn to wine. I know I'll be in Mateo's bed again tonight, and maybe I'll feel a bit better about it if I manage to get drunk first. I wish I had the nerve to take what Vince has, but the sexist assbags only give women wine at dinner, no hard liquor.

Which, I call bullshit, because we *need* hard liquor to deal with them.

Once Mateo finishes his salad, I push back and stand to clear his plate.

Vince's hand shoots out, grabbing my wrist before I'm all the way up. I freeze, not sure what to expect.

"I want you to bring my dinner," he states.

Swallowing, hating the impulse, I look to Mateo. I catch mild surprise on his face before he clears it, his gaze moving to mine, watching to see what I'll say.

"Okay," I say uncertainly.

Mateo, probably not pleased with my response, meets Vince's gaze. "Why?"

Vince's eyes meet his, full of resentment. "Why *not*?"

Not one to be challenged, Mateo gives a deceptively casual shrug. "Well, I'm the one fucking her each night, I'm the one waking up with her tangled in my arms every morning, doesn't seem to me there's much reason—"

Vince's chair flies back and I jump, gasping. Mateo already had the attention of half the table with his boastful assholery, but the few at the far end who hadn't been looking are now.

"Fuck that," Vince says lowly. "Fuck. That."

"Vince," I say, glancing over at Mateo. I don't disagree, but I don't think it's even *safe* to make a scene telling Mateo to fuck off at family dinner. I envision Mateo pulling out his gun, the one that's been inside me, and shooting Vince without remorse, just because he fucking can. I envision shocked faces around the dinner table, but all of us too afraid to defy Mateo, so we finish our dinner while Vince's body grows cold right there on the ground next to us.

"No," Vince says, his finger in my face. "You shut up."

I do, not because I'm obeying, but because I'm a little shocked.

"Fuck this," Vince says again. "She's mine. I never gave her up; I never said I didn't want her... No."

Mateo doesn't respond, and Vince doesn't give anyone else a chance to. Locking his hand around my wrist, he drags me out of the dining room.

My heart pounds as I scurry to keep up with him, glancing back nervously. "Are we allowed to do this?"

"Everyone else takes what they want, why the fuck should I care?" he mutters.

"I don't think we're allowed to leave Sunday dinner," I point out.

"Fuck Sunday dinner."

This feels more than a little reckless to me, but I don't get the impression he's interested in my opinion. I don't know what's going to happen, not right now, not tomorrow, but I guess I'm along for the ride either way.

When we get to his room, Vince slams it shut, then backs me up toward the bed. My heart's racing, doubtful about this whole thing. He said he couldn't even look at me, so how's this going to work?

Also, he still looks angry. Here he is, with me in his bedroom, our bodies close enough to touch, but there's a fire behind his brown eyes, burning up any tenderness I might have hoped to see there.

He doesn't speak to me. I think he's going to, but it looks like he changes his mind. Instead, he grabs the bottom of my dress and hikes it up, startling me.

Hands on my hips, he lets his gaze rake over my body. I glance down, noticing bruises on my thighs—marks left by Mateo.

It seems to settle on Vince at the same time. His gaze frozen on my marked thighs, he swallows and takes a step back.

I don't want him to retreat, and I feel sick that he had to see that, but I don't want him to pull away, so I take a step toward him.

"Don't think about it," I say quietly.

"How?" he asks. "It's all I *can* think about."

"I didn't want him. Doesn't that count for something?"

His lips curve up, his smile bitter. "Thing is, Mia, I don't believe you."

"You don't *want* to believe me," I accuse, not understanding why. "How is it so hard to believe—?"

"You were sitting in his study visiting with him when Adrian told him about a pick up this weekend. He *let* you sit there—and no one was forcing you to be there."

"I was just trying to get along. I just wanted things to be amicable, I never thought… I never thought he'd actually force himself on me, Vince."

"Mateo doesn't trust anyone, Mia. Least of all someone he's giving reason to hate him."

"He wasn't trusting me, he was setting me up," I say, a little irritably. "For this, right here. You were right all along, he never intended to let me go because I saw you walk out of that goddamn house. Instead of telling you no, for whatever reason, he said as long as you want me, and then immediately began sabotaging us. I should've believed you. I don't know… if it would've stopped this from happening, but maybe then you'd at least believe me."

"Now you know how *I* felt, trying to tell you what he was like and you not believing me. Calling me *paranoid* and crazy—treating me like I'm the asshole, when all I was trying to do was protect you."

"I get that now. I didn't then. I have no frame of reference for this, Vince. I've never known people like that. I didn't know how to navigate this world. I'm supposed to keep you happy, I'm supposed to be careful around him—I'm so fucking twisted up between the two of you."

His jaw locks again, and I can see his anger seeping out again. "I can't *stand* to think about his hands on you. You've slept in his bed the past three nights—apparently you wake up *tangled* in his motherfucking arms every morning."

"He only said that to hurt you."

"Well, it fucking worked," he says, raising his voice. "Why did you stay, Mia? If he hurt you, if you didn't want him, if you were so goddamn afraid of losing me, why did you stay with him?"

Shaking my head, I try to come up with an adequate explanation. "I didn't think you wanted me to come back. I didn't have anywhere else to go. It's not like I get to leave here if you cast me aside, Vince. It's not like I have *options*."

"You think I don't know that?" he demands irritably. "It weighs on me every fucking day. It has since he brought you here, but now? Now I get to lie in my own goddamn bed with images of you spreading your legs for him, of his mouth on you—and you enjoying it."

I open my mouth to say I didn't, but I can't. Obviously the first two times I did enjoy it, I just… didn't know it was him.

He moves in again, giving me a light shove. I drop to the bed, scooting backward uncertainly. "Right here," he says, pointing to the bed. "Is this where you let my cousin fuck you?"

"You're not being fair," I tell him.

"What about this morning, huh? Before you put on this pretty dress and came down to serve him dinner, did he fuck you then?"

I close my eyes, unable to look at him, torn by too many different feelings—not least of all, shame.

"He did," he says slowly. "He's been inside you *today*, hasn't he?"

"Please stop," I say, not liking this.

"Then get it out of my head!"

"I don't know how!" I cry, wishing I did. "You have to *want* to, Vince. I'm not a goddamn magician. Tell me how to make it better!"

"Promise me he won't touch you again."

With a bitter laugh, I shake my head. "How? How can I promise that? I can promise if he does, I'll fight, but how do I promise you he won't force me? You act like this is my doing. If I could stop him, I would have already!"

"I'm gonna kill him," he says, jaw locked as he spins around.

"Don't say that," I say, immediately. "You don't mean that—"

Spinning back around, he gapes at me in furious disbelief. "Are you fucking kidding me? Don't you fucking defend him to me, Mia."

Stomach sinking, I shake my head in denial. "No, I wasn't. That's not what I... that's not what I meant."

It's on the tip of my tongue to point out that Cherie said there are cameras everywhere but the bathrooms, that I've been thinking about it over the past few days and I think maybe he *does* watch them. It's awfully coincidental that as soon as Vince tells me he doesn't want kids, Mateo decides to fuck me with no condom.

But Vince isn't listening—he's enraged, climbing across the bed in my direction. I skitter back, nervous, and he catches my leg, yanking me down near him.

"Vince, Wait—"

"You tell me he fucking forces you and then you have the *audacity* to be protective of that son of a bitch?"

"No, I wasn't—"

He doesn't let me finish, jerking my dress up around my waist and shoving me down on the bed. I panic, trying to get back up, but he pins me to the bed just like Mateo has.

"Is that what you like? Am I not *dangerous* enough for you, Mia?"

"Vince, stop," I cry, tears leaking out of my eyes now. "That wasn't what I was—I'm not protective of Mateo—"

"Stop fucking talking about him," he bites out, grabbing my bruised thighs and wrenching them apart.

"Please, Vince, not like this."

"I know I'm not the Morelli who last had his dick inside you in this bed, or even today, but I'll have to fucking do."

I sob, dropping my face to the pillow as Vince shoves inside me. I'm already so sore from Mateo and he's being so mean that every thrust burns like hell. I can't stop crying the whole time, and when he finally finishes, I realize he's not wearing a condom either. I don't know whether he was so angry he forgot, or he figures if I do wind up pregnant, at least now there will be a sliver of a chance he's the father.

He doesn't curl up next to me when he's done, he just gets off the bed and goes to the bathroom, leaving me half-naked and alone.

When he comes back out, he's still angry. I can't look at him, but I can tell by the way he's slamming shit.

Finally moving, I pull my legs together and curl up on my side, tucking myself into a ball.

Vince stops pacing around the room after a few minutes and walks over to the bedside, watching me. He sits on the edge of the bed with his back to me, running a hand over his face and through his hair.

"I shouldn't have done that," he finally says.

I don't know if he means brutalizing me or the lack of condom, and he doesn't clarify.

He's close enough now that I don't have to speak loudly. "The cameras."

Vince frowns, not understanding.

"I just didn't want him to hear you say that on the cameras. Didn't want him to take it as a threat. He'd hurt you."

He's dead silent so I glance up at him, watching understanding dawn, then morph into dull horror as he realizes his mistake. "You weren't…?"

I shake my head no. I can see he's about to sink under the realization, and I don't have the mental capacity left to deal with it today, so I ask, "Will you hold me?"

Understandably surprised, he asks, "You want me to?"

"It's been a rough week," I point out. I could use a little comfort, and there's really nowhere else to get any.

Sighing heavily, he yanks back the comforter and climbs on the bed. First he drapes the blanket over my body, like it can cover up what he just did, then he settles in behind me, pulling me into his arms. I lean into him, closing my eyes and wondering how the hell my life got turned upside down so completely in such a short stretch of time.

# CHAPTER TWENTY SIX

VINCE HOLDS me for the rest of the night. I half expect someone to come summon at least one of us, but it never happens. I fall asleep sometime before the sun rises, but I'm still exhausted when I hear Vince's alarm.

I wait for him to turn it off, but after a minute, I roll over and see he isn't there. I reach over to turn the damn thing off myself, rubbing my temple as my head throbs. It's going to be a long day.

Elise brings me breakfast, which she normally doesn't, so I figure one of them must have told her to. I don't ask which one. I don't care.

I can't feel anything again today. Maybe I'll snap out of it once I wake up, but right now? Nope.

I don't seek anyone out for a ride to school. There's enough time to walk and I could use the fresh air.

I'm halfway to school when I hear the car behind me, slowing to a stop. No stop sign in sight, so my stomach sinks with dread, expecting to look over and see Mateo, or at the very least, Adrian.

When I look, however, there are two men I don't recognize. My heartbeat skitters, wondering if these are Morelli flunkies, here to finish me off.

There are two men in the sleek white car, one in a black leather jacket and a complexion a shade or so darker than Cherie's with a bushy black mustache and pudgy apple cheeks. The other man has ruddy cheeks and wears a black leather jacket, his gut hanging over a pair of extremely unfashionable blue jeans.

"Mia Mitchell?" Potbelly says.

I cut a look in their direction, clutching my phone in my pocket.

"Ma'am, are you Mia Mitchell?"

"No," I reply.

Pressing his lips together, he says, "Ma'am, we know you are."

"Then why ask?" I respond, picking up the pace.

The other man speaks up, "Miss Mitchell, we just need to ask you a few questions."

I finally stop, stomach dropping as Potbelly holds up a badge for me to see. "Now, please."

"Why?" I ask, even though I can guess.

"We have a few questions, ma'am, just a few questions. It'll only take a few moments of your time."

Swallowing, casting a gaze over my shoulder, I tell him, "I'll be late to school."

"Hop on in, we'll give you a ride."

My eyes widen in horror. "No! No, not... I can't."

"Let me make it easy for you, Miss Mitchell. You can get in the car with us now and answer a few questions, then be on your way to school, *or* we can take you down to the station for questioning instead. Whichever's easiest for you."

I remain on the sidewalk, my eyes searching the road behind me, making sure Mateo didn't send anyone to follow me. Fear pierces the veil of numbness, ripping a hole down the middle and shedding it.

"I can't talk to you. I don't know anything."

Throwing the car in park, Apple Cheeks waits while Potbelly opens the car door. "All right, down to the station it is."

"No," I say quickly, heart hammering. "No, I'll get in the car."

I look one last time before I open the back door and climb inside. Shifting my backpack in my lap, I try to calm my racing heart, afraid they'll be able to see how nervous I am.

"I didn't do anything wrong," I say.

"No, we didn't think you did, Miss Mitchell. Thing is, it's come to our attention you've been spending time with the Morelli family lately."

"Is that a crime?" I ask.

Potbelly chooses his words carefully. "Well, no. But it might not surprise you to hear they're being investigated for several cases of wrongdoing. We looked into you, Miss Mitchell, and it just happens that you live right next door to one of those investigations."

Fear ties my stomach into knots, thinking of Vince. Thinking of the night of the fire, then the night he broke in to threaten me. God, what I'd give to go back to *that* being the scariest part of my day.

"I don't know what you mean," I tell them.

He reads off the address to the house next door to mine. "There's nothing you could tell us about the fire that happened at that address?"

"It was tragic," I say, unhelpfully. "I heard they were doing drugs or something."

"Actually, they were drug *dealers*. For a, I guess what you'd call a 'rival' family. Odd coincidence, isn't it?"

"I don't know anything," I state, hugging my backpack against my chest. "I didn't know my neighbors well and I had no idea they were any kind of rivals or whatever to… anyone, so I'm afraid I can't be much help."

"What's your relationship to Vince Morelli?" Apple Cheeks asks.

"He's my boyfriend."

"And as your boyfriend, I can see how you might feel badly talking to us about him, but this is important, Miss Mitchell. If you don't want to help us, things could get bad for you."

"I did nothing wrong. You can't threaten me."

"That's true," Potbelly drawls. "However, turns out your mom came into some money pretty unexpectedly, and… well, as much as I'd hate to have to involve her, it might be worth looking into."

Narrowing my eyes, I reiterate, "I don't *know* anything about the fire."

"That's too bad. What about anything else? Even if you don't know about the fire, maybe you know something else that could help us? Why don't you think real hard? Anything."

Apple Cheeks chimes in, a little softer. "We can keep you safe, Mia. If your concern is that there would be retaliation, we can guarantee you that won't happen."

Shaking my head, I say, "You can't guarantee that."

"We can. There are programs in place to protect people like you, Miss Mitchell. We could keep you safe all the way up to testifying, and forever after. With your help, we could put Mateo Morelli behind bars, and you and your family would never be in a lick of danger for it."

Easing back in the seat, I mull over those words. What if that's true? There's witness protection, right? What if I really could give them dirt on Mateo, and just like that, he'd be out of my life?

Vince would probably go down with him, though. Even after last night, I don't want that.

But Mateo.... Mateo would deserve it.

They'd probably go easier on Vince than him anyway—Vince is small potatoes. Mateo's the one they want. Maybe they would even work with me to spare Vince in exchange for giving them Mateo. And I probably could—with what Adrian said in front of me. I could tie Mateo himself directly to it.

*"I know you're angry right now, hurt, scared, but you should know this doesn't change anything. Like me or hate me, you will remain loyal to me. You speak a word about anything you shouldn't, and I will end you."*

The memory of Mateo's threat—uttered mere moments after violating me—causes gooseflesh to rise on my arms.

"I'm sorry," I say, lowly. "I don't know a single thing that could be of use to you."

"Ma'am, your mother—"

"Investigate her if you have to," I interrupt, shoving open the door. "I can't help you."

I hope it's over once I'm outside of the car, but Potbelly holds out a business card for me to take. "Well, why don't you take this, just in case you remember anything? Maybe you'll hear something we can use in the future."

I stare at the card, but I know I can't take it. Forget the possibility of somebody finding it—if I have that in my possession and Mateo assaults me again, I might be tempted to call.

Swallowing, I shake my head and walk away.

**Don't go to the bakery after school. Taking you to dinner. Wear whatever you want.**

I get the text from Vince at lunch.

My initial response is uncertainty—it's already been a hell of a day, and I haven't even left school yet. I don't really want to face Mateo though, particularly after last night, so I don't reject his offer.

Cherie takes me home after school, and since I know I'm doing dinner with Vince, I go to our room to do my homework.

A little after four, Vince shows up.

"You ready to go?" he asks.

"Sure," I say, flipping my textbook closed. When I stand and turn to face him, however, I'm caught off guard. Vince's eye appears to be swollen, and his lip is split. Rushing over to him, I reach out a hand to touch him, but stop short, figuring it might hurt. "Oh, my God, Vince. What happened?"

He shakes his head like it doesn't matter. "I'm fine."

"Did someone hit you?"

"I'm *fine*. It was nothing."

"Who did this?" My first thought, honestly, is Adrian. He seems to be the only decent one around here, and even he isn't decent enough to stop any of it. Then again, I don't know if he'd actually *hit* Vince. He doesn't tread carefully around the Morelli men like everyone else, but that may be taking things too far.

"It was just sparring," he says dismissively.

"Sparring?" I ask, quirking a skeptical eyebrow.

"I think Mateo just really wanted to punch me in the face. It was at the gym. It's fine."

I'm surprised to hear it was Mateo, though I guess maybe it's payback for his little scene at the table yesterday. If so, it's a light enough retaliation. I guess that's why Vince doesn't care.

"I feel like for future reference, not sparring with him would be a good idea," I advise.

Rolling his eyes, he says, "He'd still punch me if he wanted to. Mateo does what he wants, Mia. Don't worry about it. At worst, it may get ugly in a couple days." Nodding toward the door, he says, "Let's get out of here."

Grabbing my purse from the floor, I follow him out. "Where are we going?"

"You'll see," he tells me, surprising me by reaching down and taking my hand.

I offer a tentative smile when he looks over at me, but I'm confused.

## Accidental Witness

We haven't been out on an actual date since I moved in, and obviously last night he was *not* in the mood to wine and dine me.

I think he feels guilty. Which... well, I guess he should.

I watch out the window as he drives, trying to guess where we might be going, but I have no idea. When he finally pulls into a parking area, it's outside an apartment complex.

"This is where we're eating?" I ask, confused.

Instead of answering me, he takes me by the hand again and leads me inside.

I'm surprised again when he pauses outside room 602 and uses a key.

Then he opens the door and gestures for me to go inside. Thoroughly confused, I look around. It's sparsely furnished, but as soon as I spot the kitchen, I see pots and cans of food, a bag of flour, spices, and some kind of silver machine with a crank handle. Across the kitchen in the corner there's a small round table with two chairs, an unlit candle at the center, already set for two.

A smile spreading across my face, I ask, "What is this?"

"I asked Joey if I could borrow his apartment for the evening. I seem to remember we're *way* overdue for a spaghetti dinner."

Recalling the time he bought my groceries and then I asked him to leave, I nod my head. "I guess we are."

"And I know you just use the readymade stuff, but I can't eat spaghetti sauce from a jar. It just isn't right."

Rolling my eyes, I say, "Don't be a spaghetti snob; it's good!"

"Well, I'm going to show you how to make your own spaghetti sauce, *and* we're making our own pasta. We'll see which one's better."

"This is nice," I tell him, feeling lighter than I have in a while.

Taking my hand, he lifts it and places a light kiss to my knuckles. "Good. After dinner, we've got the living room to ourselves—any movie you want. At least, any movie that Joey *has* that you want."

"I'm sure I'll be overwhelmed by the selection," I assure him.

"I hope you like Jason Statham."

Snorting, I respond, "Who doesn't?"

A few minutes later, washed up and ingredients sorted, Vince and I start dinner.

"I've never cooked with a guy before," I tell him, mincing garlic.

"Weird, me neither."

I roll my eyes at him. "That's because in your family only women cook."

Lifting an eyebrow as if to admit his inability to argue that, he says, "Well, this is my mom's recipe, so I know it's good."

"You never told me about your mom."

His demeanor dims a little, and I feel him want to retreat. To his credit, he doesn't. "Like most Morelli women, she got trapped into a relationship with one of us bastards and couldn't get out."

"Ah," I murmur, nodding. "How did she die?"

"Pills. Killed herself."

My head snaps up. "Oh, Jesus. I didn't know, I'm sorry."

He dumps a can of diced tomatoes into the pot. "I always told myself I wouldn't be like him. Swore it. I didn't want to become someone I hated."

I'm not sure if he's talking about Mateo or his father, but I really don't want to bring up the former if he's not talking about him, so I guess, "Your dad?"

He nods. "I'd never let him meet you. He's garbage."

"Well, I'm sure you're not like him, then," I say easily, lifting the chopping board and taking it over to the pot, scraping the garlic in.

"I was last night," he states, quietly.

Putting the cutting board and knife down on the counter, I wrap an arm around him and give him a squeeze. "No."

"Yes. Eighteen years ago, he did to Maria what I did to you, and every day I see Cherie it's a reminder of the kind of man I don't want to be."

That stuns me. Mateo had filled me in on their relation, but he certainly hadn't indicated it had been non-consensual. I just figured he had an affair with the maid—typical.

"Your dad and Maria weren't...?"

"She hated him," Vince states. "He wanted her anyway. Morelli men take what they want."

I don't know what to say to that. It's not like I haven't seen proof of precisely that since joining their fucked up family.

"I don't want to be like that, Mia."

"Then don't," I say simply.

"I'm so sorry for last night," he says, meeting my gaze.

"I know. It's okay. We don't have to… It's over. I forgive you. We're okay. I just want us to get past everything. I don't want to dwell."

"No matter what happens, nothing like that will ever happen to you again at my hands."

Offering a supportive smile, I nod. "I know."

"And you were right about what you said, too. Mateo can't get between us unless we let him. I'm not gonna let him anymore."

"Neither am I," I state.

Leaning in to touch his forehead against mine, Vince asks, "Can I kiss you?"

Smiling slightly, I tell him, "Always."

# CHAPTER TWENTY SEVEN

IT'S EASIER to stay out from under the cloud of gloom now that I'm out of Mateo's room and back in Vince's. I still think about the possibility of cameras all the time, because there aren't any *visible* in Vince's room, which means there are hidden ones. Vince hasn't touched me again, giving me time to heal, but I think about it when we're lying in bed. Will Mateo be able to watch? I guess I shouldn't care so much. Voyeurism would at least be less intrusive than what he's already done.

Between school, the bakery, and hiding out in Vince's room, I don't have to see Mateo again until Wednesday night.

Maria comes to tell me Mateo wants to see me in his study before dinner. She brings a garment bag, but I don't even open it.

"What if I don't go?" I ask. I don't know why I think she could anticipate his reaction, but I really, really don't want to find myself alone with him again. Especially not right now, when I have no idea of his mental state. Is he pissed that his little plan didn't work? That I'm back with Vince? Will he redouble his attempts to break us up? I know Vince is fighting to stay with me now and to keep Mateo out of our relationship, but I'm not sure how we will hold up under the reality. If Mateo decides to keep me as a plaything, will Vince be able to handle it? Will I?

Warily shaking her head, Maria said, "You don't say no to Mateo."

"But what if I do?"

"I think you can guess," she states. "He isn't alone. Adrian is with him."

That makes me breathe a lot easier. He may be a creep, but I don't *think* he'd rape me in front of Adrian.

"Why does he want to see me?"

She merely shrugs, leaving the room.

In a small act of defiance, I don one of the dresses Vince gave me.

I don't know where Vince is, but I wish I did. I really don't want to go to Mateo's study without telling him. We haven't discussed how we'll deal with this, but my instinct is that I should be as open as possible when I'm going to be around him. Secrets will only make him stop trusting me again.

I haven't decided how that openness will work concerning sexual activity. I hope to God it never comes up again, but I have no idea how to handle it if it does.

When I show up in the study, Adrian is still there, so I breathe a little easier. Mateo's leaning against his desk, drink in hand, and he allows his eyes to move over my body. I expect him to react to my not wearing whatever dress he must have sent up, but his perusal of my body only turns up pleasure.

"Mia," he says warmly.

Staying by the door, I square my shoulders. "Maria said you wanted to see me."

"Correct. You can come closer."

"I'm all right."

Cocking his head to the side, he gives me about two seconds, then he pushes off the desk and strides over to me. I fall back a step, but I know I can't leave. He stops in front of me, looking down at me, seeming to shrink me with his gaze. After several long seconds, he reaches behind me and shoves the study door closed.

"Just because I'm letting you sleep in Vince's bed, Mia, don't get confused and think you're allowed to start defying me." Furthering his point, he drags the back of two fingers across my collar bone, dipping threateningly toward my cleavage.

Body taut with tension, I offer a barely perceptible nod. I don't relish the reminder that whatever victory it feels like we've achieved, we only have it because he's allowing it.

His hand leaves me, but the tension doesn't leave my body.

"Tomorrow night I'm hosting a poker game. I want you to come."

"I don't know how to play poker."

That makes him laugh. The bastard gives me another warm smile, like he just finds me goddamn delightful. "No, you won't be playing. You'll be there to help out. To look pretty," he adds with a wink.

"Will Vince be there?"

"No."

I hesitate, not wanting him to take my next statement as any sort of challenge. "He won't want me to go."

Mateo rolls his eyes. "Obviously."

I really don't want to put Vince through this. I mean, I don't want to do it to begin with, but I certainly don't want to leave him all night to wonder if Mateo's doing… Mateo things.

I don't know how to say any of this. There would be no point. It's nothing he doesn't already know; he just doesn't care. What I *don't* want to do is make him feel he has a point to prove about my obedience.

I wish I could make him promise me I'll be safe, but he doesn't have to. He wasn't requesting my presence, he was telling me where I would be going. Finally, I nod. "All right."

This pleases him, and he gives me another agreeable smile. My stomach turns over, because for some sick reason, it brings me relief to have pleased him.

"Is that all?" I ask, wanting to get out of here.

"Yes," he says, easily. "Cherie will get you ready. I believe Maria already brought something up for you to wear." Barely pausing a second, he adds, "I'll give Vince something to keep him occupied. Tell him where you'll be or don't."

A shiver goes down my spine at that, at the secrecy implied. I don't want to have secrets with this man, especially not secrets from Vince.

Ignoring that temptation, knowing it would just blow up in my face later, I say, "No. I'll tell him."

He shrugs, unconcerned. "Suit yourself."

Our business complete, he allows me to leave. On the other side, I lean heavily against the wall, my mind racing a million different ways. I was dreading seeing him again, being alone with him—have been, since Sunday night. It feels bizarrely comforting, despite his casual threats, that everything was… fairly normal. He didn't seem angry at me. He didn't seem resentful or put out. His reaction is nothing like Vince's— and I feel so relieved. It doesn't make sense, but I don't dread the next time I'll see him as much.

But *that* distresses me. Relief distresses me, because I shouldn't be relieved. I *hate* him. He's a terrible human being who manipulates and controls everyone around him—and I'm damn sure no exception.

There's something… addictive about him though. Something that leaves me craving the approval of a man I hate.

How fucked up is that?

More unsettled than I had been when I knew I was coming to meet him, I head for the dining room to get ready for dinner.

---

Vince sits on the edge of the bed, watching Cherie curl my hair.

Nobody speaks. Well, occasionally Cherie, when she has to tell me to tilt or not move my head, but Vince and I are both silent.

Finally finished, she grabs hair spray and coats my hair.

"Is that necessary? She's not going to the fucking prom," Vince says, understandably aggravated.

I'm sort of regretting not taking Mateo up on his offer to keep Vince busy. Maybe I should have asked him to, even though I was telling Vince. It's not helping anyone to have him sitting here, watching Cherie doll me up on orders from Mateo, none of us knowing exactly what I'm walking into, but *all* of us aware of what could happen.

Cherie understands, so she doesn't say anything in response.

"Let's grab the outfit. Where'd you put it?"

"It's still in the bag," I tell her. "I put it in the closet after dinner last night."

A few minutes later, the outfit is out of the bag and I am horrified. Vince's temper, thus far controlled, seems like it's going to explode any second.

"That's what you're supposed to wear," he says, each word angrier than the last.

I understand why. Unlike the classy dresses he bought me for dinner, this outfit is just plain trash. The fire engine red corset top is… well, a corset. There's a skimpy black skirt that may not even cover my ass, and a pair of thigh-high, fishnet stockings to finish off the "$25 for a blow job, $100 for an hour" look I'm apparently going for.

"He's just goading you, probably," I tell him.

"They're just clothes," Cherie adds, trying to help.

Vince is unimpressed by our attempts.

I'm not at all looking forward to putting this on, so I take it in the bathroom, wanting to see the damage first. It's not good. I do what I can to loosen the corset and take the attention off my boobs, but it's ineffective. Even a gay man would have to look right at them on sight.

Why is he doing this?

Giving up on the impossible, I open the bathroom door and march out to the firing squad.

Vince's eyes get the lusty look I recognize, but it's struggling with his short fuse, and the short fuse is winning.

"It doesn't matter," I tell him, shrugging like it doesn't even bother me. "It's just an outfit. It's fine."

"Don't go."

"Vince..." I sigh, because he knows that's not an option.

"He's gonna... he's not going to keep his hands off you, Mia."

Gathering up her things quietly, Cherie says, "I'm done here, so... I'm gonna leave you guys to... all this."

I don't blame her. I wish I could bail, too.

Placing my hands on Vince's shoulders, innocently pressing my boobs against his chest, I say, "Let's fight the battles we can win. Mateo's going to be busy playing poker with his buddies. We won't be alone."

"What if I rip it? You can't wear it if it's damaged."

"Don't," I say, stilling his hand as it skates toward my corset. "Please. I don't want to provoke him. Just... it's just an outfit. It'll be over in a few hours."

"I'm waiting up," he states, like I have any power over when we'll get back.

"Don't torture yourself. I'll wake you up to let you know I'm home safe if you want me to."

"I'm not going to be able to sleep."

Reaching for his hand, I state, "We're not letting him do this, remember? I know it's hard, trust me, it's not easy for me either, but..."

"How am I supposed to send you off to him, knowing what's going to happen?"

I take a slow breath and let it out, wondering the same thing. But I know the answer. "Because we don't have any alternative."

"How are we supposed to live like this?" he asks, causing my hope to plummet. This is the *first* Mateo-sized bump we've come to since swearing we wouldn't let him get to us, and he's already getting to Vince. If we can't survive one, how will we keep going?

"It's the only way. We can't keep going in circles. We already know where it ends up, and I don't want to go back to that."

Mainly because 'that' is Mateo's bed, and if Mateo is my strongest lifeline? I'm super fucked.

He looks down, shaking his head. "No, neither do I."

"I'll be fine. He won't touch me."

We both know it's a lie, but Vince wants it to be true, so he nods like he believes it.

"Why don't you bring that ass over here, sweetheart?"

As degrading as I feared tonight would be, it's worse. Just not for the reason I expected.

Mateo isn't the problem.

The other creeps trickling in to play poker are.

It's still Mateo's fault, I suppose. Dress me up like a hooker, I guess you can't blame the guys for thinking I am one.

Six men sit around the table, draining glass after glass of liquor, smoking cigars, and occasionally pushing obscene amounts of money around the table.

Two hours of leering, two hours of their eyes all over my body. I need to shower for a week straight after I leave here tonight.

This one's drunk though, I can see it in his face. His cheeks are ruddy, his eyes have the gleam of drunkenness, and his big bald head shines as I reluctantly approach him to give him more alcohol.

As I go to pour it, his hand creeps up under my skirt and over my ass. I gasp, jumping, alcohol sloshing out of the decanter as I try to right it in motion.

"Hey," Mateo barks.

The laughter in the room dies, smiles falling from faces as they all look slowly in his direction.

I swallow nervously, looking at him myself.

His gaze is still on baldy, but then he looks at me. "You're not gonna make me sit here thirsty, now are you?"

It's a sad day when I'm so eager to get away from someone, I welcome approaching Mateo, but I scurry right over to him.

He watches my hand shake as I dump some of the alcohol into his tumbler. As soon as I finish, he picks up the cigar he's been fiddling with for a couple of rounds and glances at me.

Finally, he holds it out to me. I take it but I don't know why, and my uncertainty must register on my face. Before I have a chance to ask, his hands are on my hips, yanking me into his lap, adjusting me until I'm straddling him.

It's harder to breathe, but I'm not scared. Just… confused.

He hands me the lighter, but my eyes can't seem to move away from his.

Then with all the casualty of someone who does so every day, he plants his hands on my nearly-bare ass cheeks and pulls me against him.

He's hard, and I'm sick, because my loins stir at the contact.

He plucks the cigar from my fingers, placing it into his mouth, and I realize he wants me to light it for him. I fiddle with the lighter, hands still unsteady, until I manage it.

Mateo gives me a slow smile and a little wink. "Thanks, sweetheart."

My blood runs hot and cold, confusion and overstimulation wreaking havoc on my peace of mind. Not like I had much coming into tonight, but I get the feeling I'll be leaving with significantly less.

He lets me off his lap a few minutes later, and I'm not immediately sure why he did it… until I notice the other guys barely even look my way again. I still bring them drinks or snacks or cigars, but no more leering to make me uncomfortable, and *definitely* no more groping.

He marked me as his.

I'm obviously not, but the knowledge does little to remove the mantle of guilt around my shoulders.

When I can get away, I text Vince to let him know everything's going fine. I had to leave my phone in the other room, since my outfit leaves absolutely nowhere to store it. I also want to tell him that now, while it's still true.

A little later, there's a pounding on the door. Having seen too many movies, it scares me, and I think the game's being busted or something.

Nobody else is concerned though.

"Probably Conroy's lazy ass," Mateo says to the table, before nodding at me. "Let 'em in."

I wish everyone would've arrived before Mateo did his little cigar performance, but I guess someone will clue any newcomers in if they start to act stupid.

Yanking the door open, I open my mouth to welcome them, but I stop short, mouth hanging open, because I recognize the two men at the door.

The cops who stopped me on my way to school Monday.

# CHAPTER TWENTY EIGHT

MY MOUTH goes dry and my mind races. The party *is* being busted—and what the hell is going to happen now? I'm going to be hauled into the police station, no clue how to get out of talking, *Mateo* is going to be arrested—this is a fucking disaster.

Then Potbelly brings a finger to his lips, indicating I should be quiet.

It's too late to warn them anyway. It's too late to tell Mateo... I don't even know what I could tell him, because this is it.

They've got him.

I should feel relieved, but... I don't.

Potbelly takes a step forward and I stumble back several steps, but then he moves past the door, in Mateo's sight, and I'm baffled because he hasn't even pulled a gun.

"There you are, you lazy bastard," Mateo says, congenially.

One of the other guys groans and jokes, "Aw, the boys in blue. We're gonna have to take it down a few notches, guys."

I don't know what the look on my face must be right now, but some mash-up of disbelief and what-the-fuck is my guess.

"Mia," Mateo says, nodding at me. "Grab them cigars."

I turn slowly, trying to make sense of things—and fast. Mateo obviously knows they're cops, and it does make sense that he would have some on his payroll, but... the potbellied cop obviously knew who I was at the door, when Mateo *couldn't* see them, and he told me to be quiet.

My blood runs cold as I realize they're double-crossing him.

They're obviously here as friends, cops on his payroll, but when they're not here, they're trying to turn people close to him to testify against him.

I don't know what to do. I could wait and see how things shake out, but what if Mateo, guard down, says something in front of them they could use?

He'll find out they talked to me. He finds out everything. And they've seen me here tonight, so they'll never believe me again if I tell them I don't have anything to offer them. They'll come after *me*, and because I can't turn on him… what's going to happen to me?

My hands are on the cigars, but I can't move. The whole world is suddenly crashing down around me and it's hard to breathe. It's hard to see a way out of this.

I drop the cigars.

I turn around and look once more at the table.

Then, before I can talk myself out of it, I walk over to Mateo. "You're out of cigars."

With a perplexed frown, he says, "No, I'm not."

I nod. "Are there more in the back? Can you show me?"

His expression clears and he leans back, giving me a probing look. Quietly, he asks, "You want me to take you to the back room, alone, to show you where the cigars are?"

Sighing to myself, I say, "Yes."

He nods once, then moves to stand. "You gentlemen'll have to excuse me for a minute. I have to help the lady locate some more cigars."

I wish he'd hurry the hell up. Those stupid cops probably know what I'm about to do, and we'll all be lucky if they don't stop me before I can.

My hope is that they're outnumbered, with no back-up outside. That's the only way this works.

At the same time, I don't even want to think about what Mateo's bound to do to them if they're on their own.

As he follows me into the back room, he says, "I have to admit, this surprises me."

"Trust me, it's a last resort."

But he's had even more to drink than usual, and he's relaxed. His hands drop to my hips and he moves closer, not aggressive, just… strangely playful. "You want to play, Mia?"

"No," I say, removing his hands, but surprised that he lets me.

"Oh, come on." He leans in, the scent of his cologne hitting my nostrils as his lips move to my neck. My sensitive, sensitive neck.

I grab his hair, tugging his mouth away from my body. "Stop. I need to tell you something."

"That you like hair-pulling?" he asks with a sensual smile. "Thank you. I approve."

He reaches a hand toward mine, doubtless to give it a tug, but I grab his wrist. "Mateo, those two guys that just came in are cops."

His eyebrows rise, but he does not look impressed by my intelligence. "Yes, I know. That's why I give them money. Don't get too excited though, they won't arrest me."

He's still teasing, and while it's a little refreshing, there's no time for this. "Yes, they *will*," I say, a little desperately. "Those guys are not your friends, Mateo. They stopped me Monday before school. They asked me questions about you. They wanted me to give them information, to… testify against you."

All amusement vanishes from his face, and a scary stoicism takes its place. "Monday?"

Swallowing, I bob my head.

"You didn't tell me."

*Fuck.* "No. I… I didn't tell them anything, I told them to leave me alone. I probably should've told you, but… it was just… there was a lot going on."

The way he studies me makes me squirm. There's usually some trace of amusement when he looks at me, whether because he thinks I'm being a naïve idiot, or because he's enjoying the game only he knows he's playing with my life. But right now, he's dead serious, and it sends fear like I've never known traveling down my spine. If he would've looked at me like this the first time he pulled a gun on me, I probably would've dropped dead from a heart attack and saved him the trouble.

"I should've told you," I say, quietly. "But… I don't think we can dwell on that right now. What do we do?"

His hand slowly moves to my neck, his thumb brushing my jaw, and then he leans in and kisses me. My hands go to his chest, pushing against him. "Mateo," I say, against his mouth. "Stop it. This is so *not* the time."

But he's not pushing, and…he's smiling.

Meanwhile I'm frowning, confused, wondering if he's lost it.

"You're something else, Mia," he tells me, touching my face again, but kindly, like he finds me adorable.

I can only stare, wide-eyed.

"They are my friends," he states. "I sent them to talk to you Monday."

"What?" I ask, faintly.

Shrugging, he says, "I had to see what you'd do. I had to see if you'd turn on me or remain loyal." Cupping my face in his hand, he says, "You passed."

Shock courses through me as his words sink in. Sheer horror follows, realizing he'd been testing me, and if I would've talked, if I would've told the men who swore they could protect me about the information he let Adrian share in front of me....

How long had he been setting me up for this?

My mouth is still gaping open when his mouth finds my neck again, his hand moving between my legs. Arousal stirs at the touch of his fingertips and I push him away again, shaking my head.

"You... you..."

"Mm hmm," he verifies, catching my wrist and going back to my neck.

"But... but... they tried to give me the number to the police station. They said they could keep me safe if I..."

His lips leave my neck and he moves closer to my ear, whispering in a rough, silky tone, "Sweetheart, if you ever betray me, God Himself won't be able to keep you safe."

Relief should be pouring through me, but it's only a trickle. I'm stuck in horror, because I can remember sitting in that car, *wanting* to talk.

"But you didn't, so you won't," he continues. "I built you up, broke you down, took everything from you... and you didn't turn on me."

A sickening thought gets lodged in my gut. I've seen how Mateo works now, I've been manipulated according to his designs, and now I'm wondering...

"When did you...?" I shake my head, pulling back from the kisses he's leaving along my neck. "How long have you...?"

I don't know how to ask, but he doesn't make me. Mateo pulls back so he can look at me, and while he doesn't exactly move away, he does stop advancing on me.

"Mia, *anybody* with a gun to their head is going to tell you they won't talk. It's survival, plain and simple. I'm the predator, you're the prey. I have my teeth to your throat, you'll promise me anything I want to try to make it out alive. You may even think you mean it. But when it comes down to it, when it really comes down to it, you can't know unless it happens. Vince wanted to keep you alive. He was a pain in the ass about it from the get-go, but I wasn't about to take that chance. You're young, fragile; I never thought you'd hold up under the pressure. I had to trap you. I had to take everything away from you. I had to ruin your life, betray you—I had to make you despise me, make you *want* to see me behind bars more than you wanted anything."

"You did all of this just to see if you could make me talk? You… *raped me* as part of a *plan*? As a *means to a fucking end*? To make me hate you—which I had every right to!—to…to…?"

"Yes," he says, not allowing me to finish the in-progress implosion of my brain. "And despite having every motivation to, you didn't talk. You passed. Congratulations."

"Do I get a fucking ribbon?" I ask, dumbfounded.

He smiles. "Better. You get your freedom."

That knocks the fight right out of me. I don't think I heard him right—or I misunderstood him somehow. "What?"

"I'm never the most trusting guy in the room, but… you've shown me I can trust you not to say anything against my family. You don't have to be afraid of Vince leaving you anymore. If he does, you're free to move on with your life, removed from the Morelli family. Or, if you're hooked, you can give me a call," he says, winking.

"Vince… he was in on this? Sunday night…?"

"No," Mateo says, his smile disappearing. "No, that…" He pauses. "I did not anticipate that he would… That was a surprise. I mean, it certainly helped, but no, that was all him."

"So, you've only been toying with me for *this*? It was never real, it was… you were just… manipulating the circumstances until you did enough damage to test me?"

He takes a few seconds before he answers. "Well, yes and no. Obviously, it really happened, but my main motivation was this. I didn't think you'd enjoy rape, but I thought you'd probably enjoy murder far less. Made a judgment call."

I don't know what to feel anymore. There's logic to what he says, but I don't know how to process the implications. I don't know how to file away everything that's happened to me, or my observations about him as a person. He's tormented me and Vince, all in the name of testing some theory—an admittedly solid theory, but… wow.

I don't even notice he's caught my hand until he presses it against his cock. He's hard beneath the soft fabric of his pants, and though I'm foggy with confusion, it registers.

"I can think of a way for you to thank me," he says playfully, his lips brushing my earlobe, sending shivers of pleasure all along my nerve endings.

"Mateo…"

"Don't worry, I can take away your choice," he says, tugging me close. "I prefer not to. I confess, while I didn't hate myself for a single time I fucked you, Mia, I would like to experience you fucking me because you want to, actually knowing it's my cock inside you."

I release a breath, knowing I need to get the hell away from him. That goddamn dirty mouth does things to me it shouldn't, and I don't want him, I want Vince.

"You said it was all a game. Game's over," I remind him.

Rubbing my hand against his cock, he tells me, "There are always other games."

"With you, yeah, I bet there are," I say, with a shaky, unconvincing laugh.

I haven't pulled my hand away, though, and I probably could have. He's still holding my hand, but if I tried to break his hold, I don't think he'd stop me.

So why am I still stroking him?

Why can I feel myself getting excited?

"I need to go," I say quietly.

"I'll take you home after the game's over," he says, moving between my legs.

"Mateo," I say, my heart pounding with a mix of panic and something else. It's the something else that's the problem. "You have to stop."

"Why delay the inevitable?" he asks, his hand sliding up the inside of my thigh. "Vince is a good kid, but he's a kid. You need a man."

"No," I say, yanking my hand from his cock to grab the one moving between my legs. "What I need is to get away from you."

"To go back and live at my house, where you'll see me day in and day out. I will fuck you, Mia, it's just a matter of when."

"Jesus Christ," I mutter, and even though I'm me, and I have control over this situation, I can't help but believe him.

I don't know how to explain what I feel for Mateo. It isn't yearning, it isn't want. I wouldn't even call it lust, but he calls to me in some way. I don't *want* him, but I'm ensnared all the same.

*Feel* isn't even the right word. It's not an emotional response, it's a force of nature. Mateo Morelli is a black hole, and no matter how I feel, no matter what I want, I can't escape from being sucked into him.

As I think that, his finger moves inside my panties.

"Stop."

He doesn't, sucking on my neck before saying, "No, don't tell me to stop. We've already played that game. I want to play a different one."

"It wasn't a game to me," I remind him, soberness piercing whatever fuckery he's practicing on me right now. "It was real to me."

His hand cups my neck again, and it feels so tender—too tender. "Come on, sweetheart. Don't hold a grudge."

I about sputter at his minimizing it to a grudge, but then he's kissing me and I don't know what to do. I push against his chest, but he pushes between my legs and a moan slips out of me.

"Fuck," I say, shoving him harder. "Stop it. Stop it! Stop playing games with me."

"Just give in. Play with me, not against me."

I shake my head, scooting closer to the door. "I'm going back out there. I will finish this stupid *poker* game bullshit, but this is the only game I'm playing with you tonight."

He sighs, but doesn't move to stop me as I reach the knob of the door. "Another night, then."

I freeze.

I could move. I want to move. He won't stop me, but his words keep me right where I stand.

Because I *can't* play this game another night.

I don't know where it will go, or what the new stakes will be, or who will get destroyed in this one, but I know someone will. And I consider it *highly* unlikely it will be him.

No, it will be me and Vince. Again. It will *always* be me and Vince. Anytime we go up against this man in any capacity, whether in earnest, in a battle of wits, of wills… he is always going to destroy us. Maybe not even on purpose. It's just what he does. How he plays. He's a lion trying to play with a kitten—the kitten will always get hurt.

I want Vince, I want to see what we can become, but there's one thing I know for certain: we will not survive Mateo. We can fight as hard as we want, but he'll win every time. Whatever Vince and I promise each other, regardless of what we want, Mateo will always wreck it.

Since I haven't moved, he asks, "Change your mind already?"

"I can't do another night." I shake my head, looking down at the floor, baffled by how I could be in this situation right now. "What is wrong with me? I know the truth about you, so why do I still want to believe the lies?"

"Because you're human," he says, coming up behind me. His hands come to rest on my hips again. "And you're sweet. And young. And *so* idealistic."

"This isn't fair to Vince. Why won't you just *stop*? Just leave us alone? Let us see if we can build something together."

"That's what you want?"

"*Yes.*"

He mulls it over a minute before saying, "I might have a proposition for you."

This already feels like a trap, so I sigh, hanging my head. "What now?"

"We both know you'll end up back in my bed eventually—probably sooner than later, if we're being realistic. And painfully, for Vince. He'll have to watch it all unfold again. I've charmed you before; you know if I set my mind to it, I'll do it again."

"I don't know that," I mutter.

"Sure," he says, unconvinced. "What if we skip all the foreplay? I get you tonight. Once. You give yourself to me one last time, and in doing so, save Vince plenty of torture. It's a favor, really."

"No," I say. "I don't trust you."

"Smart."

I roll my eyes.

"I'll give you and Vince your own place."

Turning to face him, I say, "What?"

"It's proximity to me that wears you down. You live in my house, you're under my rule. You go where I say, when I say, and do what I say when you get there. That wasn't an act; that's your life in my house. What if you didn't live in my house? What if I gave you and Vince your own space, let you move out?"

Let us get away from him.

Vince's words run through my mind: *"I want something of my own, something to… get me out from under his thumb."*

Monday night comes back to me, how lovely it was just the two of us at Joey's apartment, making dinner, snuggling as we watched movies, no pressure. Mateo didn't even exist there.

"We wouldn't have to see you at all?"

"Well, Sunday night dinner. But you come, you eat, you leave when you're ready—not like living there. I won't rock your boat. If you want to try with Vince…this is how."

God, that's tempting. "I… I can't do that to Vince."

Sighing like he can hardly handle how pedestrian I am, Mateo asks, "Do you know why people lie, Mia?"

"Because they're cowards," I reply.

He smiles at the insult. "Because it's *easier*. Stop doing everything the hard way. Just lie to him. He'll love you for it."

"You'd just tell him," I toss back.

"I wouldn't. I won't. You have my word."

I snort, and he scowls.

Catching me at the small of my back, he yanks me against him. I gasp, caught off guard, and he says, "Now, now. I've never given you my word before. I do have *some* honor."

"If you did, I don't think you'd be holding your erection against me right now."

"If I didn't, I wouldn't have offered you an out at all and I could hold my cock against you whenever I feel like it."

I can't really argue that.

Just like I can't argue against the way my body is reacting to him.

When it has every reason to be repulsed by him, the damn thing is somehow turned on instead. I want to believe in myself, in Vince, but there's too much evidence to the contrary. Vince's reaction to how Mateo dressed me up tonight—the first time Mateo fucks with him again, and he reacts just the way Mateo intends. He can't stop letting him under his skin.

And a tiny part of me points out, Vince believed as much as I did that Mateo would forcibly fuck me tonight.

Would this be so much worse?

"You *promise* you wouldn't tell him, *and* you would give us our own place away from you?"

"I do."

"Do you have a condom?"

He smiles like the devil, about to acquire a shiny new soul. "I do."

Swallowing once, twice, three times, I meet his gaze, still afraid he'll screw me over…but more afraid of the alternative.

"Okay," I say, stomach falling even as the word spills out of my mouth. "I'll do it."

# CHAPTER TWENTY NINE

ONCE THE words are out, I feel almost light-headed, already wondering what I've just done.

I only get a brief glimpse of his victory—he extinguishes the sparkle in his eyes before he scares me off. His track record at this point does nothing to recommend him, and I could very well be digging my own grave right now instead of an escape tunnel.

Wisely, he doesn't give me any more time to think about it. Once his hands slip beneath the scant fabric of the skirt, cupping my ass and pulling me against him, all ability to think drains right out of me. Knowing all I do about him should make him unattractive, unappealing, repulsive—but somehow it only makes knowing he wants me, even if only for a game, strangely thrilling.

Mateo dips his head to the overflowing cleavage spilling out of the corset. As his lips brush the exposed skin, pleasure moves through my veins, leaving on a breathless sigh. He's still forceful, grabbing me to pull me closer. I shouldn't like it. I *really* shouldn't like it.

Backing me up against the door, he lifts my arms above my head, a shadow of last time. My heart does a flip, but he doesn't hold them there, instead letting his fingers skim down the undersides until he's holding my hips again.

*Fuck me*, he makes things feel good.

*When he's not making things feel terrible*, I remind myself.

He kisses me again, and my arms wind around his neck, tugging him closer. Excitement makes my stomach feel light, like I'm flying downhill on a rollercoaster. I guess I kind of am.

His hands roam all over me while we kiss. Caressing, digging, pulling. I'm panting when he finally pulls away, and only then to yank my panties off.

"Tell me what you want, Mia."

I don't know what he wants me to say, and I'm too reluctant to answer honestly. I don't want to want any of this with him. Giving voice to it feels so wrong.

His hand moves between my legs, rubbing a finger across my opening. A shaky breath escapes me, but I won't answer him.

"Come on," he coaxes, slipping his finger inside of me, using my slickness to tease me. "Do you want my cock, Mia? Do you want me to bend you over and fuck you like a nasty little slut?"

Something like a squeak slips out of me, but I still won't answer.

"Or do you want my mouth first? Do you want me to lick that pretty little pussy until you're crying out my name?"

"Jesus, Mateo."

He grins like the devil he is. "Mouth it is."

I push out a breath, uncertain, but there's nothing hesitant about this man. Planting his hands under me, he lifts me up and carries me over to a white couch along the wall. He lets me slide down his body once we get there, then he pushes down on my shoulders until I'm sitting.

Forget second thoughts, I'm on eighth and ninth thoughts, but then Mateo Morelli, all-fucking-powerful Mateo Morelli kneels on the ground between my knees, and I can't think anymore. Shoving up the tiny skirt, he leans down and gives me the most intimate of kisses, starting slow, teasing me, enjoying every impatient breath, every shift of my hips. He picks up the pace, his tongue relentless against my clit, and in no time at all, just like he promised, I'm gasping his name as jolts of pleasure shoot through my body.

I sag against the couch, but he comes up and gives me a fiercely sexy look that states without words there will be no breaks here. I scoot as he comes down on the couch with me, hips between my legs, and kisses me.

Our tongues tangle for a minute, then he pulls back just enough to ask, "Do you taste your pussy on my lips, Mia?"

His hands move to his belt buckle, ripping it off and tossing it in the floor before unzipping his slacks.

I take the few seconds to catch my breath, and to my relief, he rips open a foil packet and slides on a condom.

"Touch me."

I swallow, allowing my hands to roam his body as he comes down on top of me, not entering me yet, just kissing me, giving me time to explore him. I haven't done this before, for obvious reasons, but I like it. My fingers caress muscles, skate down his flat abdomen. Feeling a little timid, I grasp his cock, enjoying the subtle sounds he makes as I guide him between my legs.

I arch as he pushes inside me, slowly, but stretching me. He doesn't want to hurt me this time, so he keeps pace, waiting for my body to adjust to his size. I'm wet, but his girth takes some getting used to no matter how prepared you think you are.

"You okay?" he murmurs.

I nod, and he starts kissing my neck again, sending shivers everywhere. My body finally relaxes under his ministrations. He pulls out slowly and pushes back in with far more ease this time. I lock my legs around him, looking into his dark brown eyes, completely aware I'm out of my league by a huge margin.

His pace picks up and he's fucking me good, murmuring things like, "You like my cock deep inside you, Mia?" and "Your pussy feels so good, sweetheart."

For the most part, I'm just trying to hold on as he buries his huge cock inside me over and over again.

"Harder," I finally challenge, burying my face in his shoulder.

Mateo chuckles, obeying *me* for once. Pounding me relentlessly until pleasure erupts and sweeps over with me with such intensity that I scream, digging my nails into his back. He hisses, still pumping into me, and then groans with his own release, thrusting his hips slowly, wringing every last second of pleasure he can from my body.

This time when he collapses on top of me, I wrap my arms around him and hold him close. My body is still weightless from the orgasm, but I know reality is just on the other side of the wall, and I'm not ready for that.

I knew I would be entertaining at a poker game tonight, but I didn't know the bet with the highest stakes would be mine.

A few minutes pass, then he finally musters the energy to push up off the couch. I watch him as he heads over to the counter, grabbing a paper towel to clean up.

"Condoms are lame," he informs me.

"Condoms are necessary," I disagree. Then, since there's probably not going to be a better time, I go ahead and ask, "What if I'm pregnant?"

He shrugs, dropping the soiled napkin into a garbage can and walking back over to me. "I still need a son."

"That's not funny."

"I'm not joking," he informs me, but lightly.

I want to point out it could be another daughter, but this whole topic makes me sweat, so I drop it.

Mateo rights himself, straightening his clothes and raking a hand through his hair. "This was fun. We should do it again sometime."

My face falls, a ball of dread dropping into my stomach.

He glances back at me over his shoulder. "Just kidding."

"You're a bastard," I inform him, still a little uneasy.

"In every sense of the word." Finally he walks to the door, pulling it open. "When you're presentable, come back out. We'll wrap this up soon and I'll get you home."

It's a little surreal and I'm still afraid to trust it, but at this point, what choice do I have?

The excitement of the night has worn off, and by the time I'm slogging back to Vince's bedroom with my heels dangling from my fingers, smelling strongly of sex and cigars, nervousness has moved into the space containing all my hope when I struck a deal with the devil.

I don't know if I did the right thing. I don't know what will happen tonight. I don't know what I'm coming home to.

It's close to three am, so I shouldn't be surprised to see him on the couch, asleep, failing in his mission to wait up for me.

I'm so relieved. Stripping the clothes off and shoving them in the dirty laundry basket, I tiptoe to the bathroom and take the opportunity to scrub Mateo off my skin. I stay in the shower, scrubbing until my skin's red and agitated, letting the hot water beat on me until there's none left.

My mind swims with guilt and fear, but I don't want to psych myself up. I told Vince I'd wake him up when I got home, so I still have to face him tonight, and I don't know how.

I put on one of his T-shirts to sleep in, part of me a little afraid it will be my last chance to. Balancing the world's weight on my narrow shoulders, I approach the couch and get down on my knees beside it. I just want to look at him. His face so peaceful in sleep, reminding me of the time that felt so long ago when he snuck into my house, just to hold me in his arms. I ache for the two kids who snuggled in bed, so blissfully unaware. I ache for the girl who thought he just didn't want to be tied down, and that was why he refused to give her a label. That girl could never be where I am right now. That girl wouldn't have just spent 40 minutes trying to scrub another man off her, she wouldn't have let him fuck her while she wore the $800 heels he bought her.

That girl was free to have a $5 spaghetti dinner with Vince, able to meet his eyes without the strain of guilt, never knowing how much that was worth.

I'm not that girl anymore.

I'm *this* girl.

And I hope that's good enough, because it's all I've got.

Reaching out a hand to tenderly brush a lock of dark hair off Vince's forehead, I give myself one more moment before I give his arm a little shake.

His eyes open, squinting at the light first, but then he sees me. Brushing the sleep away, he pushes himself up in the seat and looks around for his phone. "What time is it?"

"Late. Or, early, I guess," I tell him with a tentative smile.

His gaze moves over me, taking in whatever he can. "Are you okay?"

"Mmhmm," I say, nodding. "I'm good."

"Did he hurt you?"

I shake my head, meeting his gaze, but feeling my heart plummet as I do. I try to be convincing, knowing I have to sell it—he can never know what actually happened, and now that I know we don't have to worry about it again, I'd prefer he just think nothing did.

He frowns, as if unconvinced.

I've already anticipated this, so still kneeling on the floor, I touch a hand to his thigh. "Something good happened tonight."

"Something good?" he asks skeptically.

Nodding, I say, "I didn't tell you on Monday because we were having such a nice time and I just wanted us to enjoy ourselves, but on my way to school, I got stopped by these two guys. Cops."

Concern jumps in his eyes then, and I'm not sure for whom—his family, himself, me? "Cops?"

I nod. "They asked me a bunch of questions, wanting me to turn on you guys. Promising me safety if I did."

"Jesus, Mia," he says, pushing up even more, his alarm growing.

I hurry up the conclusion, not wanting to cause him any further stress. "They were on Mateo's payroll. He sent them. Obviously I didn't know that, but…"

He sinks against the couch, dread growing instead of dissipating. "He was testing you."

I nod again. "But I passed."

His eyes are still trained on me, full of alarm and confusion. "So…what does that mean?"

"It means I pleased Mateo. Surprised him," I amend, grimacing at my clumsy wording. "He said he believes he can trust me now. If I would've talked, it would've been then, when things were so… terrible."

His gaze drops as he probably remembers how he helped make things terrible for me that particular morning.

I reach for his hand, pulling his attention back to me. "But the really, really good thing is, he's giving me my freedom back. My life isn't tied to us anymore, and… and he's rewarding us."

Knowing Mateo, he doesn't appear convinced. "How?"

"He's going to give us a place of our own. He's going to let us move out, so things aren't so hard. So we have a chance to just… be with each other. We'll have something of our own. Something he won't touch."

"Something he won't touch?" he reiterates, understandably doubtful.

"He gave me his word. Said the game's over."

Vince is still frowning. "The game's over?"

"We'll come for Sunday dinners, but that's it. No more of… all this."

I wait for him to accept it, but he doesn't. I can understand why. It'll take time, probably for both of us. I just want us to actually *get* that time.

"If you don't *want* to, I guess maybe I could just go back to my mom's. I know they're moving in with Brax soon though, so they won't have a room for me."

"No," he says, shaking his head. "No, I... I want to, I just... I don't understand why he would do this. This isn't his style. Mateo doesn't let people out without a heavy payment for it. It's for the most part unprecedented, and the only time I can think of him actually doing it is in exchange for *five years* of someone's life. He's letting us out because you didn't talk? There's no reward for not talking, just a penalty if you do."

I shift on my knees, wishing he wouldn't dig into it. "I think he felt bad for all he's put us through."

That only causes his scowl to deepen. "He doesn't feel remorse."

"I don't know what to tell you," I finally say. "But can we just enjoy this? Who cares why?"

He meets my gaze, searching, and I'm terrified he's going to find something. I can't keep the fear from my eyes. I try belatedly to disguise it, but I start to feel sick, knowing I wasn't fast enough.

Once he finds what he's looking for or gives up searching for it, he leans back against the couch, his head falling back, and stares up at the ceiling. I feel hot all over, and not from the scalding shower I just took. I can't come this far, do this much, only to lose him before we even have a chance.

But I can't even blame him if he can't do this with me. It's a lot to handle, and we're way too young for this shit.

Without looking at me, still staring at the ceiling, he says, "Tell me something, Mia."

My chest feels hollow, knowing what's coming. I don't want to lie, but I can't tell the truth. Mateo's words come back to me and I'm so conflicted, I feel sick.

"Of course," I murmur, hating how hesitant I sound.

Now he sits forward again, leaning on his thighs, and stares me straight in the eye. "Do you love me?"

Relief pours through me that *that's* the question. "Yes," I say immediately, grabbing his hand between mine. "Yes, I do."

"Do you want to put Mateo behind us?"

I almost can't breathe with how much. "So, so badly."

Nodding slowly, still holding my gaze, he says, "Then let's do it."

I can hardly contain my joy, moving forward on my knees, wanting to kiss him. But I stop, because as much as I want to, I still feel so… soiled. If he had the images of Mateo's mouth crashing against mine earlier that night, he wouldn't want my kisses.

But he doesn't, so he leans in and gives me the kiss I'm too hesitant to give him. I wrap my arms around his neck, rising up to reach him better. As I'm kissing Vince, and his arms wrap me in a hug that makes me think he's as afraid as I am of what could come between us, I know the only way is to let it go. That's why I did all this to begin with—so we could have our freedom. We're not free of Mateo if I carry him with me.

I'll lie. If he ever asks, I'll lie.

And he'll love me for it.

# CHAPTER THIRTY

I CLIMB the three concrete stairs of the porch, using my hands as shields around my face so I can peer into the window of our new living room.

Amusement drips from Vince's words. "You know there's a key."

"I like the carpet," I tell him, ignoring his logic. "It looks soft."

"And if we use this key here, we can go in and see if it is."

I pull back from the window, placing a hand on my hip, and turn back to give him a discouraging stare. "This is our first place. Let me enjoy this."

He rolls his eyes, but he's smiling. I enjoy the lightness in him once more—it's been a long time.

Mateo stands right next to Vince, hands shoved into the pockets of his long black coat. I'm surprised by how similar they look from here, both with their dark heads, similar heights, similar features.

At least if I would've been pregnant, it would've been hard to tell which one was the father without a test. Thankfully, it won't be an issue.

I sigh, full of lightness myself.

"The carpet's new," Mateo remarks, smiling faintly at my enthusiasm. "And it *is* soft."

"I love soft carpet," I state, grinning and coming back down the steps to stand in the yard with them.

I stand by Vince and look back at the house. It's a converted duplex, so only half the house is ours, but we don't have to pay Mateo any rent.

"The other unit's full at least through the summer. You can keep the rent from that one—that way you'll have a little money to live on."

Glancing at his cousin, Vince says, "You don't want a cut?"

Mateo shakes his head. "I don't need it. You will. It's clean and in good repair, but it's a far cry from what you're used to."

"No pool?" Vince asks, mockingly.

Smirking, Mateo says, "No pool."

"I'm so okay with that," I announce. "I've got by on a shoestring budget before, I can do it again."

"You'll have to teach me," Vince says lightly.

Quirking an eyebrow, I say, "*You'll* have to eat jarred spaghetti sauce."

Clutching his heart, he asks, "Why do you wound me like this?"

I smile, leaning in and brushing a soft, impulsive kiss across his lips. "I'll make it up to you."

"Ooh," he says, clearly approving.

"Okay, I'm gonna get out of here," Mateo states, interrupting our flirting.

Vince smiles at me, winking before wrapping an arm around me and turning so we're both facing Mateo. "Well... thank you for this," Vince says.

Mateo nods, but there's a spark in his eye I don't like, and his eyes are on me. "Don't thank me, thank Mia."

Unprepared, I lose my smile, but Vince is still holding me in such a way he wouldn't have seen. I paste it back on, a little less exuberant, and try to murder Mateo with my eyes.

"For not talking," Mateo adds, after far too long a pause.

"Right," Vince says, dryly.

Mateo doesn't keep poking. Instead, he hands Vince the keys. "There's not much in the way of furniture, but a truck will be by later with a bed, a couch, a TV—just enough to get you started."

It feels real, maybe for the first time, when Mateo walks to the car waiting for him alone, and looks back to say, "I'll see you both Sunday."

For the first time in what feels like a lifetime, I'm not going to see Mateo at breakfast the next morning. I won't pass his study, or walk the halls of his house wondering if I'll see him around the next corner.

Vince holds up the keys, dangling them in front of me. "Our own place."

I smile, aware of Mateo's car pulling away. "Yep."

"Ready to go in?" he asks.

"I think so."

Vince smiles at me, taking my hand as we walk up the steps. "It's going to be so empty."

"But full of love," I joke.

Pulling a face, he says, "Ew, gross."

I elbow him in the side and he pulls me close, giving me a squeeze.

The living room is tiny, but perfect, since we won't have much to fill it with. Since there's no furniture, I sit down on the floor and cross my legs, looking around.

Vince sits down with me, following my gaze as if to see what I'm looking at.

"I think we put the TV over there," I announce, nodding confidently.

Vince agrees, jerking a thumb toward the wall behind us. "Couch back here."

"Yep. We're not going to be able to afford cable, so we should borrow all of Joey's Jason Statham movies."

Snorting, he wraps his arms around me and tugs me back against him. "I can think of far better uses of our time."

I let him pull me back, pulling a thoughtful face, resting my chin on my hand to really sell it. "Like what?"

In response, he leans down and brushes a soft kiss across my lips. I kiss him back, wrapping my arms around his neck at the awkward angle, and before I know it, we're tugging clothes off and christening our brand new living room.

Afterward, curled in each other's arms on the floor, I announce, "The carpet *is* soft."

Vince snorts, tucking my head under his chin. "Good thing."

We stay just like that for a long time—too long. We were supposed to bring in the stuff we had packed and brought over in Vince's car, but before we even get dressed again, the furniture truck pulls up outside.

Scrambling to get dressed before they come up on the porch, I tell Vince, "Our first purchase has to be curtains."

Since we never made it past the living room, Vince goes to make sure the path to the bedroom is clear for the movers, and I head out to the truck.

"Vince Morelli?" the man asks, glancing at his order sheet.

## Accidental Witness

"Yep, this is Vince Morelli's house."

The second man rolls up the back of the truck, placing a ramp there. I move around to the back to look at the stuff, since Mateo never asked, just ordered it himself. It's mostly what I expect as I watch them unload—a queen bed, a mid-size television with a stand, a charcoal gray sofa. Then the unexpected: a short three-shelf bookshelf and a single rectangular box.

Vince is down the hall, putting sheets on our new bed, so once the men bring it in, I take a moment alone to open the mystery box.

It's my box of graphic novels.

On a gold-rimmed, cream colored card, scrawled in the handwriting I didn't recognize the first time, it reads:

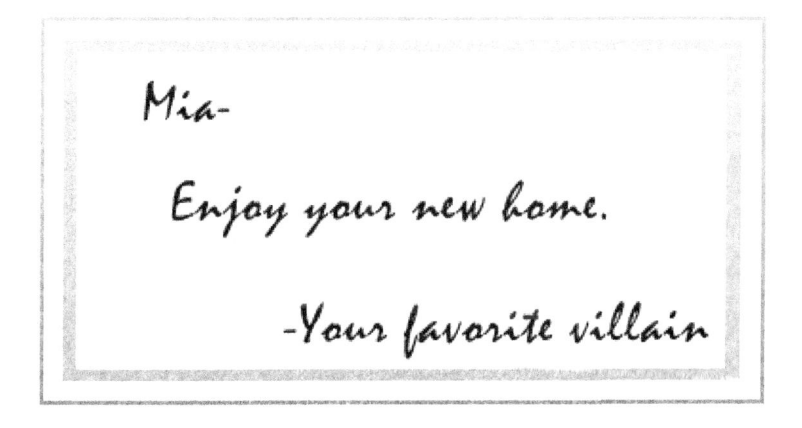

> Mia-
>
> Enjoy your new home.
>
> -Your favorite villain

I can't help smiling as I read it.

"I did it!" Vince calls, his voice louder as he comes down the hall. "All by myself. We don't even need a maid."

I stand, crushing the card in my fist and shoving it in my pocket, since we don't have a garbage can yet. "Good job, baby," I say, with a teasing wink.

"Those corners are no joke," he states, glancing past me at the box. "What's in there?"

Shaking my head dismissively, I tell him, "Oh, just some books."

That doesn't excite him in the least, so the box is already forgotten. Grabbing my hand, he tugs me down the hall. "Come look at how good I did."

I grin at him, allowing him to pull me along. "I bet there's never been a more neatly made bed anywhere, ever."

"I can't wait to mess it up," he tells me, flashing me a smirk.

Checking the imaginary watch on my wrist, I say, "Then why should we? I got nothing else to do today."

"Oh, you do now," he assures me, pulling me in for a kiss as we back into the bedroom, then kicking the door shut behind us.

# Accidental Witness

# ABOUT THE AUTHOR

Sam Mariano has been writing stories since before she could actually write. In college, she studied psychology and English, because apparently she never wanted to make any money!

Sam lives in Ohio with a fantastic little girl who loves to keep her from writing. She appreciates the opportunity to share her characters with you; they were tired of living and dying in her hard drive. (The Morellis actually *did* die in her old hard drive, but she resurrected them so you guys could meet them! You're welcome, or she's sorry, depending on how you feel right now.)

Feel free to find Sam on Facebook, Goodreads, Twitter, or her blog—she loves hearing from readers! She's also available on Instagram now @sammarianobooks, and you can sign up for her totally-not-spammy newsletter!

If you have the time and inclination to leave a review, however short or long, she would greatly appreciate it! :)

Printed in Great Britain
by Amazon